**Also available from
RaeAnne Thayne
and HQN Books**

Haven Point

Hope's Crossing

For a complete list of books by RaeAnne Thayne,
please visit www.raeannethayne.com.

RaeAnne Thayne

RIVERBEND ROAD

HQN™

ISBN-13: 978-0-373-78983-2

Riverbend Road

Many people play a vital role in bringing a book to life, from the first tiny seeds of an idea germinating in my imagination to the final creation. I am deeply grateful to every single person at Harlequin—from the art department for their stunning cover designs to the tireless marketing team to the fabulous HQN editors (especially the incomparable Gail Chasan, who has been with me through more than fifty books now!). Thank you to Sarah Burningham and Katie Olsen of Little Bird Publicity, my agent Karen Solem, my assistant Judie Bouldry, my review crew, and all the bloggers and booksellers who work so hard to help my books reach my wonderful readers.

For *Riverbend Road* in particular, I must thank Michael Lynch for the invaluable research help. The former small-town police chief and big-city homicide detective is a quiet everyday hero who has lived a far more fascinating life than any fictional character I could write! Also, I am indebted to my friend Jill Shalvis, for helping me through some sticky plot points and for always having my back.

Finally, I must thank my husband and three children. You fill my life with joy.

CHAPTER ONE

"THIS WAS YOUR dire emergency? Seriously?"

Officer Wynona Bailey leaned against her Haven Point Police Department squad car, not sure whether to laugh or pull out her hair. "That frantic phone call made it sound like you were at death's door!" she exclaimed to her great-aunt Jenny. "You mean to tell me I drove here with full lights and sirens, afraid I would stumble over you bleeding on the ground, only to find you in a standoff with a baby moose?"

The gangly-looking creature had planted himself in the middle of the driveway while he browsed from the shrubbery that bordered it. He paused in his chewing to watch the two of them out of long-lashed dark eyes.

He was actually really cute, with big ears and a curious face. She thought about pulling out her phone to take a picture that her sister could hang on the local wildlife bulletin board in her classroom but decided Jenny probably wouldn't appreciate it.

"It's not the calf I'm worried about," her great-aunt said. "It's his mama over there."

She followed her aunt's gaze and saw a female moose on the other side of the willow shrubs, watching them with much more caution than her baby was showing.

While the creature might look docile on the outside, Wyn knew from experience a thousand-pound cow could move at thirty-five miles an hour and wouldn't hesitate to take on anything she perceived as a threat to her offspring.

"I need to get into my garage, that's all," Jenny practically wailed. "If Baby Bullwinkle there would just move two feet onto the lawn, I could squeeze around him, but he won't budge for anything."

She had to ask the logical question. "Did you try honking your horn?"

Aunt Jenny glared at her, looking as fierce and stern as she used to when Wynona was late turning in an assignment in her aunt's high school history class.

"Of course I tried honking my horn! And hollering at the stupid thing and even driving right up to him, as close as I could get, which only made the mama come over to investigate. I had to back up again."

Wyn's blood ran cold, imagining the scene. That big cow could easily charge the sporty little convertible her diminutive great-aunt had bought herself on her seventy-fifth birthday.

What would make them move along? Wynona sighed, not quite sure what trick might disperse a couple of stubborn moose. Sure, she was trained in Krav Maga martial arts, but somehow none of those lessons seemed to apply in this situation.

The pair hadn't budged when she pulled up with her lights and sirens blaring in answer to her aunt's desperate phone call. Even if she could get them to move,

scaring them out of Aunt Jenny's driveway would probably only migrate the problem to the neighbor's yard.

She was going to have to call in backup from the
state wildlife division.

"Oh no!" her aunt suddenly wailed. "He's starting
on the honeysuckle! He's going to ruin it. Stop! Move
it. Go on, now." Jenny started to climb out of her car
again, raising and lowering her arms like a football
referee calling a touchdown.

"Aunt Jenny, get back inside your vehicle!" Wyn
exclaimed.

"But the honeysuckle! Your dad planted that for me
the summer before he… Well, you know."

Wyn's heart gave a sharp little spasm. Yes. She *did*
know. She pictured the sturdy, robust man who had
once watched over his aunt, along with everybody else
in town. He wouldn't have hesitated for a second here,
would have known exactly how to handle the situation.

*Wynnie, anytime you're up against something big-
ger than you, just stare 'em down. More often than
not, that will do the trick.*

Some days, she almost felt like he was riding shot-
gun next to her.

"Stay in your car, Jenny," she said again. "Just wait
there while I call Idaho Fish and Game to handle things.
They probably need to move them to higher ground."

"I don't have time to wait for some yahoo to load up
his tranq gun and hitch up his horse trailer then drive
over from Shelter Springs! Besides that honeysuckle,
which is priceless to me, I have seventy-eight dollars'
worth of groceries in the trunk of my car that will be

ruined if I can't get into the house. That includes four pints of Ben & Jerry's Cherry Garcia that's going to be melted red goo if I don't get it in the freezer fast—and that stuff is not exactly cheap, you know."

Her great-aunt looked at her with every expectation that she would fix the problem and Wyn sighed again. Small-town police work was mostly about problem-solving—and when she happened to have been born and raised in that small town, too many people treated her like their own private security force.

"I get it. But I'm calling Fish and Game."

"You've got a piece. Can't you just fire it into the air or something?"

Yeah, unfortunately, her great-aunt—like every-body else in town—watched far too many cop dramas on TV and thought that was how things were done.

"Give me two minutes to call Fish and Game, then I'll see if I can get him to move aside enough that you can pull into your driveway. Wait in your car," she ordered for the fourth time as she kept an eye on Mama Moose. "Do not, I repeat, do *not* get out again. Promise?"

Aunt Jenny slumped back into her seat, clearly disappointed that she wasn't going to have front-row seats to some kind of moose-cop shoot-out. "I suppose."

To Wyn's relief, the local game warden Moose Porter—who, as far as she knew, was no relation to the current troublemakers—picked up on the first ring. She explained the situation to him and gave him the address.

"You're in luck. We just got back from relocating a female brown bear and her cub away from that campground on Dry Creek Road. I've still got the trailer hitched up."

"Thanks. I owe you."

"How about that dinner we've been talking about?" he asked.

She had not been talking about dinner. Moose had been pretty relentless in asking her out for months and she always managed to deflect. It wasn't that she didn't like the guy. He was nice and funny and good-looking in a burly, outdoorsy, flannel-shirt-and-gun-rack sort of way, but she didn't feel so much as an ember around him. Not like, well, someone else she preferred not to think about.

Maybe she would stop thinking about that *someone else* if she ever bothered to go on a date. "Sure," she said on impulse. "I'm pretty busy until after Lake Haven Days but let's plan something in a couple of weeks. Meantime, how soon can you be here?"

"Great! I'll definitely call you. And I've got an ETA of about seven minutes now."

The obvious delight left her squirming and wishing she had deflected his invitation again.

Fish or cut line, her father would have said.

"Make it five, if you can. My great-aunt's favorite honeysuckle bush is in peril here."

"On it."

She ended the phone call just as Jenny groaned. "Oh. Not the butterfly bush too! Shoo. Go on, move!"

While she was on the phone, the cow had moved around the shrubs nearer her calf and was nibbling on the large showy blossoms on the other side of the driveway.

Wyn thought about waiting for the game warden to handle the situation but Jenny was counting on her. She couldn't let a couple of moose get the better of her. Wondering idly if a Kevlar vest would protect her in the event she was charged, she climbed out of her patrol vehicle and edged around to the front bumper. "Come on. Move along. That's it."

She opted to move toward the calf, figuring the cow would follow her baby. Mindful to keep the vehicle between her and the bigger animal, she waved her arms like she was directing traffic in a big-city intersection. "Go. Get out of here."

Something in her firm tone or maybe her rapid-fire movements finally must have convinced the calf she wasn't messing around this time. He paused for just a second then lurched through a break in the shrubs to the other side, leaving just enough room for Great-Aunt Jenny to squeeze past and head for her garage to unload her groceries.

"Thank you, Wynnie. You're the best," her aunt called. "Come by one of these Sundays for dinner. I'll make my fried chicken and biscuits and my Better-Than-Sex cake."

Her mouth watered and her stomach rumbled, reminding her quite forcefully that she hadn't eaten anything since her shift started that morning.

Her great-aunt's Sunday dinners were pure decadence. Wyn could almost feel her arteries clog in anticipation.

"I'll check my schedule."

"Thanks again."

Jenny drove her flashy little convertible into the garage and quickly closed the door behind her.

Of all things, the sudden action of the door seemed to startle the big cow moose where all other efforts—including a honking horn and Wyn's yelling and arm-peddling—had failed. The moose shied away from the activity, heading in Wyn's direction.

Crap.

Heart pounding, she managed to jump into her vehicle and yank the door closed behind her seconds before the moose charged past her toward the calf.

The two big animals picked their way across the lawn and settled in to nibble Jenny's pretty red-twig dogwoods.

Crisis managed—or at least her part in it—she turned around and drove back to the street just as a pickup pulling a trailer with the Idaho Fish and Game logo came into view over the hill.

She pushed the button to roll down her window and Moose did the same. Beside him sat a game warden she didn't know. Moose beamed at her and she squirmed, wishing she had shut him down again instead of giving him unrealistic expectations.

"It's a cow and her calf," she said, forcing her tone into a brisk, businesslike one and addressing both men in the vehicle. "They're now on the south side of the house."

"Thanks for running recon for us," Moose said.

"Yeah. Pretty sure we managed to save the Ben & Jerry's, so I guess my work here is done."

The warden grinned at her and she waved and pulled onto the road, leaving her window down for the sweet-smelling June breezes to float in.

She couldn't really blame a couple of moose for wandering into town for a bit of lunch. This was a beautiful time around Lake Haven, when the wildflowers were starting to bloom and the grasses were long and lush.

She loved Haven Point with all her heart but she found it pretty sad that the near-moose encounter was the most exciting thing that had happened to her on the job in days.

Her cell phone rang just as she turned from Clover Hill Road to Lakeside Drive. She knew by the ring-tone just who was on the other end and her breathing hitched a little, like always. Those stone-cold embers she had been wondering about when it came to Moose Porter suddenly flared to thick, crackling life.

Yeah. She knew at least one reason why she didn't go out much.

She pushed the phone button on her vehicle's hands-free unit. "Hey, Chief."

"Hear you had a little excitement this afternoon and almost tangled with a couple of moose."

She heard the amusement in the voice of her boss—and friend—and tried not to picture Cade Emmett stretched out behind his desk, big and rangy and gorgeous, with that surprisingly sweet smile that broke hearts all over Lake Haven County.

"News travels."

"Your great-aunt Jenny just called to inform me you risked your life to save her Cherry Garcia and to tell me all about how you deserve a special commendation."

"If she really thought that, why didn't she at least give me a pint for my trouble?" she grumbled.

The police chief laughed, that rich, full laugh that made her fingers and toes tingle like she'd just run full tilt down Clover Hill Road with her arms outspread.

Curse the man.

"You'll have to take that up with her next time you see her. Meantime, we just got a call about possible trespassers at that old wreck of a barn on Darwin Twitchell's horse property on Conifer Drive, just before the turnoff for Riverbend. Would you mind checking it out before you head back for the shift change?"

"Who called it in?"

"Darwin. Apparently somebody tripped an alarm he set up after he got hit by our friendly local graffiti artist a few weeks back."

Leave it to the ornery old buzzard to set a trap for unsuspecting trespassers. Knowing Darwin and his contrariness, he probably installed infrared sweepers and body heat sensors, even though the ramshackle barn held absolutely nothing of value.

"The way my luck is going today, it's probably a relative to the two moose I just made friends with."

"It could be a skunk, for all I know. But Darwin made me swear I'd send an officer to check it out. Since the graffiti case is yours, I figured you'd want first dibs, just in case you have the chance to catch them red-handed. Literally."

"Gosh, thanks."

He chuckled again and the warmth of it seemed to ease through the car even through the hollow, tinny Bluetooth speakers.

"Keep me posted."

"Ten-four."

She turned her vehicle around and headed in the general direction of her own little stone house on Riverbend Road that used to belong to her grandparents.

The Redemption mountain range towered across the lake, huge and imposing. The snow that would linger in the moraines and ridges above the timberline for at least another month gleamed in the afternoon sunlight and the lake was that pure, vivid turquoise usually seen only in shallow Caribbean waters.

Her job as one of six full-time officers in the Haven Point Police Department might not always be overflowing with excitement, but she couldn't deny that her workplace surroundings were pretty gorgeous.

She spotted the first tendrils of black smoke above the treetops as she turned onto the rutted lane that wound its way through pale aspen trunks and thick pines and spruce.

Probably just a nearby farmer burning some weeds along a ditch line, she told herself, or trying to get rid of the bushy-topped invasive phragmites reeds that could encroach into any marshy areas and choke out all the native species. But something about the black curl of smoke hinted at a situation beyond a controlled burn.

Her stomach fluttered with nerves. She hated fire calls even more than the dreaded DD—domestic disturbance. At least in a domestic situation, there was some chance she could defuse the conflict. Fire was avaricious and relentless, smoke and flame and terror. She had learned that lesson on one of her first calls as a green-as-grass rookie police officer in Boise, when she was the first one on scene to a deadly house fire on a cold January morning that had killed three children in their sleep.

Wyn rounded the last bend in the road and saw, just as feared, the smoke wasn't coming from a ditch line or a controlled burn of a patch of invading plants. Instead, it twisted sinuously into the sky from the ramshackle barn on Darwin Twitchell's property.

She scanned the area for kids and couldn't see any. What she did see made her blood run cold—two small boys' bikes resting on their sides outside the barn.

Where there were bikes, there were usually boys to ride them.

She parked her vehicle and shoved open her door. "Hello? Anybody here?" she called.

She strained her ears but could hear nothing above the crackle of flames. Heat and flames poured off the building.

She pressed the button on the radio at her shoulder to call dispatch. "I've got a structure fire, an old barn on Darwin Twitchell's property on Conifer Drive, just before Riverbend Road. The upper part seems to be fully engulfed and there's a possibility of civilians inside, juveniles. I've got bikes here but no kids in sight. I'm still looking."

While she raced around the building, she heard the

call go out to the volunteer fire department and Chief Gallegos respond that his crews were six minutes out.

"Anybody here?" she called again.

Just faintly, she thought she heard a high cry in response but her radio crackled with static at that instant and she couldn't be sure. A second later, she heard Cade's voice.

"Bailey, this is Chief Emmett. What's the status of the kids? Over."

She hurried back to her vehicle and popped the trunk. "I can't see them," she answered tersely, digging for a couple of water bottles and an extra T-shirt she kept back there. "I'm going in."

"Negative!" Cade's urgency fairly crackled through the radio. "The first fire crew's ETA is now four minutes. Stand down."

She turned back to the fire and was almost positive the flames seemed to be crackling louder, the smoke billowing higher into the sky. She couldn't stand the thought of children being caught inside that hellish scene. She couldn't. She pushed away the memory of those tiny charred bodies.

Maybe whoever had tripped Darwin's alarms— maybe the same kids who likely set the fire—had run off into the surrounding trees. She hoped so, she really did, but her gut told her otherwise.

In four minutes, they could be burned to a crisp, just like those sweet little kids in Boise. She had to take a look.

It's what her father would have done.

You know what John Wayne would say, John Bailey's

voice seemed to echo in her head. *Courage is being scared to death but saddling up anyway.*

Yeah, Dad. I know.

Her hands were sweaty with fear but she pushed past it and focused on the situation at hand. "I'm going in," she repeated.

"Stand down, Officer Bailey. That is a direct order."

Cade ran a fairly casual—though efficient—police department and rarely pushed rank but right now he sounded hard, dangerous.

She paused for only a second, her attention caught by sunlight glinting off one of the bikes.

"Wynona, do you copy?" Cade demanded.

She couldn't do it. She couldn't stand out here and wait for the fire department. Time was of the essence, she knew it in her bones. After nearly five years as a police officer, she had learned to rely on her instincts and she couldn't ignore them now.

She was just going to have to disregard his order and deal with his fury later.

"I can't hear you," she lied. "Sorry. You're crackling out."

She squelched her radio to keep him out of her ears, ripped the T-shirt and doused it with her water bottle, then held it to her mouth and pushed inside.

The shift from sunlight to smoke and darkness inside the barn was disorienting. As she had seen from outside, the flames seemed to be limited for now to the upper hayloft of the barn but the air was thick and acrid.

"Hello?" she called out. "Anybody here?"

"Yes! Help!"

"Please help!"

Two distinct, high, terrified voices came from the far end of the barn.

"Okay. Okay," she called back, her heart pounding fiercely. "Keep talking so I can follow your voice."

There was a momentary pause. "What should we say?"

"Sing a song. How about 'Jingle Bells'? Here. I'll start."

She started the words off and then stopped when she heard two young voices singing the words between sobs. She whispered a quick prayer for help and courage then rapidly picked her way over rubble and debris as she followed the song to its source, which turned out to be two white-faced, terrified boys she knew.

Caleb and Lucas Keegan were crouched together just below a ladder up to the loft, where the flames sizzled and popped overhead.

Caleb, the older of the two, was stretched out on the ground, his leg bent at an unnatural angle.

"Hey, Caleb. Hey, Luke."

They both sobbed when they spotted her. "Officer Bailey. We didn't mean to start the fire! We didn't mean to!" Luke, the younger one, was close to hysteria but she didn't have time to calm him.

"We can worry about that later. Right now, we need to get out of here."

"We tried, but Caleb broked his leg! He fell and he can't walk. I was trying to pull him out but I'm not strong enough."

"I told him to go without me," the older boy, no more than ten, said through tears. "I screamed and screamed at him but he wouldn't go."

"We're all getting out of here." She ripped the wet cloth in half and handed a section to each boy.

Yeah, she knew the whole adage—taught by the airline industry, anyway—about taking care of yourself before turning your attention to helping others but this case was worth an exception.

"Caleb, I'm going to pick you up. It's going to hurt, especially if I bump that broken leg of yours, but I don't have time to give you first aid."

"It doesn't matter. I don't care. Do what you have to do. We have to get Luke out of here!"

Her eyes burned from the smoke and her throat felt tight and achy. If she had time to spare, she would have wept at the boy's quiet courage. "I'm sorry," she whispered. She scooped him up into a fireman's carry, finally appreciating the efficiency of the hold. He probably weighed close to eighty pounds but adrenaline gave her strength.

Over the crackles and crashes overhead, she heard him swallow a scream as his ankle bumped against her.

"Luke, grab hold of my belt buckle, right there in the back. That's it. Do not let go, no matter what. You hear me?"

"Yes," the boy whispered.

"I can't carry you both. I wish I could. You ready?"

"I'm scared," Luke whimpered through the wet T-shirt wrapped around his mouth.

So am I, kiddo. She forced a confident smile she

was far from feeling. "Stay close to me. We're tough. We can do this."

The pep talk was meant for herself, more than the boys. Flames had finally begun crawling down the side of the barn and it didn't take long for the fire to slither its way through the old hay and debris scattered through the place.

She did *not* want to run through those flames but her dad's voice seemed to ring again in her ears.

You never know how strong you are until being strong is the only choice you've got.

Okay, okay. She got it, already.

She ran toward the door, keeping Caleb on her shoulder with one hand while she wrapped her other around Luke's neck.

They were just feet from the door when the younger boy stumbled and went down. She could hear the flames growling louder and knew the dry, rotten barn wood was going to combust any second.

With no time to spare, she half lifted him with her other arm and dragged them all through the door and into the sunshine while the fire licked and growled at their heels.

CHAPTER TWO

SHE MADE IT only a few steps out of the burning structure into the blessedly sweet air and blinding sunlight before strong hands reached to take both boys.

"Careful of Caleb's leg. I think it's broken," she mumbled, not even sure who was helping her and very much afraid she was going to be sick now from a combination of the smoke choking her lungs, the exertion and delayed reaction.

"We've got to move, before the whole thing tumbles down around us." As her vision adjusted to the shift in light, she saw Cade, his face set and hard, carrying both boys as if they weighed no more than a couple bags of sugar.

"You coming?" he growled.

"Right behind you, Chief," she mumbled, then called on the last of her strength to follow Cade as he rushed away from the structure toward a cluster of emergency vehicles just arriving on scene.

He headed straight for the ambulance pulling in just behind the first water truck. Before they reached it, a couple of paramedics jumped out and grabbed a gurney out of the back. They were two of the best in the volunteer department, she saw with relief. In seconds, Ed Cutler had Caleb on the stretcher.

"I didn't have much time to assess the situation but it looked like he broke his ankle. He jumped out of the hayloft once the fire started," Wyn explained, keeping a careful eye on Ed's partner Terri Michaels as she hooked Luke up with an oxygen mask.

"Thanks. Sit down before you fall over," the bald EMT ordered her. "Terri, get a mask on Wyn here too."

"I'm okay," she said. "Don't worry about me. You've got enough on your hands with the boys. They come first."

"You're going to let them treat you," Cade growled. "And then you're going to explain to me why the hell you thought you could defy a direct order."

The paramedics exchanged glances and then pointedly busied themselves with Lucas and Caleb.

"I had no choice. You can see how quickly that thing flared out of control. When I rolled up, only the loft was engulfed but I knew it was only a matter of time. If I hadn't gone in, Chief Gallegos would be sending his guys in for body retrieval and we both know it!"

"Another ten seconds and they would have been looking for three bodies!"

Though the June afternoon sunshine was warm and the fire put out plenty of heat, Wyn shivered. As her adrenaline spike ebbed, the reality of the situation began to soak in like that water spraying out of the firefighters' hose.

In nearly five years of law enforcement, she'd never had such a close call. She and the boys all could have died inside that fiery barn. If she had been thirty seconds later…if she hadn't been able to move as quickly… if one of those blazing timbers had crashed to the ground.

No question about it, they had been lucky.

She swallowed, suddenly light-headed. She didn't realize she swayed until Cade grabbed her.

"Sit down," he ordered harshly, though his hands were gentle as he helped her to the ground. Terri came over with an oxygen mask and a water bottle.

"Did you call another ambulance for her yet?" Cade asked.

Terri looked wary at his clipped tone. "No. We'll check her blood gases first. Could be, we can treat and release at the scene with a few more puffs of oxygen."

"I'm perfectly fine," Wyn answered through the mask, then spoiled the words with a paroxysm of coughing.

When Wyn finished, Cade's silver-blue eyes looked as fierce and hard as the Redemption Mountains.

"If the paramedics don't ship you to the hospital, take your vehicle and clear out. You're officially suspended without pay for the next seven days."

For a moment, she thought the fire had messed with her hearing. "*What?* I just saved two lives!"

"And almost lost your own in the process."

She glared at him. "You can't suspend me! I didn't do anything wrong!"

"You disobeyed a direct order and your actions could have endangered others."

"How?" she demanded.

"You turned off your radio, didn't you? You had no idea what the status of the other responding personnel might have been. Nor did we have anybody on scene to provide status reports on the fire until the first engine rolled up."

She had no answer to that, especially not when he reached down and unclipped her radio from her shoulder. When he turned the dial up the air was immediately filled with voices and static as Chief Gallegos and his team communicated through the airwaves with dispatch about their needs.

"I made a judgment call," she said. It sounded weak, even to her. Okay, maybe she had ignored department policy, but those two boys chattering to the EMTs were proof that her judgment call had paid off.

"The wrong one. I'll see you in seven days," he answered tersely, then turned and stalked over to the fire command center.

CADE HAD NEVER been more angry.

The fury prowled through him, harsh and wild like the fire burning through Darwin Twitchell's dilapidated barn.

He had to be able to trust her to do exactly what he asked. Out of all six officers in this small ragtag Haven Point police department, he trusted Wynona most. She was smart, hardworking, compassionate and insightful.

She had natural instincts and seemed to always find the perfect way to allay any tense situation, from drunk altercations down at the Mad Dog tavern to hot tempers between neighbors.

He figured she came by those instincts naturally, since she was fourth-generation law enforcement in these parts.

He didn't want to suspend her, especially not when they were in the middle of their busiest time of the year with the summer tourist season heading into full swing. But what alternative did he have? This wasn't the first time she had ignored his orders but he vowed it would be the last. He wasn't a control freak but he had to know that his officers would follow the chain of command.

He glanced back at the ambulance. She looked so fragile and vulnerable sitting there in the grass, her cheek sooty and strands of wheat-colored hair slipping free of the thick braid she always wore on duty.

Beneath his anger lurked something else, something he didn't want to look at too closely. He only knew that he couldn't remember ever feeling that bone-deep fear that had sent him racing out of the station to his vehicle and then bulleting through town to the fire scene.

She was a police officer. One of *his* police officers. He would have worried about *any* of his guys who stopped responding while out on a call.

He put it away when he saw Erik Gallegos heading in his direction.

"What's the status?" he asked the fire chief.

"Barn looks like it's going to be a total loss," Erik answered. "Old thing was about to fall over anyway, next time a stiff wind blew off the lake. At this point, my crew is just trying to put out the flames and make sure it doesn't spread to the undergrowth."

"That a concern?"

Erik shrugged. "Not really. All the rain we've had the last few weeks has reduced the threat level for now, but you never know."

Cade hoped they had another six or seven weeks before fire season hit, especially since some places in the higher elevations were still covered in snow.

The chief jerked his head toward his EMTs. "Wynona okay?"

He followed the other man's gaze, where Wynona was smiling and saying something to the younger of the Keegan boys. "Seems to be."

He thought about leaving the situation there but figured word would spread soon anyway and he might as well get out in front of it.

"I gave her a week's suspension for disobeying a direct order and for turning off her comm."

Erik snorted. "Seriously? Harsh. You know you would have done the exact same thing."

That was different, though Cade couldn't quite pin a finger on why. "Your guys were four minutes behind her. She should have waited for somebody who could search the premises wearing proper gear."

"Four minutes is a long time for two scared little boys," the fire chief said.

Cade still knew he had made the right call. That had been four minutes of hell he never wanted to live through again, trying to raise her on the radio, then rolling up to the scene a half minute before the fire crews to find the place engulfed and no sign of her.

When she had burst out of that door seconds later

like she was some kind of freaking avenging angel, carrying two kids with smoke and flames pouring out behind her, his blood had turned as cold as a jump into Lake Haven in January.

His stomach still felt hollow and shaky.

"It could have been a hell of a lot worse, if not for Wyn. I'll take a little mild smoke inhalation and a broken ankle over the alternative."

"Yeah. I know."

"Lindy-Grace and Ron are both on their way. I asked Ed and Terri to wait a minute longer for the boys' parents to make it here before they roll out to Lake Haven hospital."

Erik gave him a careful look. "You going to refer the boys to juvie court for trespassing and vandalism?"

"We can cross that bridge eventually."

He should probably have a word with the boys before they left the scene. He could always catch them at the hospital or after they were discharged, but in his experience, time sometimes had a way of distorting the truth.

He should have remembered his duty, first and foremost. Yet another reason to be pissed at Wynona.

He headed back toward the ambulance. She had risen from the grass and now leaned into the rear of the ambulance trading jokes with the boys, who still looked small and frightened.

He had gone to school with their mom, Lindy-Grace, and considered her a friend. She was a sweetheart who threw the best barbecues in town and often dropped off baked goods at the police station.

He had heard rumors that LG and Ron were going through a trial separation. That must be tough on the boys. He didn't want to pile it on when they were already scared and one was injured, but he really did have a job to do, trying to find out what happened.

When he neared the ambulance, Wyn gave him a wary look and stepped aside, as if afraid he was going to yell at her again. He ignored her and stuck his head into the ambulance.

"Hey, boys. How we doing in here?"

The older one—Caleb—paled another shade when he spotted him. The EMTs must have given him something for the pain of his ankle, which was encased in an inflatable splint. "Are you gonna take us to jail because we started the fire, Chief Emmett?" he asked.

"We didn't mean to do it," the younger boy whimpered before Cade could answer. "It was just a junky old barn. Nobody used it for nothing. That's what our dad said. So we decided to make it our clubhouse and we were gonna roast hot dogs for lunch. We were supposed to go on a campout with our dad tonight but then he said he had to work so we couldn't go."

"Since we already had the hot dogs and stuff, we decided to have our own campfire," Caleb said.

As much as he liked Lindy-Grace Keegan, he had never much liked her husband, Ron. The guy had always struck him as a self-absorbed workaholic who didn't know a good thing when it lived in his house. The story just confirmed it.

"If you have to arrest somebody, arrest me." The older boy held out his wrists as if he expected Cade to slap cuffs on them right there. "It was my fault. All of it. I tried to start the fire and I guess I used too much kindling."

"No, I didn't make the ring good enough," his brother protested. "You should arrest *me*."

"But if I hadn't fallen when we jumped down from the loft, we could have run out and called for help. I'm the one responsible. Arrest *me*."

Wyn made a soft sound and he risked a glance down. Her eyes were suspiciously moist and he felt an answering tug of emotion. It would take a harder man than he was not to be touched at this evidence of brotherly love, each trying to shoulder the blame for the other.

Would any of his brothers step up to do the same for him? He wanted to think so but he wasn't sure. Hell, his own father would have shoved every single one of his boys in front of a firing squad if it meant he could save his own skin.

"I'm not going to arrest anybody—" he started to say, but didn't finish the sentence before a distraught female voice cried out.

"My babies! Where are they? My babies!"

"Mama," Lucas cried out and Lindy-Grace lifted her head at the sound like a bird dog on a pheasant.

An instant later, she and Ron were both there. Lindy-Grace shoved him aside to jump into the ambulance so she could hug and kiss each boy, babbling about how much she loved them. Ron, ashen-faced, stayed next to Cade.

When she finished hugging them, she frowned ferociously at both of them. "You are in *such* big trouble!"

At her words, both boys burst into tears.

"We're sorry," the younger one wailed. "We're so sorry, Mama."

"We didn't mean to," Caleb blubbered. "It was an accident. We had a fire ring and everything but then the fire jumped out onto some hay and we couldn't put it out. I knew we had to get out so we jumped down, only I fell hard and hurt my ankle and couldn't get up and Luke wouldn't go without me, even though I told him and told him to go."

"We were so scared," his brother interjected. "We couldn't get out and we were crying and praying and then *she* came in and helped us."

They pointed to Wynona, who smiled and waved weakly.

"Wynona Jane Bailey," Lindy-Grace exclaimed. "You saved my boys."

She jumped back down from the ambulance and wrapped Wynona in a tight embrace that couldn't have felt the greatest on his officer's smoke-seared lungs.

"If I live to be a hundred and three like my great-grandmother LuLu, I will never forget what you've done here today," LG said through her tears.

He knew just what Wyn was thinking when she arched an eyebrow at him. *See? Not everybody thinks I screwed up.*

She hugged Lindy-Grace for a moment before deftly extricating herself. "It wasn't a big deal. I just happened to be in the right place at the right time. Any other officer on the Haven Point Police Department would have done exactly the same thing. Isn't that right, Chief Emmett?"

He was spared from having to answer that by Lindy-Grace's effusive gratitude.

"I don't care. They weren't there. You were. Cade, I sure hope you're going to give Wynnie a medal!"

His jaw clenched and he opened his mouth to answer but one of the EMTs spoke up before he could get the words out.

"Actually, he suspended her for a week without pay," Terri Michaels offered, with a dark look in his direction.

The women in Haven Point apparently stuck together.

"What?" Lindy-Grace exclaimed. "Suspended her! Are you kidding?"

Cade ground his back teeth. How was he supposed to defend his position to the mother of the two boys Wynona had risked her life to rescue? Yes, he was glad everything had turned out relatively okay except for Caleb's broken ankle. But procedures were in place for a reason.

"It's an internal police matter," he finally said. "If you'll excuse me, I've got to get back to the scene. Boys, we're not done talking about this. But now that your mom and dad have had a chance to make sure you're okay, you need to be checked out at the hospital. I'll come by later to ask you a few more questions about what happened here and I'm sure Chief Gallegos will have a word or two for you as well."

"Yes, sir," they said in unison, looking chastened at his stern tone.

He walked away without risking another look at Wynona, wondering how he seemed to have lost control of the entire situation.

CHAPTER THREE

WYN WATCHED CADE walk away, tension radiating from him with every step.

She had worked with him for nearly three years but had never seen him like this. Usually he was calm, coolheaded, no matter the crisis. He was acting very unlike himself—being abrupt to two scared little boys, suspending her for actions he certainly would have taken himself in the same situation.

It left her feeling off balance, as if she were trying to hike up to the top of Mount Solace wearing high heels.

"Seriously, Wyn. How can we ever thank you?"

She shifted back to Lindy-Grace and Ron. She had a sudden feeling this was going to get old really quickly.

Her father had been the hero around town and people revered him accordingly. Twenty-five years as the police chief of Haven Point had earned him a reputation as a decent, caring man who would do anything for the people he served. The last difficult two years of his life had only solidified that love and respect. His funeral five months earlier had to be moved to the gymnasium at Haven Point High School to hold the crowds of people who wanted to come pay their respects.

She was no hero, just a police officer doing her job.

Her mother was going to *freak*. It was a wonder Charlene hadn't hitched a ride to the fire with Lindy-Grace to make sure her oldest daughter was okay.

"I'm just happy everything worked out," she said now to her friend.

"But a week's suspension! You saved two lives. You shouldn't be punished for that! What is *wrong* with that man?"

She couldn't begin to guess—nor did she want to discuss it with Lindy-Grace.

"It doesn't matter." She forced a smile. "The boys are safe and that's the important thing. And they're *not* going to go around starting any more fires to roast hot dogs without a grown-up present, right?"

Both boys shook their heads vigorously.

"We really need to go now," Ed said. "The docs at the emergency department have called three times trying to find out what the heck is taking so long. LG, you can ride along if you want. Ron, just follow behind at a safe speed and meet us at the hospital."

"Right."

"So I'm good here?" Wyn pressed.

Ed nodded as he took the oxygen mask from her. "Yeah. Your levels are great and I think Chief Gallegos would be fine with me releasing you. Just promise you'll go straight to the hospital if you notice any shortness of breath or feel light-headed."

"You got it."

She signed the paperwork releasing her from their care, then waved off the ambulance as it backed away through the fire crew.

By the looks of it, the entire Haven Point volunteer fire department had turned out for the excitement, though it looked like the barn was going to be a total loss. At this point, they seemed to be trying to contain the fire to only the barn and make sure it didn't spread to the surrounding vegetation.

She spotted Cade helping uncoil hose from one of the water trucks. No, it wasn't his job, but that never stopped him before. He always jumped in to do whatever necessary.

With a sigh, she headed for her patrol car. When she started the engine, he looked over. He wore sunglasses that concealed his expression but she had a feeling he was still glowering at her as she drove away.

She had left her phone inside the vehicle when she responded to the fire, what felt like another lifetime ago. It rang before she even made her way past the last fire truck and when she glanced at the screen, she saw she had missed six calls—all from her mother. She had to talk to Charlene eventually but she wasn't quite ready for that.

Just as she turned onto Riverbend Road, it rang again. This time the caller ID had her reaching to answer.

"Hey, Kat," she said as she pulled over to the shoulder of the road, grimly aware she was too shaky to talk on the phone and drive safely at the same time.

She was greeted by an excited shriek that nearly pierced her eardrums.

"Is it true?" her sister, Katrina, demanded.

As usual, her sister's bubbly energy made her feel

about a hundred years older, though less than five years separated them.

"I'm going to say yes, though I'm not sure what you're talking about."

"Sam just texted me that Michelle Hunter came into the store and said she heard from her mom who heard on the police scanner that you ran into a burning building and saved about twelve people."

Oh, the fun rumor mill in Haven Point. You had to love it.

"Don't forget all the babies and kittens. There had to be at least a hundred of them."

"Seriously?"

For about half a second, Katrina actually bought it. Wyn swallowed a laugh. She adored her sister, she really did, but sometimes Kat was a little too gullible—not a good trait in a second-grade teacher.

"No," she finally admitted. "No babies or kittens. Or puppies, for that matter. I didn't rescue a dozen people either. As usual, the facts tend to get a little distorted once the rumors start flying."

"Why bother with facts when they only get in the way of a good story?"

It was another of their dad's little sayings and she had to smile. Both she and her sister seemed to be quoting John Bailey more often now that he was gone. Maybe they were finally able to remember him as he once was instead of the distorted version they had lived with for the last two years of his life.

"It was only two little boys," she answered. "Lindy-

Grace Keegan's pair. And I was only a few minutes ahead of the fire crew."

"My sister, the hero! That's amazing. I'm so proud of you. Dad would have been too."

"Thanks," she answered, a little catch in her throat at the words.

"I mean it. Wait until Marsh hears."

Their oldest brother, Marshall, was the sheriff of Lake Haven County. What would he think about her suspension? He would probably support it wholeheartedly, especially since Cade was his best friend.

"Can I bring you dinner tonight?" Kat asked. "I was thinking about trying out a new recipe for chicken divan."

Her stomach gave a long, greasy roll at the offer. Kat was a fantastic, dedicated teacher, a good friend and a sweet, kindhearted person. She was also a terrible cook.

"I think I'm good. Thanks, though. I just need a little downtime, you know?"

"Are you sure? I'd love to bring you something. What about dessert? I've got more fresh rhubarb out back and was thinking about rhubarb-cherry tarts."

Her mouth puckered. Kat was on a no-sugar kick these days and Wyn could only imagine rhubarb-cherry tarts without it. No thanks. She had an emergency Snickers bar hidden away inside her house that was calling her name right now.

"You're so sweet, but really. It's been a crazy day and I need to chill."

It felt like another lifetime ago that she had been

rescuing Aunt Jenny from the cow moose and her baby camping out in her driveway.

"I totally get that. After teaching twenty-five seven-year-olds all day, sometimes when I get home from school I just want to sink into a chair and not move until the next morning. I don't know how I would survive without summers. Fine. But can we grab lunch or something this week? Don't tell me you're working double shifts! I won't hear any excuses."

"Okay. I won't tell you that." She didn't add that she wasn't working *any* shifts for several days. Kat would have no problem marching right down to the fire scene and giving Cade a piece of her mind. Her sister tended to lump Cade into the same category as Marshall and Elliot, just one more troublesome older brother.

She had never looked at him that way, but her sister did.

With the experience of long practice, she shied away from considering exactly *how* she looked at Cade.

"I could do lunch," she said instead. "Let's plan on it tomorrow."

"Perfect. Oh, and you're going to have to talk to Mom. She's already called me three times, trying to see if I know anything about what happened to you."

"Do I have to teach you again how to hit Ignore on your phone?"

"I wouldn't have to hit Ignore, if you would just man up and talk to her," Kat retorted.

"Yeah, yeah," she answered.

She and her sister exchanged *love you*s and ended the call.

She did love Kat. They had always been close, the only two girls in a family of rambunctious, wild boys— just not quite as close as Wyn had been to her twin brother.

Her heart twisted with the familiar sharp ache she always felt when she thought of Wyatt, gone five years now.

He would have run into that burning barn too. She knew it in her bones. He wouldn't have hesitated for a *second* and would have told his boss to screw off if the word *suspension* was even mentioned.

She would never be Wyatt—funny, brave, compassionate. No matter how hard she tried, she couldn't fill her twin's shoes.

Yeah, Charlene was going to be freaking out.

She would call her mother the moment she was home, she told herself.

She turned the patrol car onto Riverbend Road, the long, winding road that ran parallel to the Hell's Fury before it dead-ended.

As she neared her house, she spotted an unfamiliar minivan with Oregon plates parked in the driveway of a nearby house.

Oh, it would be lovely if someone moved in. The house had been cold and empty for too long, since before the river flooded the previous summer. She had always loved the little tan Craftsman house with the wide front porch and the cheery red shutters.

Moving to this area of town had been largely an accident. She had intended to rent something on the lake, similar to the house where she had grown up, but

around the time she came back to help after her dad
was injured and to take a job at the Haven Point PD,
the renters who had been living in her grandmother's
house moved out. Her mother suggested she move in
as a stopgap until she could find something else she
liked, and Wyn had fallen in love with the whimsical
charm of the stone cottage and this eclectic neighborhood along the river.

She loved that none of the houses were the same.
Her house, constructed a century earlier of stucco and
stones pulled from the river, seemed very different
from the Craftsman just down the street, which in turn
was nothing like Cade's log house just across the road.

Somehow they all seemed to work together.

She spied a bike and a tricycle propped against the
side of the Craftsman and a soccer ball resting in the
grass. Despite the toys in the yard, the curtains were
tightly drawn at the house and she couldn't see any sign
of activity, which she found a little weird.

The curtains at her own front window were wide-
open, though, and a familiar face peered out, as if he
had been perched exactly there in the deep window
seat, waiting all day for her return—which was very
likely.

When she turned into the driveway, that face—and
the furry body it was attached to in the form of her yellow Labrador retriever—lit up with excitement.

When she unlocked the door, Young Pete waited
for her just inside, his tail wagging with eagerness.
"Hold," she told him, then took two minutes to unhook
her service revolver and her badge and lock them in the

fingerprint safe in the hall closet before she rewarded Pete's patience with a hug.

"There's my favorite guy," she said. "How was your day?"

Her dog nudged his head against hers and the quiet, steady affection made her throat burn even as she felt some of the stress of the day seep away.

What would have happened to Pete if she hadn't made it out of that barn in time? She had to think Marshall or Katrina would have taken him in. He'd been their dad's dog, after all, a link to the man John had been before his traumatic brain injury two years before he died.

"Need to go out? Do you?"

The dog gave one quick bark and she opened the back door for him and walked out onto the stone patio overlooking the river.

She needed to change out of her smoky uniform and shower but right now she wasn't sure she could move from this spot.

After a moment, Young Pete finished his business then came back to sit beside her. The dog was ten years old and not young anymore but she still stuck the modifier on his name. Her dad had always called him that, in contrast to Old Pete, John's previous dog.

Birds flitted through the branches of one of the big elms in her backyard, their song mingling with the breeze rustling the leaves and the river's endless, soothing song.

She closed her eyes and lifted her face to the late afternoon sun.

She could have died today.

She wanted to think she'd had the situation fully in hand but Cade had it right. She had been foolish and arrogant to think she could take on that fire and win, especially without following protocol and keeping her radio on. It had been sheer dumb luck that she was here enjoying the beauty of a June afternoon.

The realization was sobering yet oddly invigorating, as if the heat and smoke had burned away something hard and confining.

She felt as if she had been encased in ice since her father's death in January. Longer, really. Maybe some part of her had been suspended, frozen since the terrible succession of events five years ago that culminated in Wyatt's death, when she had made the decision to go to the academy in his stead.

Each of her brothers loved law enforcement, just as their father and grandfather and great-grandfather before them. A Bailey had been keeping the peace here since the first settlers moved into the area the Native Americans considered a place of mystical strength and healing.

Her father and Wyatt had given their lives for the job. If she loved it as they had, she might have been willing to die in the line of duty. She didn't. She never had.

Her pocket jangled suddenly and she knew by the ringtone it was her mother. Shoot. She'd meant to call Charlene the moment she got home. As the widow of a fallen police officer and the bereaved mother of another, her mother had every right to her worry and Wyn felt bad for adding to it.

"Mom. Hi. I'm sorry I missed your call. It's been a…crazy afternoon."

"Oh honey. I've been frantic! I called the ER, I called the station, I called your house. Finally I called Cade and he told me what happened and assured me you were all right."

"I am. A little smoke inhalation but I was treated and released at the scene."

"So it's true. You really ran into a burning building to save a couple of juvenile delinquents."

She thought of those poor, scared little boys, each trying to shoulder the blame for the accident in order to take the burden from the other.

"Something like that."

"Oh honey."

She heard a sniffle and could guess her mother was trying to hold back the tears she had probably been crying all afternoon. Charlene had lots of practice sitting at home and worrying. Guilt pinched at her again. She should have called the moment the EMTs took away the oxygen mask.

"I'm coming over to make sure you're okay," her mother insisted.

"It's not necessary, really. I'm fine."

"You say that, but I don't believe you for a minute. I can hear it in your voice. Mother's intuition is never wrong, honey. You're upset and you need me there."

She closed her eyes, loath to hurt her mother's feelings by telling her the reality was exactly the opposite.

She loved her mother, she did. Charlene was sweet and earnest and she loved nothing more than to fuss over her family. Wynona mostly found it exhausting.

For two years, her mother had turned those energies to caring for her husband after his brain injury. Charlene visited him daily in the nursing home and had been a dedicated and selfless caregiver. Wyn admired her greatly for it. Since John's death, though, her mother had tried to shift all those caregiving energies to her children—whether they needed it or not.

She couldn't deal with Charlene today. She *couldn't*.

"I'm actually on my way out," she lied.

Charlene paused. When her mother spoke again, Wyn couldn't miss the eagerness in her voice. "A date?"

Gah. She suspected her mother thought that the very day she would turn thirty—in four months, one week and two days—she would become a dried-up old maid.

"Afraid not. I've, um, got some things to do for McKenzie's wedding," she improvised quickly. "A bridesmaid thing."

Yes. That's right. She was nearly thirty years old and still lied to her mother.

"What time will you be home? I'll bring dinner. I'm making lasagna."

She did love her mother's lasagna, flavored with fresh herbs and home-canned tomatoes and deliciousness. It was fantastic—but not quite worth everything that would come along with it.

"Thanks a million, Mom. That's really sweet of you, but I'll probably just grab something while I'm out."

"Okay. If you're sure."

Wyn could clearly hear her mother's wounded feelings in the words and she swallowed a heavy sigh.

"Aunt Jenny wants to have us all over for dinner," she offered as a salve. "I'll try to coordinate with Marsh and Kat and see when the whole gang can make it. How would that work?"

"Oh, that would be lovely. We live so close together, it's a shame we can't find more time for family dinners. Though, of course, it won't feel the same without Elliot. Don't forget Marshall's birthday next Sunday."

"Maybe Jenny can join us for that."

"I already asked her. She'll be there."

"Great. I can't wait. I've got to go, Mom. I need to jump in the shower and wash some of this smoke out. Love you."

She hung up before her mother could press her. After a quick shower and shampoo, she felt a million times better. She was throwing on a pair of shorts and a T-shirt when her phone rang again. To her relief, it wasn't her mother's customized ringtone but the one for her friend McKenzie.

"Hey, Kenz."

"Wynona Jane Bailey!" McKenzie Shaw exclaimed. "If you didn't want to be a bridesmaid for me, you could have just told me! You didn't have to risk your life and nearly die to get out of it, a month before the wedding!"

She made a face as she combed through her hair. "I didn't risk anything. Good grief. Does everyone in town know?"

"LG called me five minutes before Cade did."

Lindy-Grace worked for McKenzie at her gift shop and they were good friends, so it only made sense she would let her know what happened.

"You will be at the top of Lindy-Grace's Christmas list for the rest of your life," McKenzie went on. "You know that, don't you?"

"Lucky me. She gives the *best* presents."

"And the top of ours as well. Ben and I have a very soft spot in our hearts for those boys. We would have been devastated if anything had happened to them. The whole town would have been devastated."

"Everything ended well and now we can all move on."

She was already tired of all the hullabaloo, especially for a decision that she was beginning to accept might not have been the smartest one she'd ever made.

"Not everything. I understand Chief Emmett suspended you from the department for a week without pay."

Ugh. Small towns! A dog couldn't pass gas without people talking about it.

"Does everybody know that too?"

"Cade called to tell me personally before the rumors started flying."

Of course. McKenzie was the mayor of Haven Point and Cade technically reported to her. Apparently he had been very busy on the phone all afternoon, between her mother and her dear friend.

"I told him that didn't sound like a good idea to

me," McKenzie said. "I can word my opposition more strongly, if you want."

"Heavens no! I don't need my friends fighting my battle for me."

"Your *friend* happens to be his boss, in a round-about way."

"All the more reason to keep your mouth shut. Please, Kenz."

"It doesn't seem right to me. You saved the lives of two boys and shouldn't be punished for that."

"I'm looking at it as a nice vacation," she lied. "I'll finally have the chance to catch up with things around here. Plus, it will give me more time to help Devin with the final plans for your bridal shower."

"You two are taking this bridal shower *way* too seriously. It's beginning to scare me."

"Don't worry. This is just practice. You and I can do the same for Dev and her sexy rancher when they tie the knot."

"Good point," McKenzie said and Wynona could hear the smile in her voice. In the background she heard someone else talking to her friend and a moment later, McKenzie came back on the line. "I've got to go. Somebody is here to make a special floral order."

"No problem. I have to go too. Young Pete needs to go out again."

"I'm just going to say this again. It's time you dropped the descriptor. Young Pete has prostate issues, like other dudes of a certain age," McKenzie muttered.

She smiled and hung up after exchanging goodbyes, deeply grateful for her friends. Yes, she had been a bridesmaid five times in the last two years—it would be six after Devin's wedding in a few more months. She was getting a little tired of it, but she would be lost without her friends, who had lifted her through more than they even knew.

"You might not be young anymore," she told Pete, "but you're still worth a dozen puppies."

He wagged his tail, still standing by the door, patiently waiting for her to open it.

"You know what we both need?" she decided on impulse. "A little walk to clear our heads. Somewhere out of cell range, preferably."

Pete seemed to be in full agreement, especially when she slipped on her walking shoes and grabbed the little pack she always kept stocked with a flashlight, water bottle and granola bar.

She decided to head for their favorite walk, along the Mount Solace trail that would take them across the Hell's Fury River and up into the mountains above town. The bridge that led to the trailhead was just on the other side of Cade's house so she didn't bother with Pete's leash, though she brought it along and stuffed it in the pack.

The dog stayed by her side as they walked down the street with the sound of the river accompanying them. When they reached the little Craftsman, she saw a slight woman with auburn hair unpacking groceries from the minivan, aided by a little boy of about four and a girl a few years older.

Pete, ever friendly, wandered over to say hello with his tail wagging a hundred beats a minute. The boy let out a shriek and hid between his mother and the minivan.

Shoot. She should have used the leash. She forgot there were new people in the neighborhood who didn't adore him yet like everybody else did.

"Pete, get back here," she called. After a reluctant moment, the dog wandered back to meet her as she approached the little family and she gripped his collar tightly.

"Sorry about that," she said. "He loves to meet new people and can be a little too friendly sometimes. Hi. I'm Wynona Bailey. I live just down the street in the stone house with the green shutters. Welcome to Haven Point."

The woman didn't answer her smile. Her features were closed, unapproachable, her green eyes arctic.

"Isn't there some sort of leash law in Haven Point?" she asked in a stiff voice.

So. Not the friendliest of new neighbors. Too bad. The kids were adorable, with auburn hair like their mother's. The boy's was curly and the girl wore hers in two long, thick braids.

"Technically, yes," she answered. "I've got a leash here. But since we were just walking from our house to the trailhead just up ahead, I decided not to use it."

"My son is afraid of dogs. Especially big, ill-behaved, dangerous dogs."

She had to blink at that. No one in his right mind could possibly call a big, furry sweet-tempered guy like Young Pete dangerous *or* ill-behaved. He only wanted to say hello, for heaven's sake.

"Sorry again. I'll try to keep him out of your way. Come on, Petey." She grabbed the leash out of the pocket of the backpack and clipped it on him. The little boy had emerged from behind his mother and gave her a tentative smile and she couldn't help smiling back.

"It was great to meet you all," she said, even though she hadn't really met them. *Meeting someone* implied an exchange of names, which the woman had quite pointedly not shared.

She waved at the children. The boy waved back and it looked like his sister wanted to, but at the last minute she stuck her hand in her pocket. Their mother had turned away to unpack groceries.

Wyn gave a mental shrug and headed past Cade's log home to the beginning of the trailhead up into the mountains. As soon as she and Pete crossed the bridge, she unclipped his leash with a defiant look back at the family, but they had disappeared into the house.

CHAPTER FOUR

IT DIDN'T TAKE long for the sheer beauty of her surroundings to siphon away the unpleasantness of the encounter with her new neighbors.

She had grown up hiking the foothills all around Haven Point but this was indisputably her favorite walk. The trail to Mount Solace was an easy but steady climb through stands of fragrant pines and firs and a thick forest of aspens with leaves that fluttered and danced on the slightest breeze. Amid the trees were several wide meadows bursting with wildflowers this time of year—columbine and kittentails, Indian paintbrush and delicate Queen Anne's lace.

She loved the solitude and the serenity she always found in the mountains and as she walked, she felt the tension in her shoulders begin to ease. Pete enjoyed it, too, sniffing from tree trunk to flower patch to granite boulder.

An hour later, she felt much more centered and calm. Yes, she had a close call today. Yes, it probably had been a mistake to run into that barn and especially to turn off her comm while she did it, but she would never regret rescuing Lucas and Caleb, no matter what Cade said.

The sun was beginning to slide behind the mountains and her stomach reminded her she still needed to think about dinner.

"What do you think? Should we go home, Petey?"

The dog's ears perked up and he inclined his head down the trail, just in case she had forgotten the way back.

She had to smile. "Thanks. Lead on."

The dog obediently took point and they made their way back down. She loved the uphill trail for the burn it gave her quads and thighs and the sense of accomplishment, but the real reward came from the walk back down, when she caught occasional glimpses through the trees of the lake and the silvery twist of river and the town she had sworn to serve and protect.

She had hiked higher than she intended, she realized, as the shadows lengthened and the temperatures began to drop. She picked up her pace. Just before she hit the relatively flat part of the trail that paralleled the river, she heard voices ahead of her—unhappy voices, by the sound of it. A couple of upset children.

Remembering her new neighbors, she called Pete over to her and clipped his leash onto his collar.

"Sorry, dude. Better safe than sorry, right?"

Pete huffed out a breath but he was so easygoing that he never minded the leash much. They continued walking along the trail that curved with the river, following those voices.

Finally, they rounded a bend where she discovered the new occupant of the cute Craftsman sitting on the trail with her right leg stretched out in front of her and her children hovering close.

Wyn did a quick situation assessment and saw the woman's ankle was swollen and beginning to bruise. She had a vague sense of déjà vu. Apparently this was her designated day to deal with injured limbs.

Her children knelt beside her in the dirt. The little boy's face was streaked with tears and the girl was holding her mother's hand, though she also looked pale and frightened.

The woman caught sight of Wyn and her distressed features closed up.

"Oh. It's you."

The woman tried to struggle to her feet as if she didn't want to be caught in any kind of vulnerability and Wynona hurried forward.

"Please, don't get up. That looks nasty!" Grateful for the impulse she'd had to put on Pete's leash, she moved closer so she could have a better look at the injury. "I'm guessing the rock over there was the culprit. I stumbled over the same one on my way up."

She pointed to one of those basketball-sized rocks that sometimes seemed to spring out of the ground overnight along these mountain trails, like mushrooms after a rain.

"We were watching a pretty bluebird on the trail and my mama didn't see the rock. She says she sprained her ankle," the girl offered.

"That was probably a mountain bluebird. They're my very favorite bird."

"I liked it too," the girl said. "It sounded nice. I like your dog. She's pretty."

"She's a he, actually. This is Young Pete and I'm Wynona Bailey. Wyn."

"I remember. You said so before. My name is Chloe Montgomery. This is my brother, Will, and my mom, Andrea. I'm six years old and Will is four. My mom is thirty."

Ah. Andrea Montgomery. That was the name of the woman who was now frowning at her daughter like she had just revealed state secrets.

Or maybe Wyn was being too suspicious. Maybe the woman was merely grimacing in pain.

"Do you mind if I take a look?" she asked Andrea Montgomery. "I'm a police officer here in Haven Point, trained as an EMT too."

This was the second time that day she had been grateful that Cade insisted everyone in the department go through the necessary basic training in first aid. Haven Point was a small town, he had always explained, and sometimes his officers were on an accident scene alone for several minutes before the volunteer fire department could mobilize. A little knowledge might even mean the difference between life and death.

If she hoped the other woman would be relieved to find out she had basic medic experience, Wyn would have been sadly disappointed. If anything, the woman's features tightened even further and she avoided Wyn's gaze.

"That's not necessary, Officer Bailey. It's not broken. I only twisted it a little. I was catching my breath a moment before we head back home. I'll put some ice on it when we get home."

"I'm not an expert but that looks like a sprain to me. Even if it's only twisted, you might have some tendon and ligament damage. You could make it worse, if you're not very careful."

"I'm fine, really. Sorry we're in your way. You can just go around me."

As if Wyn could ever leave a neighbor—even a prickly one—sprawled out in the dirt. The woman obviously didn't want her help but beneath the coldness, she sensed something else, a hint of another emotion that smelled to her cop's nose suspiciously like fear.

She couldn't begin to guess why her neighbor might be afraid of *her* but it made her intensely curious.

"You've got at least a quarter-mile walk back to your place. Even if the ankle is only twisted a little, that's going to be a long, hard slog with two kids by yourself. You won't make it before dark. Do you have a flashlight?"

The woman still continued to avoid her gaze but shook her head, just as Wyn would have guessed.

"Look, at least let me try to find a walking stick you can use for support."

After a pause, Andrea Montgomery relented slightly. "That might be helpful."

"Great. Kids, can you help me? I'm looking for a walking stick that's about this tall and this big." She held her hand at shoulder height and made a wide circle with her thumb and forefinger.

The boy—Will, his sister had said—found one first and produced it triumphantly.

"That looks great," Wyn exclaimed.

"Thanks, honey," Andrea said with a soft smile for her son that contrasted starkly with her attitude toward Wynona. "Let's see if it works."

She gripped the walking stick and used it to pull herself to her feet. "Look at that. Perfect."

Her son preened as if he had just single-handedly shot down the Death Star and Wyn had to smile. Yeah, Andrea might be a cool customer to *her* but the woman seemed like a loving mother.

"Thank you," the woman said. "I think we'll probably be fine now. You don't have to wait for us. I'm sure you have somewhere to go."

"Not at all," she answered, which was the unvarnished truth, though it was a little depressing.

She had no one to blame but herself for that state of affairs, really. Kat had offered to bring dinner and so had Charlene. McKenzie likely would have been more than thrilled to come over. Given half a chance, Lindy-Grace probably would have thrown a parade down Lakeside Drive.

She had shut everybody down, so it was her own fault she had no dinner plans.

"Young Pete and I aren't in a hurry," she assured her new neighbor. "We were taking our time ambling home with no particular schedule and a few moments more won't matter to us. I don't feel good about leaving you here when you're injured. If you don't mind, I'll just stick with you so I can be sure you make it home."

The woman looked as if she minded very much but she must have realized Wyn wouldn't back down. She finally gave a shrug and started making her painstaking way down the trail.

It was clear after just a few steps that Andrea Montgomery was in considerable pain but she stubbornly continued on.

They walked slowly back with Andrea leading the way and Chloe behind her, holding her brother's hand. The boy seemed to be warming up a little to Pete and no longer looked completely panic-stricken, though he continued to keep a safe distance between them. Wynona, in the rear, kept up a running commentary with the children, identifying some of the birds that flitted through the trees and different varieties of wildflowers they passed.

They still had several hundred yards to walk before they reached the bridge when Andrea stumbled again and let out a gasp of pain.

Wyn decided it was time for a little more firm intervention.

"Chloe, I know your brother isn't very crazy about dogs," she said. "What about you?"

"Oh, I love them," she declared. "We used to have a big dog named Magnus but my dad found him a new home without kids after he bit Will when he was little."

This earned the girl a swift look from her mother, whose features were white with pain. Was it because the girl mentioned her dad? Where *was* the man? And was he the reason Andrea Montgomery seemed determined to keep her distance?

"That's good to know. Do you think you could hold on to Pete here while I help your mom?"

"Oh yes!" Chloe exclaimed. "May I?"

"I don't need help," Andrea said stiffly.

Wynona ignored her and handed Pete's leash to the eager girl, then stepped forward to the woman's side.

"Don't be a hero. Trust me, that gets old after a while. Just lean on me. I'll help you back to your house. I know you don't know me, but, I promise, I'm harmless. I'm only trying to help. I don't want you falling again and making things worse for yourself."

The woman's mouth tightened, whether from irritation or pain, Wyn couldn't tell. She had a feeling she was better off not knowing. They made their way to the bridge and over it, then only had the short distance to the family's new house. By now, the children were in front of them and both of them were giggling at Pete. Will seemed to have completely warmed up to the dog— Pete's sweet nature had a way of winning over even the wariest of hearts.

"Your children are adorable," Wyn said after a moment.

Andrea's features softened. "Thanks. I'm pretty crazy about them."

It was another point in her favor, along with her strength and stubbornness, which seemed more than a little familiar to Wynona.

If Andrea hadn't made it so clear that she didn't want to have anything to do with her, Wyn might have thought they had a good chance of becoming friends.

"I'm sorry your introduction to the Haven Point

backcountry didn't end well. When your ankle feels better, you'll have to try the trail again. It's a little bit of a climb but Mount Solace is stunning this time of year. If you keep going up this trail, you'll eventually come to a beautiful waterfall. It's not huge but it's definitely worth the effort."

"I'll keep that in mind," she answered.

"Another good trail is Crimson Ridge," she went on, mostly to distract the woman from the pain of hobbling along on her sprained ankle. "The trailhead for that one is just past Redemption Bay. It's one of my favorites, especially in late summer when it's wild-blackberry season. In the fall, the sugar maples up there turn amazing colors, which is where the trail gets its name."

"Are you…from here?" Andrea Montgomery asked. Though pale, she didn't falter once. Another point in her favor.

"Yep. Born and raised. It's a really nice community, full of good people."

"If everyone here is good, why do they need a police department?"

She laughed. "Okay, *most* of the people are good. We've got a few bad eggs but they're the minority."

Andrea's new house was in sight now, which seemed to give the woman a little extra strength.

"You picked a great time to move here," Wynona continued. "In a couple of weeks, we'll have our annual Lake Haven Days and wooden-boat show. Your kids will love it, trust me. There's a pancake breakfast, a big parade, a craft fair and all kinds of activities for children.

They can even make their own wooden boats and have races in the marina."

"Sounds…nice."

"Oh, it is. And at Christmastime, you can't miss the Lights on the Lake Festival. People come from miles around to see local boat owners decorate their watercraft and parade from here to Shelter Springs and back. It's quite a spectacle."

"We'll plan on it."

"So where are you from and what brings you and your family to Haven Point?"

She meant the question to be casual and conversational, a subtle little probe, but Andrea Montgomery instantly tensed.

"The Pacific Northwest," she said, the words as sharp as pine needles.

That was certainly deliberately nonspecific. The polite thing would be to let the subject rest but that wasn't in her nature, police officer or not.

"What part?" she asked.

For a long moment, the other woman didn't answer. She glanced at the children then back down in front of her.

"Near Portland," she finally said.

"Oh, that's a beautiful area," Wyn said, hoping to put her at ease again. "I drove through there when I was in college on the way to the coast with friends. I loved it. I especially remember how green it was and all the beautiful gardens. I was struck by the gorgeous masses of flowers in baskets hanging from the streetlamps."

As she hoped, Andrea seemed to relax. "It's an easy place to grow flowers, as long as they like a lot of moisture. I love the wildflowers here."

They talked about flowers and gardening a little—not Wyn's area of expertise, as evidenced by the scraggly flower gardens outside her house. She waited until they reached the driveway of the Craftsman before she slid the next question into the conversation.

"And what brings you to our beautiful neck of the woods? Do you have family close by?"

The woman gripped the walking stick with white knuckles—from pain or tension, Wyn couldn't tell. "We needed a change," she said tersely.

She obviously wasn't going to add anything more and Wyn knew she had pushed her hard enough.

"Haven Point is a nice place for a new start," she said, offering up a calm smile, "especially with the new Caine Tech facility opening up. We've had many new people move in already and expect even more. We're happy to have you all."

"Thanks," Andrea said as they walked up the driveway. Wyn helped her struggle up the few steps. "And thank you…for your help."

"You're very welcome. That's what neighbors do. Are you sure you're okay from here?"

"Yes. Fine."

Wynona gestured to the other woman's swollen ankle. "You probably know this already but you should elevate that and ice it. RICE, right? Rest, Ice, Compression and Elevation."

"Got it."

"And if it's still swollen and giving you trouble in the morning, you may want to see a doc. My friend Devin Shaw is an excellent family doctor and is wonderful with children and grown-ups alike. Hold on, and I can write down her name and number for you."

She reached into the front pocket of her backpack for the little notebook and pen she always kept there, just in case. Her best moments of inspiration for solving cases often came while she was hiking and she hated to lose her train of thought. She jotted down a few things then ripped out the paper and handed it to Andrea.

"Here you go," she said. "That's the number and address for Devin's clinic. I also put down my cell number. If you need someone to drive you to the doctor or the grocery store while you're laid up, I'm more than happy to help."

The other woman looked both shocked and wary at the offer. "Thank you."

"You're more than welcome. The third number is the other essential thing you need to know—the secret delivery number for Serrano's. That's the best restaurant in town and they have pizza, sandwiches, whatever kind of comfort food you need and if you tell them I referred you, they'll deliver it right to your door. They don't do that for everyone but will help out in an emergency."

"That's very kind of you."

Andrea looked overwhelmed but grateful too.

"Seriously, I'm just up the street if you need anything." She grabbed Pete's leash from Will, who apparently was now completely over his fear of big dogs—at least *her* particular big dog. "I'll see you guys later. Take care of your mom, okay?"

"'Bye, Officer Bailey," Chloe said.

"'Bye," Will said with an adorably enthusiastic wave that would have scared away any mosquito within a square mile. "'Bye, Pete."

Wyn walked back down the driveway then waited until the woman and her children were safely inside the house. The blinds moved as if someone had made sure they were closed tightly.

Something wasn't right with this family. The impression settled on her shoulders and refused to lift. The woman wasn't simply unfriendly. She was a bundle of nerves and had the hollow-eyed, furtive look of someone with something to hide.

What? Was she afraid, guilty or both?

A dozen possibilities flitted through her mind, none of them good. Wyn turned, barely registering the lovely lavender dusk that smelled of cut grass and someone working the charcoal grill.

It wasn't any of her business, she told herself. Didn't she have enough to worry about without taking on someone else's problems?

Her gaze landed on Cade's SUV with the HPPD logo on the side, parked in the driveway of his log home across the street. Like him, she was a police officer. Taking on other people's problems was sort of in her job description.

She really *should* mention her concerns about the new neighbor and ask him to keep an eye on things here, just in case trouble showed up in the middle of the night.

As a side benefit, perhaps she could persuade him to reduce her suspension by a few days. It was worth a try, anyway.

CHAPTER FIVE

THIS WAS THE craziest damn day he'd had in a long time and right now all he wanted was a steak, a cold Sam Adams and a nice, relaxing baseball game on the big screen to help him unwind.

Though he had a perfectly serviceable gas grill and it was fine in a pinch, he preferred the rich flavor from the traditional method so Cade spent a moment lighting the charcoal on his old-fashioned Weber. Yeah, he was a two-grill guy. Sue him.

Once the coals were smoldering, he headed inside to turn on the game and pulled the two rib eyes marinating in the refrigerator. Since it was as easy to grill two as it was one, he always cooked an extra and used the leftovers for fajitas or a steak omelet.

He had a very limited skill set in the kitchen, he would freely admit. Most of it involved flames and protein of some sort, though he tried to add fruit and veggies where he could.

He set the steaks on the counter and reached back into the refrigerator for a beer. He was just grabbing the bottle opener when his cell phone rang.

Sometimes he wanted to grab the thing and toss it into the middle of the Hell's Fury.

As much as he would have liked to ignore the blasted ringing, he knew he couldn't. It might be an emergency. He was the chief of police and had a responsibility to the people of Haven Point, like it or not.

A quick check of the caller ID showed it wasn't a problem in his community but still something he couldn't ignore. His sister-in-law wasn't in the habit of calling him for no reason.

"Hey, Christy," he greeted her. "What's going on?"

She uttered a particularly succinct epithet that basically summed up Cade's own prior delightful twenty-four hours. "Guess who just called me from jail again? That's right, you guessed it. Your idiot asshole of a brother!"

And this day just kept getting better and better.

He closed his eyes and pressed the cold bottle to the tension headache brewing at his temple. A familiar sense of helplessness settled in his gut, the same feeling he always had when dealing with certain members of his troubled family.

"I've had it. Do you hear me? I told him the next time would be the last time. I told him if he can't keep his sorry ass off a bar stool, there's no freaking *way* I was going to bail it out of jail again."

"DUI?" he guessed, though it didn't take any particular detective skills.

"What else? Third one in four months." She swore again. "It's like he's been on one long bender since he lost his job."

Marcus was the brother just younger than he was, with barely two years between them. He was also the

Emmett brother who seemed determined to follow in their father's wobbly, drunk-off-his-ass footsteps.

Until a few months earlier, things had been going well for Marcus. Though his brother had only graduated high school by the skin of his teeth, he immediately moved to Boise and went to work in construction and eventually made a good living driving a cement truck.

He and Christy had a rocky start, marrying young after she got pregnant, but seemed to be making things work and had even added a few more kids to the mix.

Earlier in the year, Marcus's company had run into financial trouble and he was laid off and everything seemed to implode.

"I can't do this anymore, Cade. I just can't," Christy said. Her voice wavered and he could hear the tears just below the surface. "When he's here, he just mopes around doing nothing but snapping at me and the kids."

"Being unemployed is tough on a guy like Marc, who's used to taking care of his family."

"I get that. Believe me, I get it. But instead of going out to find another job, he goes out and buys more booze. What is *wrong* with him?"

Cade didn't know how to answer. Christy wanted him to fix his brother. He felt as if he'd spent his entire life trying to duct-tape together the jagged pieces of his broken family in one way or another. Hell of a lot of good that had done over the years. He hadn't been able to prevent his mom from getting sick when he was eleven and he couldn't keep anybody else out of the hot mess of trouble they always seemed to land in.

"What do you need from me?" he asked.

"How about a phone number for a good divorce attorney?" she countered.

That would be a disaster for their three kids, who adored their father. On the other hand, living with an unreliable, unstable, angry drunk wasn't a great alternative.

"I can't help you there, Christy. He might be an ass but he's still my brother. He would be devastated to lose his family. You know he loves you."

"Does he? Really? He's losing his family right now. He's just too plastered to notice!"

Was she only calling to complain or did she really think he had some power to change his brother's behavior? He couldn't decades ago when they were kids. He certainly couldn't now.

"I'm not bailing him out this time," Christy went on. "I'm dead serious. I'm working my fingers to the bone, trying to keep food in my kids' mouths and shoes on their feet. I'm not going to use my hard-earned money to bail him out of jail one more time. As far as I'm concerned, he can rot in there."

Maybe that would be the wake-up call his brother needed, the stimulus to get off his butt and make a change. Or maybe Marcus would perceive Christy's inaction as proof she didn't love him, which might send him slipping further into the depression that seemed to have caught hold.

"I understand where you're coming from."

"Do you?"

Yes. Hell, yes. After his mother died, Cade had tried

his best to help his father but had finally had to accept his father loved Johnnie Walker far more than he could ever love his sons.

Marcus wasn't Walter. He was a good man going through a rough stretch.

"I can try to talk to him, see if I can convince him to go into rehab."

Christy paused and he heard more sniffling on the line. "Don't you think I've tried that? Only about a thousand times. He won't listen."

"It's worth a shot."

"Maybe you'll have better luck. He respects you more than any other man he knows."

"I can't make any promises," he warned. "Any change has to come from him."

"I appreciate the effort anyway. You've been a good brother to him."

He would beg to disagree. A good brother would have been better at keeping his siblings out of trouble.

"It might be a few days before I can get over there. I've got to work double shifts for a while since I'm short an officer this week." He grimaced at the reminder of Wynona Bailey and her foolhardy stubbornness.

"That's fine with me. Let him stay in there and stew about the mess he's created."

"I should be able to squeeze out a few hours toward the middle of the week to drive to Boise."

"I hope you can talk sense into his hard head."

"So do I."

She was silent for a moment and he heard more sniffling on the line and a muffled sob. "Why does he have to make it so hard to love him?" she finally burst out.

If his brother had been there, Cade would have had no problem pounding him, badge or no badge. Idiot. He had a good thing going. A wife who loved him, kids who needed him. Why would he throw all that away?

Cade's own beer—the bottle from the single six-pack he allowed himself per week—suddenly tasted flat and bitter.

None of them had been given much of a chance, with an abusive drunk for a father and a weak mother who didn't take care of herself and ended up with liver disease because of it.

With such a screwed-up childhood, it was a wonder Marcus had been able to maintain a good relationship with Christy all these years.

"You take good care of yourself and those kids."

"That's what I'm trying to do. But you know Marcus won't see it that way."

He feared she was right. "Do you need help with bills?" he finally asked quietly.

Christy was silent for a long, awkward moment. "You've done more than enough, Cade."

He didn't mention to her that Marcus had come to him asking for help paying the mortgage the last few months. He had a feeling she knew and was too proud and stubborn to ask for more.

He would send a check anyway and hope she accepted it, for the kids' sake. Losing their home wouldn't help the situation right now.

"I'll talk to you later in the week to see how things are going," he said.

"Thanks, Cade. I didn't know what else to do but to call you. I needed to vent to someone else who loves that idiot as much as I do."

"I'll do what I can," he promised.

After they said goodbye, he leaned his head back against the wall and closed his eyes, exhausted suddenly from the crazy day. Marcus and his latest DUI seemed like just one more thing he couldn't fix.

The world was filled with problems he couldn't solve, which sometimes seriously sucked.

The doorbell rang while he was still trying to figure out how he could slip Christy the extra money for her mortgage—which happened to be the one problem he *could* remedy.

He might get to that steak at some point that evening, but he was beginning to wonder.

"Coming," he called out.

He headed to the front door and pulled it open. All thoughts of Marcus and Christy, DUIs and mortgages, flew completely out of his head.

Wynona Bailey stood on his doorstep with her wheat-colored hair pulled back into a thick braid and tan shorts revealing a surprisingly long stretch of tawny legs.

Yeah. The world was really good at throwing unsolvable problems at him.

His mind snapped back to that nightmarish moment when he had pulled up to the fire at Darwin Twitchell's barn and found her patrol vehicle empty and no sign of Wyn, and then an instant later she burst through the doors of the barn with a kid in each arm and flames exploding behind them.

He had run through that moment in his head dozens of times in the last few hours and still couldn't figure out the emotion he'd experienced, when he knew she was safe and unharmed.

Something had changed. That's all he knew. Or maybe it had been there forever but was only now growling to life.

"What are you doing here?" he asked, then realized how rude the words sounded when her hesitant smile slid away.

But what was he supposed to say? Though she lived at the other end of the street, they didn't socialize at each other's homes outside of work. He could count on one hand the times he'd been to her place, usually to drop off paperwork. She stopped here just as seldom.

Why was that?

He didn't know the answer and it seemed odd now. They were friends and had been for years, even before she came to work for him after her father's injury. Her brother was his *best* friend.

He had been to all his other officers' homes several times. Barbecues. Birthday parties. It had never been a big deal to socialize outside of work, especially in a small police department like Haven Point. But something about Wyn Bailey was...different.

Maybe he could blame the same something that had sent him rushing to the scene of a fire after she stopped responding to the radio, with his heart hammering and his foot pushing hard on the gas pedal.

"I'll tell you why I'm here but I'd rather not do it standing on the porch," she said. "May I come in?"

He had no choice but to step back and open the door wider for her.

A familiar canine followed her in and he couldn't help a smile, despite the tension that popped and sparked between them like a bad wire.

"Hey there, Young Pete."

The dog's ears perked up at his name and he sat at Cade's feet with his tail brushing the wood plank floor of his entryway. Cade reached down and scratched Pete in the spot he remembered the dog liked, just under its left ear.

"How are you, buddy?"

He and Young Pete went way back, to the days when the dog used to be John Bailey's constant companion. The former chief had adored the puppy, the latest in a string of dogs he always named Pete.

He wasn't a puppy anymore. Gray peppered his muzzle and he walked with the same ginger care of an old man on the cusp of needing artificial knees.

"How are the lungs?" he finally asked when Wyn showed no inclination to let him know what she was doing at his house.

At her blank look he arched an eyebrow. "Smoke inhalation, remember? A few hours ago you were being examined by two of Haven Point's finest EMTs. Ring a bell?"

"Oh. Right. The lungs." She shrugged. "If I breathe too deeply, they ache a little but nothing I didn't expect."

The reality of her close call seemed to reach out and grab him by the throat all over again. He couldn't even contemplate what might have happened to her.

Yeah, he knew the risks of the job. Every day when he sent his officers out, he knew they were risking injury and even death. People thought Haven Point was a nice, quiet town where nothing much happened but those in his department knew better. The town had its share of drug abuse, domestic disturbances, assaults.

He had been standing just a few feet away when her father took a bullet to the head that should have killed him—and in a roundabout way, eventually did just that two years later.

If Wynona had joined the ranks of the fallen that included her father *and* her twin brother, Cade wouldn't have been able to live with himself.

Her mom was probably out of her head with worry.

"That was a really stupid thing you did," he said sternly.

"Yes, I believe you mentioned that when you were yelling at me in front of the entire fire department."

For a guy with a reputation for a cool head under pressure, he had done a miserable job of handling the whole situation. He could admit that now, after the fact. He should have taken her aside and reprimanded her in private. The whole public-safety community didn't need to watch him lose his temper.

Too late now. It was done and he wouldn't back down or change his mind.

"Did you come here thinking you could talk me out of the suspension? If you did, don't bother."

"You are ridiculously stubborn, Cade Emmett. Did anybody ever tell you that?"

"You. About a thousand and sixteen times."

Of all his officers, he trusted her judgment most. She wasn't afraid to call him out when he became dogmatic or unreasonable, whether during an investigation or in personnel issues. He wasn't afraid to admit when he was wrong but he knew he wasn't on this one.

"Would you at least consider reducing the number of days I'm suspended?"

"No."

She narrowed her gaze at him. "This is the worst time of year for the department to be shorthanded, with all the tourists starting to trickle in before Lake Haven Days in a few weeks."

"I know that."

She sighed. "You're hanging me out to dry as an example to the rest of the guys, aren't you?"

Yeah, that was partly true. When it counted, he needed his officers to follow the chain of command. If he ordered an officer to stand down, he needed to know the order would be heeded.

"It's not easy having to be the one who makes the tough calls."

Sometimes he was really tired of being the responsible one. Between the phone call from Christy about his brother and Wynona calling him out because of her suspension, the burden had never felt so heavy.

"I get it. You did what you had to do. A week just seems excessive to me."

"A week. No more, no less. You scared the hell out of me, Wyn."

He shouldn't have said that last part, especially not in that rough, intense tone. She gazed at him, her eyes wide and he thought he saw something there, a little flicker of awareness, before she shifted her gaze down to her dog, who was now stretching out on the floor at his feet.

"Fine. Your decision. I guess we'll all have to live with it. That wasn't really why I stopped anyway," she went on. "You have new neighbors across the street."

"Yeah, I saw a vehicle in the driveway this morning and a moving van unloading things when I came home around lunchtime."

"Do you know anything about them?"

He shook his head. "Not a thing, except what I saw earlier. They must have kids because I saw a couple of bikes out on the lawn when I came home—a boy and a girl, judging by the stereotypical bike colors. The pink bike was bigger. They drive a minivan with Oregon plates and listen to NPR, according to a bumper sticker."

She laughed. "For not knowing anything about them, you seemed to have picked up quite a bit."

It would probably sound too much like bragging to recite the license plate he'd memorized or the county in Oregon where the vehicle was registered last. "It's my job to notice what's going on in front of me."

She made a funny little sound in her throat that morphed into a cough. "Of course it is."

Did her dry tone imply there was something significant he hadn't noticed?

He frowned. "Why are you so interested in our new neighbors?"

"It's also *my* job to notice what's going on around me and something there is off. I don't know what it is but it's got my nose itching."

Her instincts were usually right on the money.

Once she called him in for backup on a routine traffic stop of a gray-haired couple driving a sedan with Ohio plates. None of his other officers would have found anything unusual about them but Wyn had caught a subtle vibe about the pair and ended up asking their permission to search the vehicle. When the couple refused, he brought in Rusty, the drug-sniffing dog from the Lake Haven Sheriff's Department, who found a quarter million dollars' worth of heroin sewn into the hollowed-out seats.

He would have said she had her father's cop instincts—except for the last few weeks he had served under her father.

"Have you met them already?"

"Yes. Well, the mom and the kids. Andrea Montgomery and two kids, Chloe and Will. I don't know if there's a dad in the picture. I didn't see any evidence of one but that doesn't mean anything. I said hello to them on my way to the trailhead. When I was coming down, I found her sprawled out on the trail with a sprained ankle. I helped her back to her house."

"You're on a roll. How many more people will you rescue today?"

She made a face. "I couldn't just leave her there."

No, she wouldn't. Wynona was like her father in many ways, full of compassion and concern.

"What makes you think something's off?"

"She doesn't seem very crazy about police officers. When I told her I worked for the local police department, you would have thought I told her I drowned kittens for a living."

"Plenty of people don't like the police. That doesn't make them criminals."

"I know that. This was something beyond dislike. More like…fear."

Perhaps she was exaggerating or had misunderstood the woman's reactions but, again, he trusted her gut. He had guys in the department who could shoot the hell out of a bull's-eye at the shooting range and one who could bench-press three-hundred-fifty pounds. None of them had Wynona's instincts with people.

"You think she's on the run?"

"Maybe. Maybe she's got an abusive ex in the background. Or maybe it's a custody case. Who knows?"

"Maybe she's witness protection." He couldn't resist teasing her a little. "Maybe she testified in a mob hit back in Oregon and now she's got a new identity here in Haven Point. Or maybe she's a superhero and her secret identity is a suburban mom."

She smacked his arm. "You can mock me all you want but something was up. My spidey sense is tingling about this one."

Cade dropped the teasing tone. "Want me to run the plates and see if anything pops?" he asked.

"That might be overkill at this point. She hasn't done anything wrong, as far as I can tell. I only wanted to give you a heads-up so you can keep an eye on things, especially since you're just across the street."

"I'll do that."

His phone timer went off and she raised an inquisitive brow.

"Just telling me the coals are ready for my dinner."

She looked shocked. "You're cooking? Really?"

"I guess you can call it cooking. Grilling, anyway. I'm throwing on a couple of steaks."

"Ah." Her stomach chose that moment to rumble with enthusiasm, so loudly that Pete looked up and cocked his head to the side. Wyn—the steadiest, most unflappable person he knew—looked flustered. Her cheeks turned pink and she gave an embarrassed-sounding laugh.

"That wasn't a hint, I swear. I've got leftover Chinese at home."

"I've got an extra steak, if you want it."

He wasn't sure which of them was more shocked by the invitation. She stared at him, eyes wide.

What was the big deal? They were friends. They had been for years, long before she ever came back to work for the Haven Point Police Department after her father's shooting and Cade became chief.

He had known her since she wore her hair in braids on either side and those light freckles had been much more pronounced. Back in the day, he used to spend every spare moment he could at the Baileys' house with his best bud, her brother Marshall. The warmth and peace there had been a foreign concept to him at first compared to the fighting and yelling at his own house but had quickly become addictive.

"Somebody ought to give you dinner," he said gruffly when she continued to look at him out of wide blue eyes. "It's not every day one of my officers runs into a burning building to save a couple of kids."

"Thank heavens for that." A dimple flashed beside the mouth he had never noticed was so lush and soft. "You don't have that many officers and you certainly can't suspend us all."

"True enough."

She appeared to consider the offer and he couldn't begin to guess what was going through her head. He seriously doubted she was entertaining the same thought that seemed to ricochet through his brain—that something had changed between them the moment he saw her come bursting through the doors of that burning barn.

"I would actually really enjoy a steak," she finally said. "I'm all dusty from the hike, though. Give me fifteen minutes to run home and change and toss a salad."

"You don't have to do that. The salad, I mean. I've got a head of lettuce in the refrigerator and can throw something together."

"I'll bring something. Just give me a few."

He was inordinately happy that she had agreed. Probably just lingering relief that the situation today had turned out so well, except for poor Caleb Keegan's broken ankle.

"They shouldn't take much time to cook. I'll wait

until you're back to throw them on. The coals can heat a little longer."

"Sounds good."

She headed for the door, whistling for Pete.

"You can leave him if you want. He can keep me company out on the deck."

Again, she looked a little surprised. "Okay. He could probably use some water. Young Pete, behave yourself. I'll be back in a few minutes."

She headed out into the soft dusk, leaving him with her dog, a couple of steaks and the uncomfortable feeling that he had just made a grave mistake.

CHAPTER SIX

DINNER. WITH CADE EMMETT.

What was *wrong* with her?

This had been a day for weird things. The whole moose debacle that she had nearly forgotten about, the fire, her suspension, their new neighbor and finally this.

She had tried so diligently to keep things casual and friendly between them. Since coming to work at the Haven Point PD, she felt as if she were walking on a knife's edge, afraid she might reveal her growing feelings for him.

Working side by side in a small, intimate department was awkward enough. She was the only female in the department and had to constantly pretend she was just one of the guys. With the rest of the officers, it wasn't an issue. She could laugh and joke, pull pranks and buy a round of beers at the Mad Dog on their downtime.

The problem was, deep in her heart lived the knowledge that she didn't *want* to be one of the guys to Cade.

She knew there was no other option. He was her boss. While she worked at the Haven Point Police Department, that was the only thing that mattered.

The day had already been surreal and she feared she

was too tired to keep up the pretense all evening. What if she did or said something that revealed the feelings that seemed to have always been a part of her but that had deepened and changed over the years?

This was going to be a nightmare.

A wiser woman would have simply thanked him for his kind invitation but declined. She was tired, it had been a long day, she should rest her lungs. She had a million ready excuses. What was she thinking, agreeing to spend more time with him, when it was taking everything she had to maintain this casual, businesslike relationship between them?

She could still back out. If she called him and told him she wasn't up for it tonight, he would probably even walk Young Pete back for her.

Or she could simply look at the evening as a simple meal shared by friends who shared a history going back to the days he used to come to the house to hang out with her brothers.

That was the safest route, she decided. She'd had plenty of practice keeping things casual between them. No reason a dinner between them wouldn't be the same.

She changed quickly out of her hiking shorts and dusty T-shirt into her favorite cropped jeans and a loose blouse then put on a little foundation and mascara and pulled her hair into her favorite messy bun, a much softer style than she would ever allow herself while she was on duty.

Here was that knife's edge again, the line she walked between looking presentable and not giving him the idea that she wanted to impress him.

Throwing the salad together took considerably less time than figuring out what to wear. She opted for a Mediterranean salad using feta cheese and Greek olives with the lettuce. Just before she headed out the door, she remembered she had several pieces of Aunt Jenny's fabulously creamy cheesecake in her freezer from the last time they had a family party. She took the cheesecake out and transferred a few pieces to a smaller container, then on a whim she cut up some strawberries she had on hand.

With a minute or two to spare out of the fifteen minutes she'd told him, she walked back to Cade's house on a cool, lovely night scented with climbing roses and honeysuckle from Herm and Louise Jacobs's place next door to her.

Cade had only been in his house a few years, had moved in some time after she moved back to Haven Point, but he had done a great deal in his off-hours to spruce it up.

Before he moved in, the logs had been faded and weather-beaten, the gardens overgrown. He had planted low-maintenance perennial gardens and spent a memorable week the previous summer sealing and re-chinking the logs—memorable to her, anyway, because he tended to work with his shirt off. Kat and Samantha had spent most of that week camped out at Wyn's place so they could watch him through the front window.

Her sister and Samantha Fremont were always trying to set up Wynona on dates with tourists they met in town or guys from Shelter Springs. She had gone with them a few times but the experiences were usually awkward affairs. Either the guys were intimidated because she was a police officer and hardly said a word all night like they were afraid she would arrest them if they spoke out of turn or they were titillated by the idea and wanted to know weird details like how she managed to frisk a guy without touching his junk.

She found both kinds equally abhorrent. She didn't even want to think about how long it had been since she had a serious relationship.

Okay, she knew. Five years. She had broken up with her last steady boyfriend the day before the fateful New Year's Eve party that had changed everything.

She pushed the memory away as she reached Cade's house.

In the moonlight now, his place looked tidy and comfortable, with that big Adirondack chair on the porch and the lavender blooming in the curving garden along the sidewalk.

It looked very different from the ramshackle shack where he had grown up. He had remade his environment just as he had remade himself.

As she approached the house, she saw lights glimmering in the back. She took a chance and decided he was probably on his deck overlooking the river.

She heard him before she saw him. At first she thought he might have a visitor or be talking on the phone. When she rounded the corner, she saw he was alone, with no phone in sight. Indeed, he was sitting on another Adirondack chair with his feet up on a matching footrest while he chatted companionably with her dog.

By the sound of it, they were discussing baseball.

She had to smile, charmed by the scene. He had created a comfortable oasis here beside the river, with big globe lights strung overhead, comfortable outdoor furniture and even a few big planters that overflowed with what looked like more perennials. She tried to picture Cade at the garden center outside Shelter Springs and couldn't quite manage it.

Young Pete sensed her first. He lifted his head and stretched his mouth in that expression that looked uncannily like a smile. A few seconds later, Cade turned, his gaze searching the darkness where she stood.

He was so blasted gorgeous, with that dark hair, the silver-blue eyes, the delicious hint of afternoon shadow covering his jaw and chin. If she didn't have her hands full of salad and cheesecake, she would have pressed a hand to her stomach and the sudden nerves jumping there.

Settle down. This was *Cade*. Her boss. Her brother's best friend. Her father's trainee. Yes, he had half the women in town head over heels for him. Yes, when he smiled that rare, bright smile, she forgot her own name. So what? She could come up with a million and one reasons she couldn't let any of that matter.

She stepped into the light and walked up the steps of the deck. For just an instant, she thought she saw something in his gaze, something hot and hungry. She felt an answering tug in her stomach but told herself she was only hungry—and completely imagining things.

"I figured you were back here."

"Where else would we be on a beautiful summer night in Haven Point?"

"Excellent point." She smiled and set down the containers of food on the patio table. "I brought salad and a couple pieces of my aunt Jenny's cheesecake I had in the freezer. It should be thawed by the time we're ready for dessert."

"Yum." He rose, all lanky, masculine grace, and headed for the grill. "I was hungry so I put the steaks on about ten minutes ago."

"Great. I'm starving."

"It won't be long now. Have a seat. I'm afraid I don't have much to drink in the house but beer."

"Ice water is great for me." Her throat had been scratchy since the fire, but she decided not to mention that for obvious reasons.

While he went inside the kitchen, she sank into the empty chair next to the one where Cade had been sitting. She reached down and petted her dog, who yawned and settled into a more comfortable position.

The night seemed soft and lovely, the kind of evening made for relaxing out under the stars.

The pine and spruce around his property lent an appealing citrusy tang to the air. She inhaled it, struck again by how very close she had come that afternoon to never seeing another glorious Haven Point sunset.

No doubt it was a reaction to the events of the day but the world seemed vibrant and new, overflowing with possibilities.

She hadn't taken nearly enough time to just sit and *be* lately. When she wasn't working, she was either helping out at her mother's or spending time with friends.

That was one more thing she intended to change, she resolved.

"It's so peaceful back here," she said when Cade brought her a glass with water with a slice of lemon in it. "I could sit here all evening, just listening to the water and the birds and the wind in the trees. If this were my back deck, I would never want to leave."

He laughed as he headed back to the grill. "Your house is two hundred yards away with the exact same view."

"Not the same at all, because of the way the river curves. You have a much better view of the mountains."

"That's only because I lost three trees in the flood."

He gestured to the river's edge, where she saw a trio of small saplings interspersed among the larger trees lining the bank.

The previous summer, the Hell's Fury rose to dangerous levels because of a dam break upstream. Everyone in Haven Point mobilized to fill sandbags and help people who lived along the river move their valuables to higher ground.

Because of the efforts of so many, local damage had been minimal, but a few properties still had been affected. She knew others whose basements had been flooded, their landscaping completely washed away.

"I'd forgotten you lost trees. They're pretty close too. You were lucky they didn't fall on the house."

"It was a near miss, actually. The branches at the crown of the biggest one brushed the house."

"Scary!"

He shrugged. "The trees were old and not healthy anymore and probably should have been taken out years ago. They obviously had weak root systems or they wouldn't have been impacted by the flood."

"It could have been much worse, for all of us. And now you have a beautiful view because of it."

"I guess that's the thing about floods and fires and other natural disasters," he said. "The damage from them can be devastating, but they can also be catalysts for change, offering entirely new perspectives."

It was an interesting way to look at things. "That's true. When I was little, we went to Yellowstone seven or eight years after the huge fires that burned more than a third of the park. I remember being so sad about all the snags of burned trees you could still see but my dad explained that the fires were necessary."

"Right. Lodgepole pinecones can't open and begin to reseed without being exposed to high heat."

"It's fascinating, isn't it? Certain plants and animals started to thrive only *because* of the fire and entirely new areas of the park were open to view for the first time in recent history."

Maybe the fire in Darwin Twitchell's barn had been *her* catalyst for change.

The thought seemed to resonate somewhere deep inside. It was true that she was seeing the world through different eyes than she had this morning. Maybe it was time to look at her *life* from a new perspective.

She needed a change.

The thought that had been swirling around her mind for some time seemed to come into clearer focus, just like a new mountain vista suddenly opening up because of a hundred-year flood or a devastating fire.

She was still thinking about it when Cade lifted the grill lid, releasing smoke and sizzle and a mouth-watering aroma.

"Looks like we're ready."

"Great." She closed the door on her jumbled thoughts and focused on food. "Much longer and I might have to start chomping on your shrubs like the moose I chased out of Aunt Jenny's driveway earlier today."

His smile flashed white in the dim light as he plated the steaks and carried them to the table.

She joined him, feeling suddenly self-conscious. Friends, she reminded herself. Friends and coworkers. That's all they were.

"So what cases are you working on that might need immediate attention while you're out?" he asked as she dished up salad and fruit into bowls.

She couldn't think of anything better to remind her of their work relationship than to bring up her suspension. Was that why he did it?

"Nothing pressing. I'm still looking for a break in the graffiti case and the copper-wire theft over at the conduit company. I've got a few leads I've been tugging. I can fill you in."

They talked about work for a few more minutes while she ate her salad. She cut into the steak and took a bite and had to pause just to savor the explosion of taste.

"Wow. That's fabulous."

"I've got a good marinade recipe. It makes all the difference."

"I need it! Who knew your mad grill talents have been wasted all these years frying up brats and burgers at the department barbecue!"

His smile was quick and genuine. "A guy needs a few skills to impress the ladies."

From the rumors she heard around town, Cade Emmett had plenty of impressive skills. She wouldn't exactly call him a player but he had a reputation for never dating the same woman more than a month—and always leaving her wanting more.

Suddenly feeling warm, she reached for her water glass and swallowed. Just her luck, the mouthful of water slid down the wrong way and she had to cough several times to clear it. By the time she finished, he was frowning.

"Throat still sore?"

It was, but she didn't want to tell him that. "No. I just drank too quickly. I'm fine."

He didn't look convinced. "What did Charlene have to say about you running into a burning building?"

"She wasn't very happy about it," she admitted.

"I can imagine. Poor woman. She's lost enough. She doesn't need to lose you too."

She felt the familiar ache for Wyatt and her father. She missed them both so much.

"Mom didn't lose me," she pointed out. "I'm still here for her to fuss and fret over and I plan to be for a long time."

"How is your mother doing?" he asked after a moment.

"I think it's been tough as she tries to adjust to being

a widow, but she seems to stay busy with her friends and her hobbies. She misses my dad, even though she really lost him two years before he died."

Cade's jaw tightened and a shadow flashed in his gaze. If she hadn't been looking at him closely, she might have missed it. A second later he became expressionless, his features as remote and stony as that mountain face up there. "The last few years weren't what anybody could call normal."

He always had the same reaction when anyone brought up her father. That dark shadow, the sudden tension, and then the careful concealment of his emotions. She didn't know if it was grief or anger... or something else.

There was something about her father's shooting two and a half years earlier that Cade refused to talk about. No matter how she tried to probe, he always shut her down until she finally got tired of the brick wall.

The night was too lovely, too perfect, for her to ruin it by trying again. She wasn't in the mood so she decided to change the subject.

"If you want the truth, she's a little annoyed that she now has three children who are over thirty—or close to it, anyway—and she doesn't have a single grandchild to show for it."

"You're not thirty yet."

"Almost. I reach that momentous milestone this fall."

He shook his head. "How can that be? Seems like just yesterday you were riding your little pink bike with the white basket and you and Wyatt were begging Marshall and me to let you come down to the river to fish with us."

She was nearly thirty years old, but was she happy?

Her life had become something she never expected. Back when she rode that pink bike and used to put baby dolls in the basket, she had wanted different things. She wanted to be a wife, a mother, and to have a job where she helped people. It seemed so silly now but when she was young she had dreamed of opening up an ice cream shop—because what made people happier than ice cream?

Did that girl even exist anymore? Wynona helped people, the way she always wanted, but not the way she had planned. And, she had to admit, they weren't often happy about her help.

She went to work every day at a job that no longer seemed right for her, then came home to an empty house. Something needed to change.

"Life has a funny way of rolling on," she said. "Before you know it, you wake up and you're almost thirty."

"Let's do our best to make sure you get there—which means no more crazy stunts like you did this afternoon."

The good food and the bite of creamy strawberry cheesecake she had tried mellowed her enough that she finally decided she should speak her mind.

"I can't understand why you're freaking out about what happened today. I'm a police officer. It's my job to put it all on the line for the people of Haven Point. Yes, this is a nice, quiet town but we both know that could change in a second. Look at my dad. His life changed forever in an instant because of one stupid junkie with a stolen handgun."

It was exactly the wrong thing to say. He tensed again, as he always did when she mentioned her dad and the shooting. He set down his fork as if he'd suddenly lost his appetite.

"Yeah. You're a police officer. *My* police officer," he growled. "It's my job to make sure you don't take unnecessary risks with your life or with civilians. The fire department was only minutes away and they were far better trained than you to extricate the boys safely."

The implication that she might have endangered the boys more somehow by rushing to get them out sent her temper flaring. "I made a judgment call—which is, again, exactly my job! We spend every day going with our instincts. Pull over this car for speeding, not that one. Stop to see what the suspicious-looking teens are trying to hide from me at the lakeshore. Take a chance and run into a burning building before the whole thing topples over. I have to be able to do my job."

"You have to be able to do your job *without harm*— to you or to anyone else."

Now she was hurt as well as angry. "I thought I had been doing that for the last two years. If you don't trust me and my instincts, maybe you ought to make the weeklong suspension more permanent."

"Maybe I should," he retorted.

His words were like a hard slap from a low-hanging branch on the trail, shocking, painful and totally out of the blue. Okay, maybe she was beginning to think it was time she considered a different career path but

she didn't need to hear it from her chief of police—
or her friend.

She took pride in her job. She was a Bailey, with all
the honor and responsibility that went along with that.
She had lost her father to the job and her beloved twin
brother. A great-uncle somewhere on her family tree
had been killed in a shoot-out with railroad outlaws.

She worked hard, she was never late, she tried to
treat the people she served with respect and courtesy.

Apparently that wasn't enough for Cade Emmett.
She rose from the table. "Are you saying you want to
fire me? What's stopping you?"

He rose as well, eyes dark with regret. "I'm sorry.
I didn't mean that."

"Seriously, don't let any sense of loyalty to my father because he was your mentor or obligation to Marshall because he's your best friend stop you. If you
don't think I can do the job, fire me and find someone
you can trust."

To her deep mortification, her voice wobbled on the
last words and she felt tears threaten. The events of that
long, exhausting, traumatic day seemed to press in on
her and she suddenly felt as hot and frightened as she'd
been crouching in that burning barn.

"I don't want to fire you, Wyn," he answered. "You're
my best officer and we both know it. You're coolheaded
in a crisis, you're dedicated and you genuinely care
about the people of Haven Point. I respect all my officers or I wouldn't have them working for me, but if I had
to pick one of them to have my back, it would be you."

"Then why are you making such a deal about what

happened today? I saved two boys' lives and all you've done is yell at me!"

"I thought you were dead. Don't you get that?"

Her breath caught at the raw intensity in his voice and she stared at him.

"When I rolled up to the scene and didn't see you, I thought you were inside that barn and we were going to find you burned to a crisp, along with the kids."

The words seemed to vibrate through the night, through her. She felt light-headed suddenly, as if she'd just run down to the lake and back.

"I had the situation under control," she whispered. She couldn't seem to take her gaze away from his, from those blue eyes that blazed with searing emotion.

"If something had happened to you on my watch, it would have destroyed me."

Destroyed him? His word choice rocked her. Yes, she might be the officer he wanted at his back in a crisis but losing her would have *destroyed* him? What did he mean?

She let out a shaky breath. "Nothing happened. I'm fine."

"Your family has lost enough. Wyatt. Your dad. The Baileys have given more than their share, don't you think?"

Ah. So it *was* about her family. "You were only worried about facing Charlene if something happened to me."

"I didn't think once about your mother, trust me."

"Marshall, Katrina or Elliot, then. They can all be pretty formidable."

"This has nothing to do with your family. I was worried about losing *you*."

She didn't know how to deal with this serious, intense Cade Emmett—and she was quickly losing her slippery grasp on the feelings she tried so hard to contain around him. In desperation, she made a lame attempt at humor.

"I get it," she said, forcing a smile, though she was pretty sure it trembled at the edges. "It's tough to find qualified cops willing to work for the paltry wages in Haven Point. You would have had to go through all the interviews, the pesky background checks, calling referrals, then finally training someone new. It's a pain."

"I wish this was only about the job," he said gruffly.

He was almost close enough to kiss her. Just another step. She swallowed and licked her lips, willing him to take it.

She had saved two lives today. No matter what he said, she knew she had done the right thing, showed a shaky but resolute courage that would have made her father proud. She had done it for the boys' sake, not because she wanted recognition or a commendation but surely she deserved *something* for her effort.

He wouldn't kiss her first, she suddenly realized—and not because he didn't want to. The complete certainty of that left her dizzy. Cade wanted to kiss her but he would never take that first step. His job was everything to him, his chance to become more than just another worthless, lazy Emmett.

She would simply have to take that step for both of them. Who said she couldn't claim her own reward?

Before she could talk herself out of it, she moved that final few inches between them, stood on tiptoe and pressed her mouth to his.

He stood frozen for only a second and then he made a low, almost desperate sound in his throat and returned the kiss with a fierce hunger.

CHAPTER SEVEN

FINALLY.

Everything inside her seemed to sigh, to turn soft and gooey.

His mouth was warm, determined, and tasted like strawberry cheesecake and mint and Cade.

She had wondered forever what it would be like to kiss the man. Now she knew—just as she knew that one taste would never be enough.

She had guessed somehow that he wouldn't be one of those sloppy, take-charge, my-way-or-nothing guys and she was absolutely right. He teased at her mouth, seduced her, seeming to know instinctively just what she liked.

He made that low sound in his throat again and pulled her closer and she couldn't believe she was really here, kissing Cade Emmett on a magical June night. She wrapped her arms more tightly around him. She couldn't get close enough and everything about him seemed to make her ache with longing.

The men she tended to date the last few years could be summed up in one word: *safe*. They were nice guys, mild-mannered, nonthreatening. She could trace the reason she gravitated toward them to one horrible night in her life when she had been helpless and afraid.

She dated them once or twice and it was easy to keep them at arm's length.

Not a single one of those men in five years had ever made her feel as if the world was new and bright and wonderful, as if *she* were new.

Cade wasn't safe. A woman would be foolish to make the mistake of thinking he was. He was hard, dangerous, and could overpower her in a second, regardless of all her self-defense training.

Despite that, she wasn't afraid for an instant. She wanted this moment, this night, to go on and on forever while the globe lights gleamed overhead and the river rushed by beyond the trees and she was aware of each precious beat of her heart.

SOMEWHERE IN THE murky corners of his brain, warning bells were sounding but Cade ignored them.

Wynona was soft, warm and tasted like heaven—like vanilla and plump strawberries and luscious, sinful cream.

He couldn't think straight when she sighed under his mouth, when she wrapped her arms around him and pressed her delicious curves against him.

She was so tough most of the time, brisk and no-nonsense in her uniform, and he found it incredibly seductive to know that beneath all the layers she showed to the world hid this warm, sweetly enthusiastic woman who trembled when he kissed her and kissed him like she couldn't get enough.

He couldn't either. He wanted more and more and more. He wanted to lay her down on the warm, moon-lit grass and lose himself inside her.

Some careful barrier he had never fully been aware of seemed to have toppled between them. The risky situation today—those terrible moments when he had been so terrified of losing her—had shattered it into ruins.

He felt some weird inevitability, as if they had both been holding their breath for a long time—years, even—waiting for this moment.

She murmured his name against his mouth on a sigh and the breathless sound of it rippled down his spine as if her fingers had trailed over each ridge.

He wanted them there, her fingers on his skin, ev-erywhere. Forget the grass. He would take her inside where he had a big, comfortable bed. They could spend all night exploring each other, learning each other's se-crets and celebrating that she was so gloriously alive.

Anticipation and hunger coiled inside him and he was just trying to work out the logistics of moving them both in that direction when his phone suddenly rang, the sound ringing through the night like a freak-ing piercer siren.

He froze, his breathing ragged and his thoughts tan-gled. She went still as well, blue eyes hazy with desire.

All too soon, his brain kicked into gear and re-ality crashed into him like an 18-wheeler. He men-tally churned through every swearword he knew and none of them seemed nearly strong enough. What was he doing? This was *Wyn* in his arms. His officer, his friend, John Bailey's daughter.

He was so totally screwed.

All these weeks and months and years of keeping his attraction to her under control and he threw everything away the moment her soft, tantalizing mouth touched his.

Yeah, she had kissed him first—for about half a second before he had devoured her.

He closed his eyes, wishing more than anything that they could stay wrapped around each other out here on a sweet June evening and forget the rest of the world existed.

The phone rang again, a harsh reminder of all the responsibilities he had just ignored for a few fleeting moments of lust.

"I...need to take that."

She eased away from him, her eyes still a little unfocused and her mouth swollen and lush from his kiss. She looked tousled and aroused and his body surged with hunger.

"Oh. Um. Right."

She leaned against the table while he pulled his phone out of the pocket of his cargo pants. He knew from the ringtone it was the police station.

"Yeah? Emmett here."

"Sorry to bug you when you're off duty, Chief. This is Jesse Fisher. Officer Fisher," the earnest rookie corrected himself. "I just got a call from Kelli Hansen down at the boat rental place that a couple from Nevada never brought their fishing boat back and they're not answering their cell phones. Their vehicle's still in the parking lot. Even though it's only just past nine and they're only an hour beyond the time they were supposed to return, I'm wondering if we should start a search party, them being tourists and all."

For about half a second, he had a hard time figuring out why he should care about a couple of tourists from Nevada when he could be kissing Wynona Bailey under a star-drenched sky but he forced himself to shove the thought aside.

His job. His town. He needed to focus on the needs of the people of Haven Point, not on his own frustrated longing for a woman he could never have.

"Have you called Chief Gallegos?"

"Not yet, sir. I wanted to check with you first."

Jesse was green, just a year out of POST. Like Wynona, he had good instincts. Unlike her, he was afraid to act on them.

"Let's start with Chief Gallegos. Have him send a couple of volunteer search-and-rescue boats to check out our side of the lake. More than likely, they ran out of gas or flooded the engine and are trying to row her to the marina. Or they could have headed up to Shelter Springs and lost track of the time. Before you call the volunteer searchers, check with the marina up there and see if they've seen a boat matching the description."

"Good idea. So call the Shelter Springs marina then send out the volunteer search and rescue if they haven't heard anything from them."

"Let's start with that. Call me if the situation changes.

I can be there in five minutes if you or Chief Gallegos decide you need me."

"Got it. Thanks. Sorry again to disturb your downtime."

He didn't want to think about how much worse he might have made the situation if Jesse *hadn't* disturbed him. He ended the call and, dreading the next conversation ahead of him, turned to face her.

"Wyn—"

She shook her head. "Don't say it. Don't apologize or say what a mistake this was."

"I *have* to. *Mistake* is too mild a word for what this was. I was out of line to kiss you. So far out of line I can't even *see* the freaking line from here."

Damn it. Why did she have to look so delectable there in the moonlight, with her lips swollen, her eyes soft and needy, strands of hair sliding out of her sexy little updo thingy.

He frowned, trying desperately to remember all the reasons he couldn't kiss her again.

"I'm the police chief, you're my officer. If the mayor or anybody on the city council found out about this, we would both lose our jobs."

"You seriously think I would blab to McKenzie?"

"She's your best friend, isn't she? You're going to be her bridesmaid in a month."

"That doesn't mean I tell her every time I tangle tongues with a guy!"

Just how often did she tangle tongues with a guy? The question was none of his business but he still wanted to know.

He suddenly realized he had no idea if she was dating anyone. How was it possible that they worked so closely together and he didn't know more about her romantic relationships? Some detective he was.

She often teased him about his love life—which wasn't nearly as active as everybody else seemed to think and had shriveled to nonexistent in recent months for reasons he couldn't have accurately identified—but she shared next to nothing about her own. The omission might have been intentional on her part, but then he hadn't asked, either, for the simple reason that he didn't really want to know.

This was so messed up.

How was he supposed to work beside her now, to laugh and joke and trade stories like they always had? He was very much afraid he would always be remembering how she tasted, that little hint of strawberries and cream, and the sexy little hitch in her breath when he licked at the corner of her mouth...

He let out a long breath. "It's been a...crazy day for both of us and I completely lost my head. Can we just chalk it up to that and forget the last few moments ever happened?"

He knew that wasn't likely on his part, now that he had tasted the silky sweetness of her mouth and discovered just how perfectly her curves fit against him. He wouldn't be able to forget anytime soon—but he was sure as hell going to try.

"You really think we can forget this?"

If they didn't, working conditions at the small Haven Point Police Department would become intolerable.

The awkwardness would be off the charts and the other officers would be sure to pick up on it.

"We have no choice, in order for us to continue working together."

She gazed at him for a long, wordless moment while the river murmured and an owl hooted somewhere downstream. Finally she tucked one of those loose strands of hair behind her ear with fingers that trembled just a little. She must have sensed it too because she quickly curled them into her palm and dropped her arm to her side.

"Fine. Whatever you say. Thank you for the steak. It was delicious. I should be going. As you said, it's been a crazy day and I'm exhausted."

She turned away and began gathering up the dishes from his patio table.

"You don't have to do that," he protested.

"I'll just help you carry them in. You can clean everything up later, when I'm gone."

They worked together in silence without any of the easy camaraderie they usually shared.

His fault.

He had taken something he wanted without thinking of the consequences, and now everything between them had changed.

Idiot man.

Did Cade really think she could pretend those moments of kissing him had never happened, after all this time of wondering what it would be like?

She was quite certain that kiss would be branded

in her brain forever. The heat of his mouth, firm and delicious. His arms around her, making her feel cherished and powerful at the same time. His mouth, teasing, tantalizing, seducing.

How would she ever be able to forget it?

She'd heard rumors, of course. Half the women in town were in love with the gorgeous, slightly dangerous police chief. It wasn't only the eligible females who pined after him. After two years of working for the department, she was finally used to the disappointed sighs from ladies, young and old, when she showed up on a call instead of him.

She was asked at least three or four times a day where that nice Chief Emmett was and sometimes she thought certain females she wouldn't mention called the police on every little thing, just in hopes he would be the one to respond to the emergency.

Now she knew the hype was not an exaggeration.

When she returned to work, she would have to sit across from him during department briefings and try not to remember the way he had kissed her with fiercely intense concentration, as if all his secret fantasies had just come true and he didn't want to miss a second of it.

Good luck with that.

She wasn't going to do his dishes for him, even though her mother probably would have reprimanded her for it. What her mother didn't know, and all that.

She helped carry the last dishes into his tidy kitchen then picked up Pete's leash. "I'll leave you the rest of the cheesecake."

She wasn't sure she would ever be able to take a

bite of cheesecake again without remembering him. That was a crying shame, since she loved cheesecake.

"Thanks," he murmured.

"I guess I'll see you in a week, then." She gripped the dog's leash and headed for the door.

To her dismay, he followed right behind her. "I'll walk you home."

Didn't he realize a girl sometimes needed a minute to herself to catch her breath after kissing a guy like him?

Or maybe that was only Wyn.

"Totally not necessary." She had a black belt in Krav Maga, for heaven's sake. She could certainly take care of herself when walking two hundred yards down her own quiet road in the sleepy town of Haven Point.

"Necessary or not, I'm walking you home."

She had no chance of talking him out of it. The man could be as stubborn as she was.

Why had she ever even entertained the idea that she might be able to convince him to ease her suspension? Once he made up his mind about something, Cade was immovable—which didn't bode well for her chances that he would ever kiss her again.

As they set off the short distance to her house, Pete took the lead, his nose sniffing all the edges where concrete met grass. She couldn't resist glancing at the house across the street. The curtains and blinds were shut tight, without even a sliver of light peeking through. The bikes and balls had been hidden away in the garage, the van pulled out of sight.

If she hadn't spoken with the woman and children

herself earlier, she might have thought the house still stood empty. It was a mystery she was determined to solve, though she accepted she couldn't do anything about it tonight.

She was painfully aware of him beside her, big and tough and gorgeous. That kiss. How on *earth* was she supposed to pretend it never happened?

"How's your family?" she asked, seizing the first topic she could find to fill the awkward silence.

If anything, his features suddenly appeared even more stark and remote in the moonlight. "Not that great, to tell you the truth."

"What's going on?"

His mouth tightened as if he regretted saying anything. He said nothing for a long moment and she had a feeling he was trying to decide whether to answer.

Finally he sighed. "Marcus is in jail again in Boise. His wife called to tell me right before you knocked on the door."

"DUI again?" she asked. He had confided in her a few months back about his brother losing his job and running into legal troubles.

"I don't think he's going anywhere for a while. His wife doesn't want to bail him out this time."

She was grateful that he could still talk to her as friends, at least.

"You're not going to, are you?"

"No, but Christy wants me to talk to him. What do I say?"

"That's a tough one."

"I just want to shake him and tell him to get over

himself and think about what he's doing to his kids. If he loves them, how can he put them through the same damn things we had to endure?"

The frustration in his voice and the echo of old pain made her throat ache. She longed to reach for his hand, to share some of that burden but knew she didn't have the right.

She could only guess at what his childhood had been like after his mother died, when Cade had been expected by his worthless father to take care of himself and his brothers. She knew a little of it, things she had figured out herself and bits and pieces she had picked up from overhearing her parents talk when they thought no one was listening.

Walter Emmett, Cade's father, had been an alcoholic, in and out of jail, who eventually died a few years ago after his latest prison stint. She knew Cade was the one who held his family together, who got his brothers off to school, helped them with homework.

When Cade was eighteen, Walter Emmett went to prison again for robbery and Cade's younger brothers were sent to live with relatives in southeastern Idaho. Her parents and Marshall tried to persuade him to move in with them for the last four months of his senior year of high school, but he refused.

Instead, barely eighteen, he stayed by himself in their run-down home in Sulfur Hollow, working after school to keep the utilities on.

The day after graduation, he left for Marine Corps basic training. Through hard work, he became a military policeman and after two deployments, he left the

Marines and came back to Haven Point to work for her father.

Cade was an extraordinary man.

Many people never managed to rise above the difficult circumstances of their youth and chose instead to re-create it in their own lives. Despite everything, he had broken the cycle to become a man who was respected by just about everyone in Haven Point, even the lawbreakers.

Was it any wonder so many women in Haven Point found him irresistible?

Including her, apparently.

She tightened her hold on Pete's leash as they neared her house. "That's what you have to say to him. Remind him of what things were like for all of you growing up and tell him he owes his children better than you had. We can't change the past but that doesn't mean we have to live there either."

"That is absolutely right."

When they reached her mailbox, Pete padded up the sidewalk and waited there for her to unlock the door for him.

"Thank you for walking me home. Can you believe we made it all this way and not a single person tried to attack us?"

He gave a mock scowl at her dry tone. "Don't press your luck, Officer Bailey. You're not inside yet and you never know who might be lurking in the bushes."

She didn't have anything to worry about from random attackers. The man walking beside her, however, was definitely a threat—at least to her emotional health.

Memories of their kiss teased at the edges of her memory and she did her best to hide her sudden shiver.

When they reached her door, he stopped and faced her, his jaw set. "I have to say this one more time, Wyn. I should never have lost my head earlier. I swear, it won't happen again but if you think you need to file a complaint with the mayor and city council, I completely understand."

She stared at him, hurt that he would even think her capable of such a thing—especially when her only complaint was that he didn't kiss her long enough!

She wanted this whole thing to go away. What had she been thinking, to kiss him like that? She hadn't been thinking, obviously, otherwise she would have realized it would change *everything*.

"I kissed *you*. I'm the one who wasn't thinking straight. I don't know, maybe smoke inhalation rattled my brain or something. It was an impulse, I acted on it and now it's done. It was one kiss. Surely our working relationship— *and* our friendship—can survive one kiss."

A muscle flexed in his jaw but he said nothing.

Did he think they *couldn't* get past this?

The kiss had affected him more than he wanted to let on, she suddenly realized. He was attracted to her and he didn't want to be.

Was she supposed to find that flattering or offensive?

Neither, she decided. It just *was*.

"Absolutely nothing has changed," she lied. "*We* haven't changed. When I return to work in a week—tanned, relaxed and well rested—things will be just as they were between us an hour ago."

"I hope that's true." He didn't look optimistic, however. He looked…troubled, his forehead furrowed and his eyes murky.

He seriously thought he had risked his job by kissing her. She couldn't do anything to help ease the stress he felt about his brother or the scars he still carried from childhood but she could help him with *this*.

"You're the one who said we should forget it. That's what I intend to do and I suggest you do the same. You've got enough to worry about right now. You're going to have to try to survive a busy June week on a lake full of crazy tourists while you're short your best officer. That problem, at least, is entirely your own fault."

He gazed at her for another long moment, then the edge of his mouth lifted into a faint smile. He looked faintly relieved at her determinedly casual attitude. "No matter how rough it gets, I'm still not lifting your suspension early. I'll see you in a week, Officer Bailey."

He reached down to give her dog a farewell pat. "See you later, Pete, buddy."

"Good night," Wyn said.

He waited until she unlocked her door and went inside before he headed back down her sidewalk toward Riverbend Road and home.

She watched him for just a moment, then headed through to the kitchen and poured water for Pete and for her. The window was open and she stopped for a moment to gaze out at the dark night and listen to the soothing sound of the endless river.

Yeah. She was a big fat liar.

She had told him nothing had changed while the truth was, she suddenly felt as if the entire world had shifted. The repercussions seemed to ripple around her like she had just jumped into that river, still icy with runoff.

How could she go back to being merely friends with him when she could no longer avoid the hard truth that she wanted so much more?

She had always felt something for Cade. When she was fourteen and he had been the rough-edged kid hanging around with her brothers, she thought it had been sympathy mixed with a healthy dose of forbidden crush.

She knew about his family, knew he had a rough home life, knew her dad had tried to mentor him and show him he could reshape his own destiny.

He wasn't the first young man John Bailey had tried to help out along the way, nor was he the last. Yet Cade was the only one who left her flustered and hot every time he came around.

Over the years, that secret crush had developed into affection and respect. She had chosen to focus on those things, not the little hitch in her heartbeat around Cade, especially after the terrible New Year's Eve when she was twenty-four, when everything changed.

She could do that now. Just put it aside and focus on her life—and on figuring out what she wanted to do with the rest of it.

CHAPTER EIGHT

Wynona quickly decided she wasn't very good at doing nothing.

Though she had gone to sleep fully intending to stay in bed all morning and catch up on reading on this, the first day of her suspension, she woke before sunrise, exhausted from a night of twisted, tortured dreams.

She only remembered the last few bizarre scenes her subconscious had spun right before she awoke. In one, she had been back in the middle of smoke and flames and fear, trying her best to comfort two scared little boys when Cade galloped through riding a moose, of all things. He had scooped up the boys and rode out with them while telling her she was going to have to stay inside the burning building for the entire length of her seven-day suspension.

The dream had shifted then and she was on his deck with the river murmuring past and the night air swirling sweet and cool around them. Cade kissed her, his mouth hot and urgent on hers. In the dream, they kissed for much longer than they had in real life, until she felt like she was as hot and breathless as she had been inside that structure fire.

He murmured to her in that low, sexy bedroom voice

that he wanted to do more than kiss her, that he wanted to do *everything* with her, but he couldn't. When she asked him why, he calmly pointed out that her clothes were on fire and he didn't want to get burned. In horror, she looked down and discovered she was wearing her full Haven Point Police Department uniform, which was completely engulfed in flames.

In the dream, she cursed at him for not telling her and letting her ruin her last good uniform, and then she ran to the bank of the Hell's Fury, ready to jump in, where she found Andrea Montgomery, her foot in a cast, floating down the river on an inner tube, her children right behind her like little ducklings.

Andrea told her she wasn't welcome there but Wyn insisted she had no choice. Couldn't they see her clothes were on fire?

She awoke right before she jumped into the icy waters.

Dreams. What the heck, right? Sometimes her subconscious was seriously whacked.

Sensing Wyn was awake, Pete padded over to be let out. She groaned and pushed the last tendrils of weirdness away as she climbed out of her warm bed and grabbed a robe.

She let him out, then stood watching the pink rim of sunrise above the mountains before letting him back inside again a few moments later. She thought about going back to bed but she was wide-awake now, too restless and unsettled to even settle back between the sheets with a good book.

Instead, she changed into work clothes then spent

several hours weeding the perennial flower beds her grandmother had planted years ago. Wyn tried to maintain them but with her hectic schedule, it was a haphazard effort at best.

She had all the time in the world now, she told herself. Might as well do it right. When she was satisfied all the morning glory and dandelions, curly dock and those pesky mallow had been ruthlessly eradicated, she turned her attention to the inside of her house and all the jobs she always claimed she didn't have time to finish.

Two hours later, her kitchen cupboards had been scrubbed and organized and her closet plucked clean of all the clothes she no longer wore. The excess now filled a couple of bags in the back of her SUV that were destined for Goodwill.

So. That was done. How she would fill the remaining days of her suspension, she had no idea but at least her house was shipshape.

A quick glance at her clock told her she had more than enough time to clean up and still make it to the regular monthly potluck lunch held at McKenzie's store.

The doorbell rang just as she was heading for the shower. She switched directions and opened it to find her mother standing on the doorstep carrying two large tote bags.

"Mom! Hi. This is a surprise. What's all this?"

Her mom headed straight back to the kitchen, completely comfortable in the home where she had been raised. "I know you told me you would grab something last night but I decided to bring dinner anyway. I came over about eight thirty but I guess I still missed you. Nobody answered the door and I couldn't find the key under the doormat."

Wyn followed her. "I'm a police officer, Mom. I don't keep my spare house key in an obvious place like under the doormat. I've told you that. The key is under Grandma's naughty garden gnome."

"Oh, I'd forgotten. You've told me that before but maybe I've just blocked it out. I can't believe you didn't throw that awful thing out after you moved here."

"It makes me laugh," she said of the little creature, forever grinning saucily while it flipped the bird to everyone in sight.

Charlene shook her head, one more way she didn't understand her daughter, but said nothing more about it as she reached into the bag and pulled out a covered casserole dish then set it on the counter. "You and McKenzie must have had a lot to talk about. Are you planning her bridal shower?"

For a moment, she didn't know what her mother meant, until she remembered she had fibbed to keep her mother from coming over and fussing over her and had told her she had plans with McKenzie.

Oops.

Guilt pinched at her, especially when Charlene unloaded more dishes onto the kitchen counter until she had set enough food for a good-sized dinner party onto the cooktop.

"Wow. That's…a lot of food."

"I know, dear, but I couldn't help myself. You know I cook when I'm upset."

Yes, Wyn could attest to that. Her chubbiness as a girl had been proof that her mother had often been upset. The stress diet Wyn had gone through after that horrible January and the rigorous regimen of fitness and self-defense classes she'd turned to before applying for the police academy had finally eradicated the last of her baby fat.

"So tell me about the shower. Where is it going to be? Is there a theme? Do you need help with the food or the decorations?"

Yeah, the truth always came out. Sometimes she was sure her mother had a built-in lie detector. Cade should seriously put her to work interrogating suspects.

"I didn't end up actually meeting up with McKenzie last night," she finally admitted.

Charlene raised a carefully shaped eyebrow. "Oh. That must be why she seemed a little discombobulated this morning and tried to make something up when I bumped into her at the grocery store and asked her about it."

Great. Now she would have to explain to McKenzie why she had shamelessly used her for a cover story.

"If you weren't with her, where did you go?"

Charlene obviously had known from the moment she walked in that Wyn had lied to her about her whereabouts. She had no choice but to tell her mother the truth now.

She went to her mom and hugged her. "I'm sorry. I told you that because I just needed to be alone. You know how I get when I'm stressed."

Her mother sniffed. "Yes. You take after your father that way."

"I ended up going on a hike up the Mount Solace trail. On my way back, I stopped to talk about a couple of cases with Cade. He was grilling steaks and he invited me over, sort of a spur-of-the-moment thing."

And then he kissed me until I couldn't think straight.

Even without knowing the last bit that Wyn kept to herself, Charlene huffed out a breath. "Well, he's got some nerve, suspending you one minute and having you over for dinner the next."

She didn't want her mother thinking poorly of Cade. Charlene adored him and fussed over him just like she did the rest of the Bailey clan and Wynona couldn't ruin that for either of them. He had too little softness and tenderness in his life and she didn't want to deprive him of any of it.

"He's doing what he thinks is best," she said softly. "I'm not saying I agree with him but he's the chief of police and it's his decision."

"Didn't you even try to change his mind while you were having dinner with him?"

She'd been a little busy, what with the kissing and all.

"You know how stubborn he can be," she hedged.

"Oh, do I ever." To her relief, Charlene let herself be distracted. "He was more hardheaded than Elliot, Wyatt and Marshall *combined*. I always said Cade had more of your father in him than any of John's own boys."

"A little stubbornness isn't a bad thing when you're

the chief of police," she said, used to the ache of sorrow burning in her throat for the man she had admired and loved so very much.

"I suppose. He does a good job, doesn't he? Your father would have been a hard act to follow for any man, after twenty-five years as the chief of police, but Cade has stepped right into his shoes."

"Yes. Dad trained him well."

She didn't want to talk about Cade—thinking about him all morning had been enough, thanks—so she deliberately changed the subject by gesturing to the containers on the countertop.

"You do remember I live alone, right? What am I supposed to do with all this food?"

"It's not that much. Only lasagna, bread sticks, salad and brownies. And, yes. I do remember you live alone. How can I forget? I just don't know why. You go on plenty of dates."

Here it was. Her mother's favorite topic. From experience, she knew enough to move off that subject quickly or Charlene wouldn't let up.

"I'm actually headed to McKenzie's for the Haven Point Helping Hands luncheon. Why don't you come with me?"

"Today?"

"Yes, as soon as I clean up. They would love to have you. I know you always said you couldn't come to the luncheons because you felt guilty leaving Dad at the nursing home by himself. Maybe it's time to start doing all these things again that you used to enjoy."

Her mother glanced at her watch, then back at her

with an oddly guilty look on her features. "I can't today. I'm sorry. I already have plans. If I'd known about it, I would have tried to make it. Maybe next time. Text me when the next one is and I'll put it on my calendar."

What plans did she have? And why did the mention of them seem to make Charlene so nervous?

"Okay. I'll let you know. Thanks again for the food. It's enough to feed a soccer team but maybe I'll freeze it."

She would never be able to eat an entire large pan of lasagna. Maybe she would invite a bunch of girlfriends over to watch a movie or something, now that she had all this free time. Devin and McKenzie had crazy schedules but would both try to make it. Katrina and her best friend, Samantha, had active social lives on the weekend but they might be available on a weeknight.

"Sounds good, dear," Charlene said. Her mother's cell phone alerted her of an incoming text and she pulled it out of her pocket then smiled a little at the message before she quickly shoved it away. If Wyn wasn't mistaken, her mother's cheeks looked a little pinker than they had a moment ago.

"Well, I have to go," her mother said. "I'll call you later. Have fun at your lunch."

"I will. And you have fun at your…other plans."

Charlene's smile seemed distracted as she let herself out.

Wyn slid the plate of brownies into the microwave to make sure Pete didn't suddenly get a hankering for them while she was gone. Plastic wrap would provide no barrier whatsoever to him but he hadn't yet learned to work the buttons on the appliances.

Whatever was she going to do with all this food?

The answer came to her while she was in the shower. When she returned from lunch, she would take it over to Andrea Montgomery's house. It would give her the perfect excuse to check on the little family and see how Andrea's ankle fared.

"Look who's here! It's the hero of the year!" McKenzie hurried forward when Wynona walked into Point Made Flowers and Gifts an hour later carrying a pasta salad and gave her a big kiss on the cheek. "Too bad we already named Mick Sargent the grand marshal for Lake Haven Days or you would have been a *lock*."

Thank heaven for small favors. She was spared that, at least.

"How fun, to have you here during the day." Devin Shaw—McKenzie's sister—beamed. "Your schedule is usually so busy at the police department."

"I've got nothing but time this week," she said.

"Why is that?" Eliza Caine asked.

Wynona didn't want to go into the whole story but her sister helpfully did it for her.

"Because Cade Emmett suspended her for a week," Katrina grumbled. "Can you believe it? She runs into a burning building to save two little boys and ends up losing a week's salary because of it."

"That's just not right," sweet Hazel Brewer exclaimed.

"I thought that boy had more sense," her sister Eppie piped up.

"Sounds like he was just jealous that he wasn't the one getting all the attention," Linda Fremont piped up with her usual negativity.

"I don't believe that was the case at all," Wyn said. Again, she was in the uncomfortable position of having to defend Cade. She didn't want her friends to think poorly of him, especially when his reasons weren't without merit.

"Chief Emmett was concerned that I jeopardized the boys' safety by going into the fire without protective gear, especially after he ordered me not to. It's a personnel issue and I would rather not talk about it."

If something had happened to you on my watch, it would have destroyed me.

His hoarse words came back to her, low and intense, sending butterflies twirling through her insides.

"What's the project today?" she asked, to change the subject and distract herself.

"We're making these handy bucket organizers to sell at our booth at Lake Haven Days," McKenzie said. "We're painting the lower part of the bucket with chalkboard paint so you can write what's inside on the side. You can be on paint duty, if you want."

Easy enough, though she didn't know why people couldn't just look inside or, better yet, keep track of where they put things.

Wyn sat down at an empty spot and picked up a brush. She didn't consider herself the most crafty of people but these gatherings, when she could fit them into her schedule, were more about hanging out and visiting with friends, as well as the warm glow of knowing she was helping someone in need.

All proceeds from sales of their monthly projects went toward benefiting various endeavors like the local food bank and the Haven Point library. Over the years, the group had raised thousands of dollars—and had tons of fun doing it.

"Has anybody met the woman who moved into the Baker house on Riverbend Road?" Wyn asked after a few moments of painting.

"That's the cute house near you that has been empty for so long, isn't it?" Eliza Caine said.

McKenzie looked thrilled. "I didn't know somebody new moved in!"

"Yes. A woman named Andrea Montgomery. She has two children, a boy and a girl. Chloe and Will."

"Is there a husband in the picture?" Linda asked with a disapproving sort of look.

"One of the kids mentioned a dad but I don't know anything about him. I've only met her and the kids."

"Pretty woman with auburn hair and two kids who look just like her?" Barbara Serrano asked.

"Yes. That's her."

"They stopped at the diner a couple of nights ago. I thought they might be tourists but she did ask me if I knew the library hours."

"Is she renting or buying?" Linda asked. "Too many new renters are moving in, now that the new Caine Tech facility is opening up."

The town's economy had greatly improved in the last nine months since Ben Kilpatrick, McKenzie's fiancé, and Aidan Caine made plans to move a branch of Caine Tech to town. Previously floundering businesses were suddenly doing much better and more were opening up all the time. Somehow, Linda Fremont still found plenty to complain about.

"I don't know the answer to that," Wyn said. "I just wondered if anybody met them, that's all. She sprained her ankle yesterday on the river trail. I gave her your name and number, Dev."

She glanced at Devin Shaw and saw a quick flash of knowledge there before the physician hid it.

"Thanks. I appreciate that" was all she said.

McKenzie didn't know if Andrea had come in to see her but she suspected so from her friend's response. Even if she had asked, Devin wouldn't have been able to answer because of privacy laws.

"I'm taking in a meal later today if anybody else has one on hand," she said.

"I do!" Eliza exclaimed. "Sue has been spending the last month putting up some freeze-ahead meals for us since she and Jim are finally taking that cruise to Alaska Aidan and I gave them for Christmas last year. They're only going to be gone two weeks but Sue seems to think we'll starve without her—and she also seems to forget that I like to cook. I was looking forward to having that glorious kitchen at Snow Angel Cove to myself, if you want the truth, especially now that I'm past the morning sickness."

It took a moment for that veiled announcement to sink in, and then everybody started exclaiming about the welcome news that Eliza was expecting a baby. She and Aidan were the sweetest couple, both completely perfect for each other. Every time she was with the two of them, Wyn was torn between delight at their obvious happiness and feeling small because of her own little twinges of stark loneliness in comparison.

"What does Miss Maddie think about becoming a big sister?" Wyn asked of Eliza's adorable daughter.

"She's over the moon, already keeping a journal filled with notes and pictures about all the things she plans to teach the baby."

"And do you know if it's a boy or girl yet?" Eppie, Hazel's sister, asked—no doubt she was planning to start work on one of her beautifully crocheted baby blankets.

"Not yet. I'm not sure we want to spoil the surprise but ask me again in a few months. Who knows? We may change our minds."

"How's Aidan doing?" McKenzie asked with a grin.

"He's gone slightly crazy, of course, already trying to improve on all the pregnancy planning apps out there. But back to your question, Wynona—I've got at least twenty meals ready to go in my freezer. I can easily spare five or six."

"Can I run out and pick them up when we're done here?" she asked.

"Of course."

"I don't want to overwhelm her. I just wanted to help her feel welcome in town."

"That sounds lovely. Just swing by the house when we're done here and you can take what you want."

The conversation turned to the upcoming Lake

Haven Days and Wyn was content to listen as she painted.

These activity lunches were one of her favorite things about living back in her hometown. Yes, there were a couple of strong personalities, the occasional tiff, a few newcomers she didn't really know yet, but in general, these women each worked hard individually and collectively to make Haven Point a warm, welcoming town.

She was thinking about it while the conversation flowed around her, not really paying attention until she heard her name.

"I still can't understand what's going on in Cade's head to suspend her," Linda Fremont said.

"If it's any consolation, he's getting flak for his decision," McKenzie said.

"I gave him an earful this morning when he came for breakfast at the diner," Barbara said. "And I wasn't the only one. All the regulars gave him the what for, I can tell you that. Ed Bybee and Archie Peralta didn't let up for a good ten minutes."

"Maybe that's why he was a real bear at this morning's public-safety planning meeting for Lake Haven Days," McKenzie said. "He growled at everybody and he nearly told Carl Palmer to pull his head out of his ass but stopped himself just in time."

Perhaps he hadn't slept well either. She gazed down at the metal bucket in her hands. Had he suffered from tangled dreams too? Some tiny part of her sincerely hoped so—which probably made her a terrible person.

"Maybe he just needs a date," Samantha Fremont

suggested impishly. "Word on the street is, Haven Point's sexiest bachelor is keeping to himself these days."

"Maybe he's seeing somebody and we just don't know about it," Devin suggested. "As much as we might like to think otherwise, we don't always know everything that's going on in Haven Point."

"Speak for yourself." McKenzie grinned.

"We might not know everything, but we do know Cade Emmett," Katrina said. "The man is a heart-breaker with a capital *H*."

"That man could leave his badge on my bedside table anytime." Roxy Nash just about purred the words.

Everybody but Wyn laughed. Wyn knew Roxy the least of all the women here, and she decided at that moment she didn't much like her.

The other woman was a project manager for Caine Tech and had moved in a few months ago near McKenzie along Redemption Bay. She was tall, lean, gorgeous. All the things Wyn would never be. She also seemed as man-hungry as Sam and Katrina. What struck her as amusing in her younger sister and her friend somehow seemed wrong coming from a woman in her late thirties with a ravenous look in her eyes.

"Word at the Mad Dog is that he's got *amazing* skills," Roxy said.

Wyn could feel her face heat and cursed her fair-skinned complexion. To her relief, nobody else seemed to notice and the conversation drifted on to other topics.

"So a week's suspension," Devin Shaw said from

across the table. "What are you doing to fill your time?"

"Right now I'm painting chalkboard paint on buckets."

"Any chance I could convince you to help me down at the community center with my yoga class?" Dev asked.

"Um, sure. I'm not really that knowledgeable but I can swing a mean Warrior Two pose."

"No doubt." Devin smiled. "I meant with that self-defense class you and I have talked about before. I've had several people request a few tips. I've tried to show them what little I know but they could really benefit from someone with your expertise."

Learning self-defense had become somewhat of an obsession after her attack. It was amazing how fear and powerlessness could motivate a person in new directions.

"Oh yes!" Eppie's wrinkled features lit up with excitement. "I want to learn a proper knee strike!"

She blinked. Did Eppie know how to implement *any* knee strike, proper or otherwise? Good grief. The woman had both knees replaced five years ago.

"Okay," she said slowly. "What day this week would work?"

"How about tomorrow?" Devin asked. "We're soaking at the hot springs the next day, which might be a good idea the day after a hard workout."

"I can do tomorrow."

"Is anybody welcome?" Roxy asked. "Every woman should learn a few basic moves to protect herself."

Everybody but Cade-hungry project managers, Wyn wanted to say. Yes. News flash. She could be a bitch.

Fortunately, Devin spoke first. "Everyone is welcome," she said. "Wednesday morning, nine a.m. at the community center, which is up near the high school."

Maybe she would casually mention that to Andrea Montgomery when she dropped off the food. If the woman *was* having trouble of some sort, she might welcome a few self-defense tips. On the other hand, with a sprained ankle, she might not be up for it right now.

At least Wyn now had one more thing to occupy her time during her suspension. She would have signed up to give a chicken driving lessons if it would keep her mind off a certain moonlit kiss.

CHAPTER NINE

So FAR HIS week was heading from lousy to miserable.

Cade drove down the quiet afternoon streets of Haven Point on a June afternoon with all the windows down on his official vehicle. Even then, the overpowering yeasty scent of beer permeated every molecule, taking him straight back to his childhood in Sulfur Hollow.

He reeked like he'd tried to take a shower under the tap, which was why he was driving home at four on a Tuesday afternoon when he had hours of work ahead of him.

Tourists who started drinking before noon ought to be dragged out of town and forever banned from the city limits, in his humble opinion.

A couple of hikers wrapping up a weeklong trip into the Redemptions had come down from the mountain ready to party. By two, they were both loaded and started picking fights with a few of the locals who liked hanging out on the Mad Dog's balcony overlooking the lake on a summer afternoon, eating burgers and shooting the breeze.

The bartender had called him to break things up and next thing he knew, he'd ended up wearing a nearly full pitcher of the nice pale ale they brewed down at the Mad Dog.

He glanced at the clock on the dashboard. He had about twenty minutes to grab a shower and a bite to eat before he needed to head back. He turned onto River-bend Road and pulled into his driveway. He was just trotting up the steps when he happened to glance to-ward the little stone house down the street—just acci-dentally, he would almost swear it—and saw Wynona heading his way with her arms weighed down by two bulging grocery bags.

Seeing her in civilian clothes always gave him a little shock—maybe because she always looked so dif-ferent than she did at work, soft and sweet and pretty. When not wearing her uniform, she favored flirty lit-tle skirts and flowery blouses or cute sundresses with strappy sandals, as if compelled to hold on tightly to that feminine side every chance she could.

She wore a skirt now in a pale salmon color with white polka dots and a soft white blouse and she looked good enough to eat.

He closed his eyes briefly, remembering the wild, *wrong* dreams that had tormented him all night—of tangled sheets and slick bodies, warm curves, and a soft mouth that tasted of strawberries and heaven. He had awakened hard, achy…and racked with guilt.

He had been a bear all day long, irritable and frus-trated. Having a full pitcher of beer thrown at him hadn't helped the situation.

So why did he suddenly feel like the sun had just come out?

He *really* needed to get a handle on this inappropriate attraction to Wynona before he did something else completely stupid.

While he was tempted to give a polite wave and head into his house, he had to ask himself what he would have done before he'd stupidly kissed her the night before.

Yesterday's Cade Emmett probably would have headed over in an instant to help her with the bulky load.

More than anything, he wanted to return their relationship to the casual, comfortable one they had always known before he'd rolled up to that fire scene with gut-twisting fear for her. He had assured her they could do it, which meant he needed to act just as he would have before the day before ever happened.

With a sigh, he pocketed his keys and headed up the road. She smiled as he approached but he didn't miss the flash of wariness in her expression.

"Can I give you a hand?" he asked.

She wrinkled her nose. "Wow. You smell like you took a bath in Bud Light."

"Yeah. That's what I get for stepping into the middle of a bar fight started by a couple of stupid tourists down at the Mad Dog."

"How many years have you been a cop, Chief? Don't you know, you wait until all the pitchers of beer have been tossed at someone *else* before you step in to break up the fight. I learned that the first week on the job."

Her teasing eased the tension as nothing else could

have and he felt a vast wave of relief. Maybe they *could* both forget that kiss eventually. In ten or twenty years.

"Sometimes a guy has to relearn all the old lessons. Don't worry, though. Haven Point is safe from beer-tossing idiots for now. The perps have been arrested and booked, so now I'm just heading home to clean up and grab an early dinner."

"In my experience, pizza always goes great with beer."

He made a face, then pointed to her bags. "Looks like you've got your hands full. Can I help?"

She inclined her head toward the house of their new neighbor. "Just making a delivery. A friendly welcome-to-the-neighborhood kind of thing."

He could see several containers of food inside the bags as well as a couple of children's books. "Nice."

"We'll see. She might throw me to the curb like you did with your early-drinking tourists. I figured it was worth a shot. Gain her trust, and all that, so I can see if she'll let me help her out of whatever trouble she's in."

He rolled his eyes. "You're a stubborn woman, Officer Bailey."

"That's funny. My mom was just saying the same thing about you."

He could imagine. He did have a tendency to stick to his guns, no matter what. He reached for the bags and took them from her. "Let me give you a hand."

"I've got this," she protested. "You have clean clothes and dinner waiting for you."

"That can all wait a few more moments."

Without waiting for her, he headed toward the Craftsman. After a pause, she followed behind him, her sandals slapping on the concrete.

"Apparently, sometimes my mother *does* know what she's talking about," she muttered, just as they reached the door of the house.

He smiled at her disgruntled tone. How was it possible that he felt better right now, beer-stained and hungry, than he had all day?

He intended to drop off the bags on the porch and return to his place across the street but the door opened before Wyn could even ring the bell. A cute kid stood there with freckles, big eyes and curly reddish hair. The kid looked like he belonged on a Norman Rockwell painting, carrying a flag and pulling a wagon filled with puppies or something.

"You're a police," the boy announced.

"I am. Hi there. I'm Chief Emmett. I live across the street from you."

The kid looked out at Cade's log home and the patrol vehicle in the driveway then back at the two of them.

"I'm Will. When I grow up, I'm going to be a police, just like my dad."

Cade exchanged a look with Wyn. "Your dad is a police officer?"

"He was. He died," the little kid said, his eyes filled with sudden shadows.

Okay, *that* caught Cade's curiosity. Apparently his new neighbor was a police officer's widow. Was that the reason Wyn thought something was wrong here?

"I'm sorry to hear that, Will. I bet you miss him a lot."

"A ton," the boy agreed. "I don't remember him very much but Chloe and my mom do."

He shifted his attention from Cade to Wynona. "Hey, where's your dog? I liked him. He was friendly and licked my hand and it tickled. He's the nicest dog I ever met."

"I'm afraid he's home," Wyn answered. "You know what? I like him too. He's a pretty great dog. He belonged to my dad, who was also a police officer. He died too. I still miss him a ton, just like you miss your dad."

Cade's throat tightened up. His own father had died six years earlier and he rarely even thought about him but he missed John Bailey every single day.

Wyn started to say something else but before she could even start the sentence, a young girl a few years older than Will with her brother's reddish hair came to the door.

"Will! What are you doing? You know you're not supposed to open the door for anybody, ever. Mom told you like a million times!"

"I didn't!" Will said. "It's not strangers. It's the lady from yesterday on our hike, only she has a police and not her dog named Pete."

Cade decided not to take offense at the boy's clear disappointment in Wyn's choice of companion. He was more interested in the girl's reaction, anyway. She seemed happy to see Wynona but he didn't miss the nervousness in her expression when she looked at him.

He couldn't tell if she was truly frightened but she clearly didn't want him there. Wyn's theory of a domestic-abuse situation didn't seem very likely, considering their father was dead, but what else might be making this girl look apprehensive?

"Hi," she said to Wynona. "Sorry, but my mom doesn't feel good and she can't talk right now. 'Bye."

She started to close the door but the fast-thinking Officer Bailey shoved her foot in before she could. That was a neat trick when a person was wearing standard-issue patrol boots but likely not so comfortable when wearing cute sandals like Wyn had on, the kind that showed toenail polish the same color as her skirt.

Wynona winced a little but held her ground. "I'm sure she'll talk to me if you let her know I'm here."

"She's on the couch and can't get up. The doctor said she has to rest her ankle with some ice. It hurts a lot. She won't say it does but I can tell."

The boy nodded. "She rested all day, even at lunch, but it was okay. Chloe and me made peanut butter and jelly sandwiches by ourselves and we hardly even made a mess."

Somehow Cade doubted the veracity of that particular statement but decided not to call the boy out in front of his sister.

"Will you please tell her we're here?" Wyn said, using that calm yet determined voice of concern he always admired. "We can come talk to her on the sofa and she won't even have to move. If you want to, you can tell her I have a gift from some of my friends to welcome your family to Haven Point."

"I bet it's in those bags," the boy said with a gleeful sort of grin. What a cute kid.

Chloe looked toward a hallway leading through the house then back at the two of them, nibbling on her lip. "I don't know. We're not supposed to let anybody in, ever, ever. Even if we know them."

Cade was all about teaching children a healthy degree of caution but this seemed excessive. He should have trusted Wyn's instincts, as usual. Something was definitely up with his new neighbors.

"How about this?" Wyn said. "We'll wait right here on the porch while you tell your mom we're here and ask her if it's okay if we come in to see her."

Chloe appeared to consider that and finally nodded. "I'll ask her. I don't know if she'll say yes, but I'll ask her."

She turned away and closed the door in their faces. If she hadn't left her brother out on the porch with them, Cade might have wondered if she had any intention of returning.

The boy stood next to Cade, gazing up at him from about waist level.

"You stink," he said after a minute, with the stark, completely unfettered honesty of children.

He glanced down at the stains on his shirt, which he had completely forgotten about.

"You know what? You're right. I had a little accident at work and somebody spilled something on me."

The boy nodded sagely. "I spill orange juice all the time. Mom always says I don't need to cry, that it's okay, I just need to help her clean it up."

"Sounds like good advice."

He *was* filthy and smelled like a brewery—probably

not the best state to be in when meeting a woman already averse to strangers.

"Maybe I'd better meet your mom another day, when I'm not such a mess."

"That might be a good idea," Will agreed, with such seriousness that Cade almost smiled. Instead, he forced his features into the same sort of solemn look.

"Listen, Will, if you ever need help from the police, I just live across the street from you, in that house right there. See it?"

Will's gaze followed the direction he pointed and he nodded. "Where your police car is."

"That's right. And Officer Bailey is just down the street, in the house made of stone with the green door, right down there."

"Okay."

"We can be here in a minute, got it?"

"I got it," Will said. "I know how to dial 911 if I have to, and I know it's only for 'mergencies."

Cade could only wish half of the adults in town understood that concept, especially the older ladies who seemed to want to call him out for everything from a mysterious noise to a missing heirloom vase they misplaced during spring cleaning.

"That's right. You help take care of your mom, especially if she has a sore ankle."

"I will," the boy promised.

"Good man."

He smiled at Will, then glanced at Wyn, who was staring at him with a warm approval that made him feel ridiculously pleased with himself.

"I'll see you later," he said.

"You don't want to meet Andrea?" she asked.

"Another day," he promised. "I'm drenched in beer, not my best look for meeting the good citizens of Haven Point. And I wouldn't want to make her more nervous."

"Good point. Well, thanks for helping me carry the bags, Chief."

"You got it. Let me know how things go."

"I will."

She opened her mouth as if she wanted to say something else but appeared to think better of it and closed it again.

He headed down the steps of the porch and then across the street. Now *his* spidey sense was tingling. Wynona was right. Something seemed off at the Montgomery household. He had no idea what, but had to trust that Wyn would be able to get to the bottom of it and ascertain somehow if the woman needed their help.

As usual, Wynona's instincts were spot-on. A good officer intuitively picked up on subtle clues in a situation and Wyn was one of the best.

His town needed her and he couldn't afford to lose sight of that.

Even if he was beginning to suspect he might need her too.

WYN INDULGED HERSELF for just a moment to watch Cade walk back to his house with that lean-hipped stride, sunlight gleaming off his dark hair.

True to his word, he acted like nothing had happened between them the night before. Okay, there might have been a moment there when he first joined her on the street, when she thought she had seen something raw and wild and *hungry* flash in his gaze. It might have been a trick of the sunlight or a figment of her entirely-too-active imagination.

She sighed. Why did he have to be so very hard to resist? He had been terribly sweet to help her carry her bags, even though they weren't heavy and she had been handling them fine. She had no problem taking care of herself most of the time, but once in a while it was nice to let someone else do it.

Cade had also struck exactly the right tone with Will, nonthreatening, interested, man-to-man. For a dude who didn't have children, Cade was remarkably good with them. She'd noticed it before, that children tended to gravitate toward him. Every year she went with him to the elementary school to give the obligatory safety talk at the beginning of the school year. Every year it was the same, with the children hanging on his every word.

Most of the teachers did the same, but that probably went without saying. This was Cade Emmett, after all.

He also went to the school once a month to read to the kids on his lunch hour, so they wouldn't be afraid of the badge or the uniform. She found that unbearably sweet.

The door suddenly opened and Andrea Montgomery balanced in the doorway on crutches, her hair flattened a little on one side where she had been resting on it.

Her skin was a shade paler than the day before and she had the tight set to her features of someone in pain.

"Oh," she exclaimed softly. "I thought… Chloe said a policeman was here with you."

"He was. Police Chief Emmett. He lives across the street."

The woman's gaze shifted to Cade's log home and the police vehicle in the driveway. "Right. Where did he go?"

"Home. He only stopped by for a moment to help me carry a few things over then he had to leave."

By now, he was probably running water for his shower. She tried not to think about that hard, hot body with droplets of water trickling down...

She cleared her throat and jerked her unruly mind back. "You were resting. I'm so sorry to bother you. I should have told your daughter to make sure you stayed put. I've been on crutches before and know what a pain they can be."

"It's fine," Andrea said, though it was quite obvious the words were a lie. "How can I help you?"

Wyn lifted the reusable grocery bags. "I'm just dropping off a few quick meals so you don't have to think about spending much time in the kitchen."

"You're...what?" Andrea frowned in confusion.

"It's not much, just a few casseroles you can heat while you're recovering and moving in. Some friends of mine put it together. I told them about you falling on the trail yesterday and people were very anxious to help. Oh, and my mom provided the delicious lasagna."

Eliza had given her the bulk of the meals but McKenzie and Letty Robles had each contributed a meal and Barbara Serrano had insisted on giving a meal from her family's restaurant as well as a couple of gift certificates and delivery coupons.

"Why?" Andrea blinked, her eyes baffled. "I don't know a soul in town except you. I don't understand. Why would people I don't know do this for us?"

Wyn shrugged. "I can't really answer that. We just try to help where we can. You picked a really nice town to move into, Mrs. Montgomery."

Andrea stared at her for another moment and then she sagged against the door and burst into tears.

Will moved closer to his mother and slipped his hand in hers. Chloe, who had followed her mother back to the door, immediately moved in front of her, as if to protect her.

"Why are you crying?" Will demanded of his mom.

"It's just… I'm… It's a shock. That's all."

"I'm sorry. I didn't mean to make you cry," Wyn murmured, wishing she knew the woman well enough to give her a hug. She could imagine Kenz and even Devin would swoop right in anyway, even to a stranger. But Wyn didn't like unexpected contact herself and tried to give people their space.

"I'm the one who's sorry. I'm not usually like this, I promise. It's just been a very hard few days and the pain medication is making me sick and my ankle is throbbing and it's been so long since someone did something so kind for me."

"Then it was past time," she said simply. "You shouldn't be standing so long. Let's get you back to where you're comfortable."

Andrea sniffled as she hobbled back through boxes to a room off the kitchen that held more boxes, along with a sofa and recliner.

"Sofa or chair?" Wyn asked.

"Chair for now," Andrea said. Wyn helped her settle in then handed over a tissue from a box she noticed on a nearby table for Andrea to dry the tears that continued to drip down her cheeks.

"Thanks. I'm sorry again about the breakdown. I'll be okay in a minute."

"Please don't worry about it. There's nothing wrong with a few tears, especially under the circumstances. I think it's amazing you're holding everything together. I would be an emotional wreck."

Instead of comforting the other woman, as she intended, this seemed to set Andrea off again. Her little boy leaned against his mother's leg, clearly upset at seeing her in distress, and she pulled him into her lap and hugged him.

"I'm okay. Don't worry. I'm okay," she murmured.

Touched at the obvious love in this little family, Wyn handed her a few more tissues.

Andrea wiped her nose and eyes and seemed to be gathering her composure.

"Who did you say this was from?"

"I'm part of an informal group of women in town called the Haven Point Helping Hands. Usually we do fund-raising for various organizations in town but sometimes we step in to help if someone's been injured, had a baby or is just going through a hard time."

"That sounds…nice."

"Some people think we're just a bunch of interfering busybodies with too much time on our hands. Really, it's mostly a good excuse to get together and catch up with each other on a regular basis. You're very welcome to come. We love new people and would be thrilled for you to join in. Everyone is eager to meet you. If you'd like to come to our next project day, it's next Thursday. Usually we only meet once a month or so but we've got a few major events coming up so we're more busy than usual. Oh, you're more than welcome to bring your kids. Everyone does. It will give you a good chance to meet new people and possibly for the kids to make some new friends."

Andrea gazed at Wyn, then down at the bags she'd set down in the kitchen. Her chin wobbled a little but she didn't cry again.

"Why are you being so kind to me?" she whispered. "I've been so cold to you."

Wyn had sensed Andrea's chilliness the day before wasn't her normal personality. Today confirmed it. She was obviously warm and loving to her children and truly seemed touched by the small gesture from the Helping Hands.

Andrea struck her as a woman who could very much use a friend.

"I can't imagine how much strength it must have taken to move to a new town where you don't know anyone, especially when you have children to worry about too," she said.

"We're making a new start," Chloe said. She was beginning to look a little less anxious.

"I'm glad you picked Haven Point," Wynona answered. "I know it's a little early but have you all eaten dinner?"

"I haven't even thought about dinner yet," Andrea answered.

"You are in luck. Now you don't have to. I brought along several delicious options in there. I can highly recommend them, especially my friend McKenzie's Gruyère mac and cheese."

"Mac and cheese is my very favorite thing in the whole wide world," Will announced. "Chloe loves it too."

"What's not to like, with all that cheesy deliciousness? Why don't I throw it in the oven for you?"

"That does sound good," Andrea said, "but you've done so much already. I think I probably can handle sliding a pan into the oven."

"It's not as easy as it sounds when you're on crutches. Please, let me help. If you want the truth, I'm happy to have something constructive to do. I've got some... unexpected time off and I'm having a hard time figuring out what to do with myself."

Andrea looked as if she wanted to argue but she finally nodded. "In that case, thank you."

"Kids, can you help me out in the kitchen? I need somebody to show me where your freezer is."

"I can show you!" Will announced. He slid off his mother's lap and raced into the kitchen ahead of Chloe, who followed a few steps behind.

"Thank you again, Officer Bailey."

"Oh, please. My friends call me Wyn."

Andrea smiled. "And I'm Andie to mine."

Wyn returned her smile, pleased to see the woman

had a little more color—and not just her red nose or the splotches on her cheeks.

"You good here? Need the TV remote or anything?"

"I have a few books and magazines. I should be fine."

After she turned the oven on to preheat, she and the children found room in the mostly empty freezer for the containers of food. When they asked if they could return to the game they were playing, she agreed—assuming their mother would as well—then returned to the family room with a glass of ice water for Andie.

"Thanks."

She noticed several boxes of books in front of a built-in shelf unit. "Do you mind if I put some of these away?" she asked.

"Oh, I'll get to them eventually."

"Keep in mind you're doing me a favor, remember? I'm on unpaid leave until Monday and I'm already bored to death."

"What did you do?" Andie asked.

Wyn sighed. "I didn't follow procedure and I might have taken an unnecessary risk with my safety and others."

While she pulled out books and set them on the shelves, she told Andrea the story from the beginning.

"It sounds as if you've known your police chief for a long time."

"Forever. He was best friends with my older brother Marshall from the time they were boys."

If she closed her eyes, she could still see him in ripped cutoffs and a too-big T-shirt, asking Charlene if he could mow the lawn for her in exchange for some of the leftovers from dinner to take home to his little brothers.

"So you've lived in Haven Point your whole life?" Andie asked.

"Most of it, except when I was away for college in Boise and police-officer training. I worked for two years for a police department just outside Boise."

Since the other woman had opened the door, she decided to walk through it. "What about you? Are you from the Portland area originally?"

Andrea tensed slightly then let out a breath. "I was raised there and that's where I met my husband. He… was a police officer too. He died eighteen months ago."

"Will mentioned that to me. Do you mind if I ask what happened?"

Her mouth tightened and she looked down at her hands. "He had an accident, sort of."

"What kind?"

"It was so like him," Andie said after a moment. "Jason was a really good man who genuinely cared about the people he served. He sounds a lot like your Chief Emmett. He was a detective. He and his…partner were working a case when a call came about a man threatening to jump from St. Johns Bridge in Portland. They were the nearest responding unit so arrived first and Jason tried to talk him down. Despite his efforts, the man ended up jumping anyway."

"Oh no."

Her mouth trembled a little. "Jason reached to grab him and I still don't know exactly what happened but

I guess somehow momentum pulled them both over. It's a long drop from St. Johns Bridge and they…both drowned."

Her husband had died trying to save someone's life, just like Wyatt had been trying to save the couple inside that stranded car during a January snowstorm.

"I'm so sorry," she said softly. "How devastating for you and your children."

"Sometimes I still can't convince myself he's really gone, you know? I wake up some mornings thinking it's just a mistake and he's only been undercover all this time, that he'll come back and make everything okay again. That probably sounds stupid."

"No, I totally understand, believe me. More than I'd like. I've lost my father and my twin brother to the job."

"Both of them, at the same time?" Andie exclaimed.

"No. Several years apart. My brother Wyatt was a highway patrol officer who was hit by a car that slid into him while he was helping a couple of stranded motorists. A bit like your Jason, actually."

She felt the same aching emptiness she always did whenever she thought of Wyatt, her best friend since they were womb mates.

"And your dad?" Andrea asked softly.

She hadn't meant to make her own losses seem worse than Andrea's. She hated when people did that but she had to finish the story now.

"He was the chief of police here in Haven Point. A drifter held up the local liquor store a few years back. When my dad pursued him, shots were fired. My dad was shot. He survived but suffered a traumatic brain injury that left him unable to talk or walk or take care of himself."

"Oh, how tragic. Your poor family."

She thought of her mother, who hid her grief by trying to pretend everything was perfect and by fussing over the rest of them.

"How can you work in law enforcement, when your family has lost so much?"

"In some families, public service is almost a sacred responsibility. I've got a brother who's the sheriff of Lake Haven County and another who is an FBI agent in the Denver field office. I guess you could say it's the family business. What about you? What do you do when you're not wrestling a couple of adorable kids and stumbling on the trail to Mount Solace?"

Andrea sipped at her water and Wyn had the feeling she was still debating whether to trust her.

"I'm a freelance commercial graphic-design artist," she finally said.

"Are you? That's terrific!"

That probably explained the elaborate computer setup in the corner. "And what brought you to Haven Point?"

Andrea paused before answering. Again, Wyn suspected she was choosing her words carefully. "In the past, I've done a great deal of work for Caine Tech. They're my major account, actually, and make up about two-thirds of my business. When I learned they were opening a facility here in Haven Point, I was immediately intrigued by the name of the town and did some research about the community. Since I can work any-

where and don't have any family holding us to Portland, I decided this would be a…a good place for a
new start."

Though what she said sounded logical, Wyn could
tell that wasn't the whole story. Something happened
between her husband's death and the Montgomery
family showing up in Haven Point eighteen months
later. What?

She had interviewed many people in her years as a
police officer, though, and she could tell by the way
Andie's expression tightened that she wasn't ready to
talk about the rest of it. Wyn would have to be content
for now with what she had learned.

"If you're looking for a safe haven, this is the perfect place," she said gently.

Andie flashed her a look. For a moment, she appeared suspiciously close to tears again, then she put
on a strained smile.

"It seems perfect. The crime rate is low and the edu-
cational system has an excellent reputation. Throw in
the abundant outdoor opportunities and the relatively
low taxes and I decided it was just what we needed."

"I'm sure you and your children will love it here."

"I hope so," Andie said softly.

The oven timer went off then and Wyn rose from
her spot on the floor by the bookshelf.

"That will be the mac and cheese. I just need to take
it out of the oven. Give me a minute and I'll bring you
a plate. Do you want the kids to eat in here with you?"

"Oh, you don't have to wait on us. I should be fine
with Chloe's help. I have to figure out the crutches any-

way, though Dr. Shaw said I should only need them
for a couple of days."

"A few days is more than enough," she said. "Can
I help you get up?"

"No. Thank you."

Wyn nodded and headed for the kitchen to pull out
the aluminum pan.

A moment later, Andrea came in on the crutches.
"That looks delicious. You're more than welcome to
stay and eat with us."

The woman who had been prickly to the point of
rudeness the day before was nowhere in evidence now,
as if the tears had washed the last traces of her away.
This warm, slightly shy woman was the real Andie
Montgomery. Wyn was certain of it.

"I appreciate the offer but I'll get out of your hair.
My dog is probably more than ready for a walk."

"Of course. Thank you again. And please tell your
friends thank you for me as well."

"I'll do that. But I would love you to come meet
them yourself next week."

"I might do that. Good friends make everything
easier."

"Isn't that the truth?"

She looked around the small but bright kitchen, clut-
tered with boxes that had to be posing a hazard for
someone trying to maneuver on crutches.

"You're not going to be able to get around for a few
more days," she said on impulse. "Meanwhile, you've
got boxes that need to be unpacked."

Andie made a rueful face. "They're not going anywhere. I can take care of them once I'm a little more mobile."

"I've only moved a few times, but I still remember how hard it is to live out of boxes for longer than five minutes. I can't imagine trying to do it with children. I'd like to help, if you'll let me. You'd be doing me a favor, actually. I told you that I have more time on my hands right now than activities to fill it."

"I can't let you do that. It's far too much to ask."

"You didn't ask. I offered," she pointed out.

"Why? I mean, I appreciate everything you've done but I…still don't quite understand why."

"I guess I feel a kinship. We both know what it's like to lose someone you love in the line of duty. We survivors are a small club and need to stick together."

"It's a horrible club," Andie said in a low voice. "I hate it."

"I can't argue with that," she answered.

It had been tough enough losing her brother and her father. She couldn't imagine the depth of Andie's pain, losing the man she loved.

Her mother had lost a son and a husband. Was it any wonder she fussed and fretted over those chicks she had left?

"So will you let me help? You won't have to lift a finger. All you have to do is supervise and tell me where to put things and I'll do all the heavy lifting. The kids can help me. It will be fun."

She could see Andie weakening. Her chin trembled and she looked as if she was going to cry again. "I don't know what to say."

How was it possible that a police officer's widow seemed so unaccustomed to simple kindnesses? In Wyn's experience, the rest of the department and their families—not to mention the community in general—stepped up immediately to provide a support network. Why hadn't Andie experienced that?

"Yes," Wyn said. "That's the only word you have to say. I won't take any other answer."

"Then yes, I suppose. The children are already tired of living in chaos and want to find all their old things."

"That's only natural. They've moved into a new house and probably want the comfort of the familiar."

"I suppose that's it."

"I'm so glad you'll let me help you. I'm teaching a self-defense class in the morning but I can be here later in the afternoon, around two, if that's okay."

That seemed to catch the other woman's interest. "You teach self-defense?"

"This is my first time, actually. Everyone is welcome, though this class is aimed toward a group of senior citizens. If all goes well, I'm considering offering classes to the general public."

"If you do, will you let me know?"

"Sure thing. You're going to have to stay off that ankle, though, so you can heal first."

The children came in looking for dinner before Andie could answer. Wyn served them plates and helped them settle at the table.

"You're not having some mac and cheese with us?" Chloe asked. "It looks really good."

"I'd better not. Pete will be wondering where I am and he's probably ready for his own dinner. But I'll see you tomorrow afternoon. I'm coming back to unpack boxes and I'm going to need your help and Will's too."

"Can you bring your nice dog with you?" the boy asked.

She glanced at Andie, who shrugged.

"I'll see what I can do," she promised, then said goodbye to the family and headed out into the warm loveliness of a June evening.

CHAPTER TEN

"THANKS FOR COMING DOWN, Chief, especially when I know you likely have a million other things more important happening in town."

Helen Mickelson, the director of the community center, appeared on the brink of angry tears. She shoved the pen she was holding into her steel-gray bun, apparently not realizing she already had two pencils jammed up there.

"Every report we respond to is important, Miss Mickelson."

"I appreciate that. I do. We've got to get to the bottom of this. I can tell you, I'm so frustrated, I want to tear my hair out. This is the third time in two months we've been hit by graffiti by some punk with a spray can and too much time on his hands."

He scanned the wall at the same message as the previous incidents here and at other places around town. Go Home Caine Tech.

"I understand your frustration. You're not the only one in town who's been hit, I can tell you that. We've had two other reports this morning, one at the marina and another on the wall in front of the supermarket. It's become something of an epidemic."

"It's total nonsense," Helen snapped. "All of it. The destruction of property *and* the ridiculous message. Caine Tech moving in to set up shop is the best thing to happen to this town in twenty years."

"Not everybody thinks so," he pointed out. "Some people don't want outside businesses moving in."

"Some people are stupid," she said tartly. "They wouldn't know a good thing if it walked up to them and handed them a birthday cake wrapped in ten-dollar bills."

"Can't argue with you there," he said.

He had always liked Helen, going back to the days when she taught his third-grade class at Haven Point Elementary School.

She had called Child Protective Services on his father once, he suddenly remembered, when he came to school with a black eye. He had tried to tell her he got it fighting with Marcus but she hadn't believed him. If he remembered correctly, she'd actually pulled Marcus out of his class to get to the bottom of it. His poor little brother hadn't been as experienced a liar as Cade yet and hadn't known what she was talking about.

Nothing had come of it. Walter Emmett had been really good at talking his way around a situation when it came to social workers. It was another story if things escalated to a police matter—at least if John Bailey happened to be the responding officer.

He studied the graffiti on the outside wall of the community center. It was about six and a half feet off the ground, which indicated a fairly tall suspect. He couldn't quite imagine a tagger carrying along a step-ladder but it was possible.

"It looks like the same suspect from the other two incidents," Helen informed him. "And Wynona Bailey agrees with me."

He raised an eyebrow at that. Did she mean the same Wynona Bailey who hadn't actually been on duty for two days?

"Is that right?"

"Yes. She pointed out the slant on the *n*'s and the way the *o*'s are shaped. As the investigating officer for the other incidents, she is quite certain the handwriting matches."

Wyn was an excellent investigator. If she went to a big city, she could make detective grade without too much effort on her part.

He could only hope that didn't happen anytime soon.

"When was Wynona here?" he asked.

Helen gestured to the building. "Oh, she's here now, teaching a self-defense class to Dr. Shaw's yoga group."

Huh. That was an interesting image. He knew Wynona worked out intensely and studied Krav Maga, Israeli combat martial arts. She had given a little instruction in basic moves to some of his other officers but he had always managed to miss her demonstrations, for some reason he didn't want to explore too deeply.

"She came by just after we discovered it," Helen went on. "I didn't see why she couldn't investigate for us, since she is familiar with what happened last time, but she told me I had to report it through proper channels. I guess that means you."

"Today, it does." The other officer on duty was investigating a car accident on the edge of town and he saw no reason to bring in the on-call officer to handle this.

"Wynona also told me I was supposed to tell the responding officer to talk to her prime suspect again. She couldn't give me a name. She said it's all in her notes that are on the server. She's ninety-nine percent certain it's the same suspect. She just needs more solid evidence to bring charges."

He knew just who Helen—and Wynona—was talking about. From the beginning, Wynona suspected Jimmy Welch, a local malcontent who wasn't happy about Aidan Caine and Ben Kilpatrick bringing a Caine Tech facility to Haven Point.

Jimmy had caused trouble before with both Aidan and Ben. He knew from briefings with Wyn on the case that she had interviewed Jimmy twice. He somehow managed to have a different flimsy alibi for each incident of vandalism but so far he'd been lucky and Wynona hadn't yet been able to break either of them.

He was going to have to talk to Jimmy again. Damn it. The man was *not* his favorite person. He reminded Cade far too much of his father, angry, belligerent, convinced the world was against him.

By the time he finished collecting evidence—taking pictures and paint samples—he knew he was going to have to talk to Wynona. She had important insight and history into the other incidents and could provide valuable help before he talked to Jimmy.

He hadn't realized until Wyn was away from the department just how much he had come to rely on her these last few years since she returned to Haven Point after John had been shot. Though not technically his assistant chief, she filled that role unofficially and he was beginning to see that each of his other officers understood that.

He respected all the guys in his department and each brought a different strength. Jason Robles was terrific with computers, Cody Hendricks had an uncanny way of persuading reluctant people to talk. George Petry had wisdom and as much experience as the rest of them combined and Jesse Fisher was the most energetic rookie he knew.

They were all great at their jobs but he had discovered the last few days that Wynona seemed to be the glue holding them all together. Each of them relied on her.

Just another reason why he needed to keep his damn hands to himself where she was concerned.

He finished taking pictures of the graffiti and collecting paint samples while Helen talked to him about her favorite cop show of the moment.

Finally, he knew he couldn't put it off any longer.

"Can you show me where Officer Bailey is now?" he asked Helen. "I should speak with her for a minute, to compare notes on the case."

"Of course. Dr. Shaw pulls quite a crowd for her seniors yoga class and they generally need plenty of room so we put them in the biggest space, up at the front where we usually set up the voting machines."

"Got it. Thanks."

"Do you have what you need? I have to make some phone calls."

"I think I'm good. Thanks. I'll let you know if there's a break in the case."

"I hope there is. This is costing us time and money. We can't afford to keep repainting over the mess made by some ungrateful idiot with an ax to grind against Caine Tech."

"I'm with you, Helen. Thanks."

He walked through the community center a few moments later and did his best to ignore the anticipation rippling through him. He had no business anticipating anything but he had realized these last few days how much he looked forward to their small interactions throughout the day and missed them when she was gone.

He had to cut that out. She was his officer, which made her completely off-limits. Beyond that, she was his best friend's little sister and the daughter of the man responsible for everything good and right in Cade's life.

The large meeting room of the community center was about half the size of a standard basketball court, with a small stage at one end for performances. He looked into the room and found the floor spread with mats and about twenty senior citizens in yoga clothes in various poses—a sight he did *not* need to see.

At the front of the room, Wyn was talking to the

class. She wore tight black yoga pants and a faded gray Police Officer Standards and Training T-shirt, her hair up in a high ponytail that made her look about sixteen.

Curious about what she was teaching, he backed up a pace so he was at an angle where he could see her but she likely couldn't see him.

"As I said earlier when I was demonstrating a few things with Devin, protecting yourself isn't a matter of being able to body slam somebody who's coming at you," she said. "The reality is, most of you aren't going to be able to do that without breaking a hip. That doesn't matter. What can be more important in these situations is learning ways to present yourself as confident and without fear—being constantly aware of your surroundings and having a thorough understanding of your capabilities and the tools at your disposal."

"You mean like pepper spray?" her aunt Jenny asked.

"That's one possibility and not a bad idea," Wyn said. "How many of you keep a police whistle and a flashlight on your key chain?"

Eppie Brewer raised her hand. "I do. Want to see it?"

Wyn smiled. "No. I believe you. That's excellent. The rest of you should follow Eppie's lead."

"What if you can't drive anymore and don't need a key chain?" Mick Sargent asked.

"You can still carry a flashlight and police whistle on a lanyard around your neck."

"Or your tackle box," Archie Peralta suggested.

"Whatever works. I've got a handout where I've

listed a few self-defense tips that start before you ever leave your house, like putting your jacket on over your purse or carrying a dummy wallet you can hand to a mugger. It's also important that before you leave your car at a store, you observe your surroundings closely, especially if the area is unfamiliar, so you know where to go in an emergency. You should also remember to walk with a purpose. Don't look at the ground or your phone or inside your purse. Keep your attention focused on the world around you."

Cade was aware of a sharp ache in his chest as he listened to her. He knew exactly why she was such a fierce proponent of people—especially women—learning how to protect themselves and why she trained in martial arts.

He hadn't known until she applied for a job in Haven Point, so she could be closer to the family. They had never once talked about it but he was aware of it every single time he sent her out on a call concerning sexual abuse.

She had been raped in college. He had read her testimony from the trial of the bastard who had attacked her and other women and Cade knew the basics of what had happened to her but she never referred to it.

"I want to see more of those cool moves you showed us before," Hazel Brewer said now. "What if somebody grabs you from behind?"

"You mean if it's somebody besides Ronald goosing you in the kitchen?" her sister Eppie asked.

Everybody laughed, even poor Ron, who had to

put up with both sisters since Eppie's husband died a few years back.

"The best thing to do in that case, if someone grabs you from behind, don't struggle and pull to get away, even though that would be the natural instinct. Instead, lean against your attacker and shove your head back as hard as you can to throw the person off balance. That could give you precious time to whip out your pepper spray and your trusty police whistle. Dev, can you help me demonstrate?"

They moved to a different part of the room, at an angle he couldn't see from his vantage point. Not wanting to miss it, he moved into the room.

Wyn spotted him instantly. She broke off what she was saying and even from the doorway, he could see a quick succession of emotions flash in her gaze—surprise and dismay and something else he didn't have a chance to identify before she quickly donned a smile.

"Chief Emmett! You're just the man I need!"

His imagination kicked into gear for one delicious moment, until he yanked it back. "Is that right?"

"I could use a helping hand over here."

With a little trepidation, he walked farther into the room. Eppie and Hazel both waved at him and Wyn's aunt Jenny grinned and winked. A wave of affection for them all washed over him, these people who had accepted and supported him, first as a police officer then the police chief after John was injured.

Nobody seemed to hold his family background against him. He had worried they would when he first came back to work for the department. If Wynona's family business was police work, the Emmett clan provided them job security, going back three generations. Renegades, outlaws, reprobates. Whatever name you wanted to use, his ancestors consistently seemed to believe themselves above the law.

His father had had a few pals on the wrong side of the law who still hassled him when their paths crossed, but the law-abiding folks had always treated him with respect and courtesy.

"How can I help?"

"I'd love to demonstrate to the class the best way for a person of smaller stature to take down someone much bigger. Nobody quite fit the physical profile here."

He raised an eyebrow. "You really think you can take me down?"

She shrugged. "No idea. It will be fun trying, though."

He wasn't sure he liked the mischievous look in her eyes. A smart man would probably take heed and back right out of the room. How could he do that, though, with all these eager senior citizens looking on?

"I'm not really dressed for a workout," he tried, gesturing to his cargo pants and HPPD polo shirt.

"You look fine," she answered, then in a low, teasing voice, she taunted, "What's the matter? Are you scared, Chief?"

She wasn't going to let him out of this easily. He tried one more time, pointing subtly to his service revolver. Understanding flashed in her eyes. She knew he couldn't leave his service revolver unattended in some corner somewhere.

"Devin would be happy to keep an eye on your piece, right, Dr. Shaw?"

"I will!" Eppie offered helpfully.

"You will not," her sister Hazel snapped.

"I've got it," Devin said, obviously trying to keep the peace between the sisters. "I'm happy to watch your piece, Chief Emmett."

"Better not let that hunky rancher of yours hear you say that," Archie Peralta said with a smirk.

Cade tried to figure out a way out, but nothing brilliant came to him. Okay, then. He could help her out for a few minutes in exchange for stealing her away from the group to talk about the vandalism case.

He unstrapped his holster and set it on the table next to Devin then followed with his ID and car keys. In the interest of a proper demonstration, he toed off his boots, grateful he'd worn fairly decent socks that day instead of the holey ones he was forced to wear when he hadn't had time for laundry in a while, then pulled out his backup gun and set it down too.

When he couldn't delay another moment, he cautiously approached Wynona on the mat, aware of the interested crowd of senior citizens watching their by-play.

She looked fresh and pretty, her eyes alight with laughter and her luscious mouth curved into a smile. As he neared her, the familiar scent of her drifted to him—citrus and vanilla and some other delicious aroma that was just *her*. Awareness sizzled through him and he wanted to just close his eyes and inhale.

This was a bad idea, he could already tell, and likely

wouldn't end well for him. She had several reasons to be upset at him—the suspension and that kiss at the top of the list, but he imagined there were others, after their years of working together.

Nothing he could do now but ride this through.

"Be careful," he murmured in a voice too low for the others to hear. "I don't want to have to hurt you."

Something he couldn't read flashed in her eyes for just a moment then she gave him a sly smile. "We'll see who's hurting in a few minutes."

"Okay, gang." She turned back to the interested senior citizens. "I know it's tough when he's wearing the proud and noble uniform of the Haven Point Police Department but I need you to pretend for a moment that Chief Emmett is a bad guy with nefarious intentions."

"Nefarious?" he murmured.

"Let's say I'm just your average woman walking down the street. What should I be doing?"

"Constantly assess your surroundings," Jenny offered.

"Wear the strap of your purse across your body so he can't use it as a weapon," the apparently bloodthirsty Eppie suggested.

"Keep your car keys in your hand to gouge out his eye," Letty Robles suggested. "My son taught me that."

"Great suggestions, all of you. I don't have any car keys or a purse. It's just me by myself when a big, scary stranger steps out of the bushes and tries to grab me from the side. Go ahead, big, scary stranger."

He moved next to her, feeling supremely stupid, though he had participated in these classes in one form or another for years. He'd *taught* these classes, for heaven's sake. Just never with Wynona.

He had to wonder why not, especially when she had undeniable expertise in the area.

Cade was beginning to realize how he had subconsciously gone out of his way to avoid situations that would put them together in uncomfortably close proximity.

Perhaps he had been afraid of exactly what had happened the other night, that the feelings he didn't want to acknowledge would come bubbling to the surface the moment his guard was down and he would do something stupid like kiss her.

She kissed you first, a voice reminded him, but he pushed it away. He couldn't think about that or he would start wondering again *why* she had kissed him and whether she might be dealing with this inappropriate attraction as well.

He didn't want to touch her. On a deep, visceral level, he was afraid if he did, he would grab her close, bury his face in her soft, sweet-smelling neck and never let go.

"Come on, Chief Emmett. Give me your worst."

Everybody was watching them. He was going to have to go through with this. He drew in a breath and came at her from the side.

A second later, he was on the mat, felled by a move he hadn't even seen coming and her foot was poised just above his gut. A few more inches south and he would be singing soprano.

"That's how you do it, people," she said with a grin. "See how I used my hand to distract him so my leg could get around his and take him down?"

"I'd like to see it again," Eppie said.

"Mind if we demonstrate that in slo-mo?" she asked him.

Yes. He minded very much. But he was now well and truly trapped. "Sure."

A second later they repeated the scene in instant replay. This time he caught just what she did but he still couldn't defend himself and he fell the same way, only this time her foot was poised right over the goods. The women tittered and a few men gasped.

"One hard stomp and he probably would be very sorry he messed with me, right?" Wyn said.

"Probably?" he murmured. She reached for his hand and helped him to his feet, where he did a little exaggerated rotation of his shoulders like he was trying to work out an injury.

"You okay?"

"It's tough work being a big, scary guy."

She snorted but didn't answer.

"Can you show us another one?" Devin Shaw asked.

"Okay. One more, then we need to let Chief Emmett get back to protecting and serving. This time I want to show you how to get away if somebody comes up behind you. Say it's late at night, you can't sleep for some reason and your dog needs to go out so you decide to take a little walk on a lovely summer night. There you are, enjoying the way the moonlight gleams like liquid silver on the lake down the hill and the sound of the river and the smell of the pines and your neighbor's climbing roses when suddenly somebody comes up behind you."

He was so busy listening to her vivid description and imagining her and Pete there enjoying the night that he didn't realize he'd been prompted until she cleared her throat noisily.

"Oh right. Sorry."

"Grab me around the throat like you want to drag me into the bushes."

What if he *did* want to drag her into the bushes? For just a moment, his mind stalled on an image of the two of them tangled together on summer-warm grass, as he had imagined that night, her mouth as sweet and welcoming as it had been in reality, her arms holding him closer, her slender curves softening with welcome while that liquid silver moonlight danced across them...

Yeah. This was a really bad idea. He swallowed and forced himself again to focus on the task at hand.

Firmly ignoring the sweet scent of her and the delectable curves he could far too clearly see in the yoga capris, he moved behind her and grabbed her around the throat with his right forearm while the other grabbed her left forearm.

She stomped hard on his foot, stuck a sharp little elbow in his stomach, and then when he instinctively released her, she turned and swept his legs out from under him in one swift movement. He landed with an *oomph* on the mat, her foot just inches above his face.

Her toes were still painted that soft shade of coral like her skirt the other day. He'd never had a foot thing before, but just now he wanted to nibble on each one...

"Oh excellent!" Jenny exclaimed. "I need to learn that one. Can you show us one more time?"

She stepped away and looked down at him in his ignominious position, her eyes bright with laughter and that mouth curved into a smile. He felt the oddest cramping around his heart, nowhere near the part of him that had been smacked to the mat.

"Up to you, Chief. Can you handle a little more?"

"Why not? I've already humiliated myself. What's a bit more torture?"

"That's the spirit."

Being so close to her *was* torture, especially when what he *really* wanted to do was snug that curvy little behind against him and keep her right there.

"That was so cool!" Ed Bybee exclaimed, after they repeated the show. "Can we practice on each other now?"

Devin Shaw stepped forward. "Find a partner and come to the mat. We'll go through the motions that Wyn showed us but we're not throwing anyone to the mat. Anybody with a broken hip can't come soaking tomorrow at Evergreen Springs."

There was a little grumbling but the class seemed to take that warning in stride.

He pulled himself to a sitting position and Wyn

reached down again to help him up. Her hand was warm and soft in his and he wanted to wrap his fingers around it and tug her into his arms.

All in all, it was probably a good idea that he hadn't done this whole self-defense demonstration with her before.

CHAPTER ELEVEN

"THANKS FOR HELPING me out. I was afraid to be too rough on any of the class members."

"Happy to help," he lied. "Though someone would have to be out of his ever-loving mind to mess with any of these old-timers here. They're a dangerous lot, especially Eppie over there."

"True enough." She smiled and it took him a minute to remember the reason he had come to the class in the first place.

"Can I steal you for a minute?" he asked.

"I believe I've just demonstrated that I'm capable of taking you down if you try."

He gave a wry smile. "Why do you think I asked first? You're nobody to mess with, as I've just been duly warned."

He wouldn't forget again.

"I just need a minute to talk to you about your investigation into whoever's tagging the community center and city hall."

"Right. Helen showed me the latest artwork. Give me just a couple minutes to answer any questions about what we showed them, okay?"

"No problem." He spent the few minutes harnessing his weapons, shoving his feet into his boots again and pocketing his ID. He couldn't seem to stop watching her as she walked among the members of the class giving a tip here or answering a question there.

Finally she joined him. "You need to talk to Jimmy Welch, but you obviously knew that already."

"I was afraid of that."

"Maybe you'll have better luck than I did cracking his alibi. I almost had him last time but the district attorney backed down because the evidence just wasn't strong enough. I tried everything I could to nail him. I even searched his garbage for empty spray cans, but couldn't come up with anything. He's usually not smart enough to cover his tracks, but this time he seems to have done a good job."

"Did you talk to the hardware store about recent spray-paint purchases?"

"Yeah. Nobody bought any of that color and Jimmy hasn't been in for weeks. It was a nonstarter. I checked all the places in Shelter Springs that sell spray paint but came up empty. All my notes are on my office computer if you want to review them. Or I can pick up the investigation again when I come back next week."

"I'll keep sniffing around and see what I can find before I head out to talk to Jimmy. Maybe I'll widen the search on the spray-paint purchases beyond Lake Haven County."

"It had to come from somewhere."

"True. Thanks for the debrief."

"Yep. I won't bother to mention that you could always lift my suspension so I can take over the case again."

"Thank you for not mentioning it," he said drily.

She smiled. "I guess I owe you for letting me take you down a few times."

"Not at all. It's good to know you can take care of yourself next time you and Pete decide to take a midnight walk, just in case there are any dangerous characters lurking on Riverbend Road."

He didn't want to leave. He wanted to stay right here and bask in her smile, though he knew she needed to return to her class.

"I haven't had the chance to ask what happened last evening at our new neighbor's house. What did she say about your little delivery?"

"She didn't turn me away, anyway. I fixed macaroni and cheese for them and we had a nice chat. I'm going back later today to help her unpack boxes."

He felt that unfamiliar tug at his heart again. She was always doing things like that, kind little gestures that made a big difference in people's lives. Wyn brought a much-welcome softness to the sometimes harsh world of the police department.

The previous summer, Wyn had been on regular patrol when she happened to see a girl in Sulfur Hollow, his old neighborhood, selling lemonade at a roadside stand. Wyn stopped for some and found out the girl was saving up to buy a new bike for her little brother because he didn't have one. Wyn had ended up not only buying a new bike for the brother but one for the girl too.

He only found out about it because the girl's mother had been an old friend of his and told him how much it meant to her daughter. Wyn had never said a word.

She was so good with the victims of crime or accidents and he knew it was because she came from a place of hard experience.

"So did you manage to wriggle out of Andrea Montgomery or the kids whether they're holed up in the witness protection program?" he asked.

"No, but I found she's one of us."

"What do you mean?"

"She's part of the law-enforcement family, anyway. Her husband was killed in the line of duty in Portland."

He frowned. "That shouldn't account for the skittishness you described."

"No, unless she just really, really hates the badge now."

"It happens. Maybe you'll learn more while you're helping her unpack boxes."

"We'll see. Good luck talking to Jimmy. Word of advice—wear your vest and take backup with you."

Jimmy did have a temper but he doubted the man would fire on the police over some misdemeanor graffiti. But one never knew.

"Thanks."

Somebody called her name from the group of senior citizens and she looked over. "I'd better go make sure Ed and Archie don't get ideas about becoming MMA headliners. Thanks again for helping me out."

"I would say *anytime*, but I'm afraid you might take me up on that."

She laughed, shook her head, then waved at him and headed back over to the mats.

He watched for only a moment longer before he forced himself to walk outside into the summer afternoon.

Their encounter highlighted just how tough a job he had ahead of him, returning their relationship to the amiable, comfortable one they had always known.

Why had he kissed her?

His life seemed composed of a string of isolated moments he would give anything to relive so he could make a different choice.

The time in Afghanistan when his convoy had been attacked and he had waited half a second too long to lift his rifle.

The nightmare incident where her father had been shot, when he had ignored his own instincts to take action before things ever got to that point.

Now he could add the soft summer night when he had kissed Wynona Bailey and changed everything between them.

WYN CLOSED THE kitchen cabinet door and shook the now-empty box. "That's the last one. You know what this means, don't you?"

From her spot on a chair at the kitchen counter with her leg elevated, Andie grimaced. "Your long ordeal of unpacking for someone else is finally over?"

Wyn laughed, delighted in her new friend. Over the last few hours, she had discovered Andrea Montgomery was nothing like the cold woman she encountered the first day. She was funny and smart and an amazing mother to her adorable kids.

"No. It means you're now officially moved in. You belong right here in Haven Point."

Andie's pretty features softened. "Oh, I like the sound of that."

"I do too," Chloe announced.

Not to be outdone, Will jumped into the air. "I love it here."

Wyn couldn't help smiling back. "Just wait. In a few weeks, you'll really love it. That's when we have Lake Haven Days, my favorite weekend of the year. We have a huge parade, a boat show, and even fireworks. And then at Christmastime, you can't miss the Lights on the Lake Festival, when boat owners decorate their watercraft of every size and shape for the holidays and float from here to Shelter Springs and back. It's so much fun."

"I think it's great that you love your hometown so much," Andie said.

She did. She would miss it so much if she made the decision that seemed to be pressing in on her more strongly over the last few days.

She thought of the phone call she had made after the yoga class earlier in the day, setting up an appointment with her old graduate-studies adviser at Boise State.

Returning to school for the master's degree she had almost completed when Wyatt died would be a huge step. She still didn't know if that's what she wanted to do—or whether she would have the guts to walk away from the comfortable life she had built here. She only knew something had to change.

She couldn't continue living in limbo. It was time to move forward with her life.

But not right now. At the moment, she couldn't imagine anywhere else she wanted to be.

She sat down at the kitchen table across from Andie. "You're going to love it here. I can't wait for you to meet everyone. McKenzie, Eliza, Barbara Serrano, Hazel and Eppie—they're sisters who also married brothers. They're real characters, just wait. They're going to take one look at these kids and want to be substitute grandmothers."

"My grandmas are both in heaven with my dad," Will said, his tone matter-of-fact.

"I'm sorry to hear that, kiddo. Mine are too. My house down the street was my grandma's and I used to love visiting with her there. She always made the *best* sugar cookies."

"I love sugar cookies," Will informed her.

"Who doesn't? I have her recipe. Maybe I'll make some for you one day soon."

"Ooh, yum," Chloe said. "Can I decorate them?"

"Maybe. I'll have to make them first."

"I can help you," Will said, sliding near her with his crayons and coloring paper. He leaned against her leg until she picked up on the not-so-subtle hint and pulled him into her lap with a smile.

Andie looked vaguely embarrassed at his forwardness but Wyn didn't mind one bit. He smelled of crayon wax and peanut butter and sweet little boy.

"What are you drawing?"

"It's your dog. Can't you tell? See, there's his tail and there's his yellow ears and his black nose."

"Sure. I can see it now. That's a great likeness!"

"You can have it, if you want," he offered, capturing her heart completely.

"Thank you!" She hugged him and he settled back against her, perfectly content, while he went to work on another drawing.

Oh, there was something about being the recipient of uncomplicated affection from a child. She wanted to sit here and hold this boy forever, to keep him safe from all the bad things the world might hold for him.

She wanted children.

It wasn't the first time the desire had manifested itself but it seemed to be happening with increasing regularity as she neared three decades.

She wasn't married and she rarely dated anyone seriously. That might pose a little bit of an obstacle to having a child anytime in the near future. She could possibly think about adopting an older child in need of love, but with all the other uncertainties in her life right now, that would have to wait.

That might be another argument in favor of going back to school. The chance to have a more settled lifestyle, with a nine-to-five job, might be more conducive to raising a child on her own.

She didn't want to do anything but enjoy the quiet peace of holding this darling boy but that would probably make her look weird to his mother.

"I think I might have some business for you," she said to Andie.

FREE Merchandise is 'in the Cards' for you!

Dear Reader,

We're giving away FREE MERCHANDISE!

Seriously, we'd like to reward you for reading this novel by giving you **FREE MERCHANDISE** worth over $20 retail. And no purchase is necessary!

It's easy! All you have to do is look inside for your Free Merchandise Voucher. Return the Voucher promptly...and we'll send you valuable Free Merchandise!

Thanks again for reading one of our novels—and enjoy your Free Merchandise with our compliments!

Pam Powers

Pam Powers

P.S. Look inside to see what Free Merchandise is **"in the cards"** for you!

We'd like to send you two free books like the one you are enjoying now. Your two books have a combined price of over $10 retail, but they are yours to keep absolutely FREE! We'll even send you 2 wonderful surprise gifts. You can't lose!

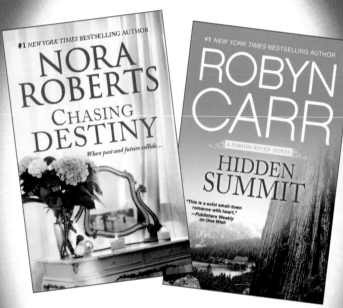

#1 NEW YORK TIMES BESTSELLING AUTHOR

NORA ROBERTS
CHASING DESTINY
When past and future collide...

#1 NEW YORK TIMES BESTSELLING AUTHOR

ROBYN CARR
A VIRGIN RIVER NOVEL
HIDDEN SUMMIT
"This is a solid small-town romance with heart."
—*Publishers Weekly* on *One Wish*

REMEMBER: Your Free Merchandise, consisting of **2 Free Books** and **2 Free Gifts**, is worth over $20 retail! No purchase is necessary, so please send for your Free Merchandise today.

YOUR FREE MERCHANDISE INCLUDES...

2 FREE Books **AND** 2 FREE Mystery Gifts

FREE MERCHANDISE VOUCHER

❑ Please send my Free Merchandise, consisting of
2 Free Books and **2 Free Mystery Gifts**.
I understand that I am under no obligation to buy
anything, as explained on the back of this card.

194/394 HDL GKCL

Please Print

FIRST NAME

LAST NAME

ADDRESS

APT.#   CITY

STATE/PROV.   ZIP/POSTAL CODE

▶ Detach card and mail today. No stamp needed. ▶

© 2015 HARLEQUIN ENTERPRISES LIMITED. ● and ™ are trademarks owned
and used by the trademark owner and/or its licensee. Printed in the U.S.A.

NO PURCHASE NECESSARY!

ROM-516-FMH16

READER SERVICE—Here's how it works:

▼ If offer card is missing write to: Reader Service, P.O. Box 1867, Buffalo, NY 14240-1867 or visit www.ReaderService.com ▼

BUSINESS REPLY MAIL
FIRST-CLASS MAIL   PERMIT NO.717   BUFFALO, NY

POSTAGE WILL BE PAID BY ADDRESSEE

READER SERVICE
PO BOX 1867
BUFFALO NY 14240-9952

NO POSTAGE
NECESSARY
IF MAILED
IN THE
UNITED STATES

"Oh?"

"My friend McKenzie Shaw is the mayor of Haven Point and she owns the floral and gift store in town where the Helping Hands meet."

"I remember. You mentioned her yesterday."

"She stopped by the community center after my yoga class was wrapping up and when I told her I was coming here, she told me to ask you if you are taking on new clients. She would like some fresh graphics for a fall ad campaign. Is that something you might be interested in?"

"Sure. That's exactly the sort of thing I do. Ads, brochures, marketing materials. Whatever a company might need. I do whatever pays the bills, if you want the truth."

She glanced at her children, who weren't paying attention to the boring grown-up conversation. "I do have survivor benefits coming in but I'm trying to save that for the kids to use for college. If we can, I'd like to continue paying our way through my freelance income alone."

"How wonderful, that you've created a career for yourself that you can basically do anywhere."

"I couldn't manage it without steady work from Caine Tech. Aidan has always been very kind to me."

"Aidan's a good man, one who certainly appreciates the importance of family."

She hadn't liked him much when he'd first purchased Snow Angel Cove and the rest of the properties that went along with it. Like others in town—people like Jimmy Welch—she had worried about what he might do to the quiet charm and easy pace of Haven Point.

She shouldn't have been concerned. Since coming to town, Aidan had infused both capital and hope into Haven Point. The downtown area was beginning to flourish, more businesses were moving in and new people like Andie were relocating here all the time.

Yes, the town would no longer be a sleepy, struggling little community beside the lake. It was growing and changing. While that worried some people, Wyn had enough faith in the people of her town that she knew the inherent character of Haven Point as a warm, welcoming place wouldn't change.

"How long have you been interested in graphic design?" she asked.

Andie launched into an explanation about her first job in high school as a retail clerk and the path that had led from that to college and beyond.

"What about you?" Andie asked. "Did you always know you wanted to be a police officer?"

"Oh no. That was the last thing on my list. I had a dozen other dreams that came first."

"What changed your mind?"

Life. Circumstances. A New Year's Eve party, a bastard with an illegal dose of Rohypnol and the horrible, helpless feeling of waking up with huge gaps in her memory, bruises on her thighs and the sick surety that something horrible had happened to her.

"Multiple things," she answered. She didn't go into the assault. She never did. "A big part of it was my brother's death. Becoming a police officer was his only dream, from the time we were kids. After he died, I guess I felt like one of us should carry on that legacy."

"You must miss him very much."

She thought of Wyatt, always laughing, always the life of the party. They looked enough alike that uninformed people often asked if they were identical twins. After a while neither of them had bothered to go into explanations about fraternal versus identical and how male/female twins biologically could only be the former.

It didn't much matter to them. They felt like two sides of the same zygote.

"He was a terrific brother and an amazing person. I'll always be sad the world lost him so young."

"I'm very sorry for your loss," Andrea said softly.

"I'm lucky enough that I still have two brothers left to boss me around. You'll probably meet Marshall. He lives in Shelter Springs but he's around Haven Point all the time."

"I'll look forward to it," Andie said.

"Well, I should get out of your hair and let you get some rest," she said. As if on cue, her phone rang.

"That must be a signal," she said with a grin. She wriggled her phone out of the front pocket of her shorts. A quick check of the caller ID had her shoving the phone back into her pocket.

"It's fine with me if you need to answer that," Andrea said.

She made a face. "It's my mom. If I answer, I'll be on the phone for a minimum of half an hour."

Andie smiled, clearly under the misconception that

Wyn was joking. "Thank you again. The words are inadequate. You've been a lifesaver."

"It was truly my pleasure." Wyn hugged Will one more time, kissed the top of his head and set him on his feet. "I'll see you all very soon."

"Will you bring Pete next time?" Chloe demanded.

"Cross my heart," she promised.

She headed out into a lovely June afternoon but waited to dial her mother back until she was planted on the back deck with some iced tea and a magazine to leaf through if the conversation dragged.

"Sorry I couldn't take your call before," she said after greeting her mother. "At the time, I had my hands full."

It wasn't a lie; she had been holding a very adorable freckled little boy with curly auburn hair and a sweet smile.

"I know how busy you are," Charlene said cheerfully. "I'm just glad you were able to find any time for me at all."

Oh, her mother. So good at laying on the guilt. Wyn forced a smile and focused on Pete, sniffing for interlopers at the edge of the yard.

"What's going on?"

"I'm just checking to see what time is good for you Sunday."

She scanned her mental calendar, trying to figure out what Charlene might be talking about. "For?" she was finally forced to ask when nothing immediately sprang to mind.

"Your brother's birthday! We talked about this."

"I'm sorry. You're right. I guess it slipped my mind, after all the excitement of earlier this week."

"I understand. It's not every day you almost die."

"No, it's not." It also wasn't every day that she saved the lives of two little boys. "So you're having a party for Marshall on Sunday?"

"Yes. Does seven thirty work? It seems late for dinner, but that's the earliest he can be here."

"That's the important part, isn't it? He's the birthday boy. Our schedules should work around his, not the other way around."

"I suppose." Charlene paused. When she spoke again, her voice had a funny little note to it. "Your uncle Mike offered to grill some of that yummy honey-lime chicken he does. Won't that be nice?"

"Yes. That sounds delicious. He always does a great job with it."

Her father's longtime widower brother had been a huge support to the whole family during the two hellish final years of John's life. Like Cade, he had visited John religiously in the care center and helped her mom around the house when Marshall, Katrina or Wynona couldn't get to things.

"Do you think you can come early to help me set up?"

"My schedule's pretty free right now, so that shouldn't be a problem."

She had only four days of suspension left—and Friday would be taken up with a trip to the campus in Boise if she kept her appointment, but she chose not to mention that to her mother.

"What can I bring?" she asked instead.

"That pasta salad you make would be perfect and would go well with the chicken."

"No problem."

"Plan for about eight people," Charlene went on.

"Eight?"

"That's right." Her mother went through the list like she was ticking off her fingers. "Aunt Jenny, Mike, me, you, Katrina and that boy she's been dating lately, and Marshall."

"That's only seven."

"Who am I forgetting?" Charlene paused to think and then spoke. "Oh Cade. That's right."

"Cade," she repeated slowly. She couldn't seem to escape him, even when they weren't working a few feet apart.

"That's right. I bumped into him at the gas station this morning, so of course I had to invite him."

"Why?" she asked. "Last I heard, you were mad at him for suspending me!"

"I know, dear, but this is your brother's birthday and Cade is part of the family. You know he's been like a brother to Marshall since they were boys."

"Right," she murmured. That didn't make him like a brother to *her*.

"So you can come early?"

"I'll be there," she answered reluctantly. She spoke a few moments more with her mother, but Charlene seemed in an unusual rush to end the call. When she hung up, Wyn leaned back on her deck, listening to the river.

She couldn't escape him.

It was bad enough that she lived down the street from the man and worked with him day in and day out. Something was seriously out of whack in the universe when she couldn't even go to her own family parties without running into the man.

When she was constantly thrust into his presence, how in the world was she supposed to convince herself she didn't have feelings for him?

CHAPTER TWELVE

COMING BACK TO this trim and tidy house on Lakeside Drive always made him feel like he was twelve again—lost, angry, hurting.

How many times had he stood on this doorstep, hoping like hell that he could come up with a good enough excuse to explain the latest bruise?

He walked up the steps, reminding himself he was worlds away from that kid who felt completely powerless to change his circumstances. No one—least of all *him*—would ever have guessed back then that one day he would be the chief of police in Haven Point.

The flower baskets hanging from the porch overflowed with blossoms and scented the air with sweetness. Like the rest of the yard, it was lush and pretty. Charlene Bailey was a master gardener who seemed to know exactly what plants went together for maximum impact. She seemed to have a particular skill for coaxing beautiful things to blossom, even in the most barren soil.

Not that he considered that a metaphor for the impact she and John had had on his life or anything.

He didn't know much about flowers, but he kept his own tidy little garden in the backyard. Everything he knew about tomatoes and beans and cucumbers, he had learned from Charlene, when she would put him and his brothers to work with her own kids, weeding a row of corn or picking raspberries or washing cucumbers to be pickled.

She would also send bags and bags of fresh produce home with Cade, both of them pretending he was doing her a favor by taking away things she couldn't use. Both of them had known it was likely the only fresh food he would have to fix for Marcus and Wes. It wouldn't have surprised him if she planted extra, just to take care of the Emmett boys.

Given the choice, he would have spent every waking moment here, where he knew his brothers could be safe and fed—especially in the summers when the days stretched out endless and bleak.

He shifted the bag of vegetables and the fruit tray he had picked up at the grocery store to his left hand so he could ring the doorbell with his right. He never knew what to bring to these things and figured produce was always a safe bet.

Nobody answered for several minutes. He was about to ring it again when the door finally opened and a vision—er, Wynona—appeared in the doorway.

She wore one of her frilly, feminine summer dresses, this one a blue-and-white flowery thing that looked like something a 1940s pinup girl would wear. Her hair was piled up on top of her head, just begging for the right guy to come along and mess it up.

All the spit dried up in his mouth and he wanted to

toss the fruit tray to the floor, scoop her up and carry her home.

"Oh. Hi." It was all he could manage.

She wiggled her fingers. "You're late. The party's already started. Lucky for you, the guest of honor isn't here yet. Marsh called ten minutes ago and he's still another twenty out. I guess he got held up by a jackknifed trailer that spilled a load of feed corn on the highway."

"I heard chatter about it on the scanner earlier."

She shrugged. "Work. What can you do? Come in. Everybody's either in the kitchen or out on the patio."

Under other circumstances, he might have given her a friendly social peck on the cheek but he didn't trust himself. Not today and not with her.

Instead, he awkwardly held out the fruit plate. After a pause, she reached for it. As he handed it to her, their fingers brushed and he thought he saw her cheeks go pink.

"You can go outside to the terrace with Katrina and her latest guy. Carter. He's a rock climber."

"Professionally?"

She smiled a little. "I haven't figured out if he actually has a job yet. He's gorgeous, don't get me wrong, but I'm beginning to suspect he's operating a few carabiner clips short of a full rack, if you know what I mean."

What kind of guy did she consider gorgeous? He had to wonder. He knew she dated here and there, but as far as he knew, she hadn't been in a serious relationship since she came home. Why not?

Because of what happened to her in graduate school?

None of his business, he reminded himself sternly, even as he felt that familiar ache in his chest.

"I should probably say hello to your mother first, before I head back to talk to Katrina and the ditzy climber. Which, incidentally, would be a really good name for a rock band. Katrina and the Ditzy Climbers."

She laughed, which he had intended, and some of the awkwardness between them seemed to ease—for the moment, anyway.

"Mom is back in the kitchen. She'll be glad to see you."

She headed down the hallway to the kitchen at the rear of the house. He did his best not to watch the hypnotic sway of her skirt.

Damn it.

He hated that everything had changed between them, all because of that kiss. Time. That's all they needed, he told himself. Soon enough, things would return to normal.

He would forget how perfectly she fit into his arms, how delicious she tasted. One day he might even be able to walk out onto his deck again without seeing her there.

The kitchen was warm and smelled of potatoes and caramelized onions. Charlene Bailey, as trim and tidy as her house, beamed broadly when she saw him. "Cade! Hello, my dear!"

Affection for her washed over him, as sweet as her hanging flower baskets. He leaned in and kissed her cheek, this woman who had mothered him and his brothers since he was twelve—and from whom he had taken so much.

"I swear, you get more handsome by the minute," she exclaimed. "However do you manage to fight off all the girls?"

"Yes, Cade. Do tell," Wynona murmured.

He gave her a dark look but didn't answer.

"What's this?" Charlene gestured to the tray. "I told you not to bring anything!"

"It's good manners, isn't it, to bring something to a party?"

He didn't add that everything he learned about good manners he'd picked up in this very kitchen from her and from John.

He held up the bag. "I've also got a couple of early tomatoes from my garden."

She looked suitably impressed. "Have you? Already? How on earth did you manage that? It's not even July! Mine are weeks away from producing anything!"

"It's an early-girl hybrid—and I started them inside in February. I've got that nice south-facing window in the spare bedroom and vegetable starts grow like crazy in there. Plus I put a water cage over my plants to keep them warm at night."

"How are your beans doing this year? Mine have got some kind of a bug."

"Aphids? Maybe cutworms?"

He broke off when he realized Wyn was gazing at him with an odd expression—a weird mix of baffled amusement and something that made him feel oddly breathless.

"What? I like growing fresh vegetables. Nothing wrong with that, is there?"

"Absolutely nothing," Wyn assured him.

"Everyone who can should grow a garden," Charlene declared. "There's nothing more calming at the end of a hard day than sticking your hands in the dirt. Wynona, why don't you slice Cade's tomatoes for us? We can add them to the salad and keep a few out for people who just want to nibble."

"I can do it. I'm the one who brought them."

"Don't be silly," Charlene said. "You're a guest here! Go visit with Katrina and her cute friend."

He was aware of a sharp pang, the same one he'd had around her for the last two and a half years, since her husband's injury. On the surface, Charlene treated him with the same warmth she showed when he was that twelve-year-old kid, but there were subtle differences he was sure no one else noticed.

Once, she had treated him like part of the family, just another one of her boys. When they got in trouble, she would yell indiscriminately. She'd dispensed hugs and discipline in equal measure.

Something had changed after John was shot, some shift in their relationship, like a thermostat that had been turned down a degree or two. Not enough to make a huge difference but enough that he couldn't help but notice.

They had never talked about it.

Did she blame him for the shooting as much as he blamed himself?

Why the hell hadn't he acted on his instincts that day...or earlier? Greasy, familiar guilt churned in his gut, especially when he only had to shift his gaze from the kitchen down the hallway, where two large portraits hung on the wall—Wyn's twin brother, Wyatt, and John Bailey. Both wore their dress blues, Wyatt in the Idaho State Police uniform and John in his Haven Point PD uniform. They both had the same nose, the same piercing blue eyes.

Wyn's twin had been her best friend. He wasn't sure she had ever really recovered from losing him so suddenly.

"When do you go back to work?" Charlene asked her daughter.

"Tomorrow, bright and early."

Charlene's jaw tightened and he saw Wynona pick it up too. She suddenly looked like she was having a tough time not grinding her back teeth.

"I can't wait," she said in a cheerful voice he suddenly realized didn't ring quite true. She studiously avoided looking at him, focusing her attention on the tomatoes she was slicing.

"No more disobeying direct orders or running into burning buildings, young lady," her mother said sternly.

The knife in her hand smacked down a little harder than strictly necessary on the cutting board.

"Right. What she said," he drawled.

She lifted her gaze from his tomatoes long enough to give him the skunk eye. "I was doing my job," she said stubbornly.

"So was I when I suspended you," he retorted. "It's my job to do all I can to make sure my officers don't take unnecessary risks."

"The key word there is *unnecessary*," she retorted. "I don't believe I did that."

"Gotta say, I'm on Cade's side on this one," someone said from the doorway to the kitchen.

"Marshall!" Charlene exclaimed. She bustled to her son and hugged him.

Marsh still wore his sheriff's department uniform. His dark hair stuck out in tufts like he'd just taken off his hat and he looked like he hadn't slept in about seventy-two hours.

Wyn and her mother hugged and fussed over him in turn—and then Katrina came in and repeated the process. When he extricated himself from the last of the women in his family, Marshall made his way to Cade, where they exchanged back slaps.

"Happy birthday," Cade said.

"Thanks for making the time."

"Are you kidding? I wouldn't miss it."

"And thanks for keeping my baby sis in line," Marshall said, with a meaningful look at Wyn. "She thinks she's invincible and always has."

"Hey!" she protested.

"True story," Katrina said.

"Oh, the trouble you and Wyatt used to get into," Charlene said. "If you weren't jumping off the roof with a blanket for a parachute, you were taking your dad's canoe out onto the water by yourself when you hadn't even started school yet. Picture me with four kids under the age of six, including twin terrors who never stopped moving."

"And you're still getting into trouble," Marshall said.

Before she could answer, their uncle, Mike Bailey, came in from the back door wearing a striped blue apron and carrying tongs.

"This chicken is close to perfect. How we doing in here?"

"We were just finishing up," Charlene answered. "I think we're ready when you are."

"Do you mind grabbing me a clean platter for the birds?"

Charlene reached into the cabinet next to the sink and pulled out a large platter with enameled cherries on it. "Here you go."

Their hands brushed as she handed it to him—just like his had with Wynona earlier over the fruit. If he hadn't been watching their interaction, he might have missed the way Charlene blushed a little and the tender smile her former brother-in-law gave her before he trotted back outside.

The air was just about sizzling with electricity between Charlene and her late husband's brother, if he wasn't mistaken.

How long had *that* been going on?

And did her children know?

Cade glanced at the others to see if any of them noticed but Wyn and Marshall were still bickering about her suspension and Kat was grabbing salad bowls to carry outside to the patio tables.

"Cade, grab those plates and take them out, will you?" Charlene asked.

He nodded and picked up the stack she indicated. Another thing that wasn't his business. Charlene had said it herself. He was a guest, not part of the family, and he would do well to remember that.

Dinner was, predictably, delicious. The only time he ever ate home-cooked meals this good was right here, at this comfortable house on the lake with the view of the Redemption Mountains.

He was just finishing up his second piece of moist, flavorful chicken when he finally had the chance to talk to Marshall.

"You've had a busy week, from what I've been hearing on the scanner," he said to Marshall.

"So have you. Boat rescues, house fires, the whole gamut."

"Summer tourist season is never boring, is it?"

Laughter rippled across the patio, and he looked over to see Wynona smiling at something her aunt Jenny said. Though it was cloudy, a shaft of sunlight seemed to find her with unerring precision. She had her head tilted to the side and some of her hair was slipping from her topknot. From here, he could see the curve of her jaw, the long, graceful column of her neck.

In that flirty, soft little dress, she looked like every fantasy he'd never known he had come to life.

As if she felt his gaze, she shifted her gaze to him. He couldn't seem to look away and he saw her lips part slightly, her breathing quicken.

"Seriously," Marshall said, jerking his attention back to their conversation, "thanks for watching out for our Wynnie."

"She's a good cop," he said gruffly.

"I have no doubt of that. She's a Bailey, isn't she? But I also would guess she hasn't changed that much since she and Wyatt were jumping off the roof with blankets for parachutes. She tends to be a little reckless and doesn't always think through the ramifications of her actions."

"She's not the only one," he muttered, keeping his gaze firmly away from her and trying not to think about that kiss that had changed everything.

Marsh had been his best friend for more than two decades. What would he think if he knew the sorts of thoughts Cade was entertaining about his sister?

He hoped to hell the man didn't find out.

CHAPTER THIRTEEN

"I'M SORRY CARTER had to leave so early," Wyn said to her sister, though it wasn't at all true.

"He's heading out first thing in the morning to take a climbing group up Teewinot in the Tetons and he still had to get his gear together."

"Oh, he guides other climbers too?"

"Among other things. He takes river trips down the Snake and in the winter, he's a ski instructor in Utah."

"He seems…nice."

"He's very nice—not to mention he looks like he belongs on the swimsuit issue of an outdoors magazine."

"I don't believe outdoors magazines generally have swimsuit issues."

"Maybe not, but if they did, I would nominate Carter for the cover," Kat said.

"So you like him?" she asked carefully.

"Sure. He's a lot of fun. Except for the part where he's a few carabiners short of a full rack," she said pointedly.

Wyn flushed. "You heard that?"

"The window was open and it was a little hard to miss. Don't worry, Carter didn't hear you. At the time, he was down at the lake trying to skip a rock with his toes."

"Still, I'm sorry. I shouldn't have said that. I don't even know the guy." She loved her little sister, even if she wasn't always crazy about her choices in men.

"It's nothing I haven't thought before."

"So why are you dating him?"

"I teach second grade in Haven Point, Idaho, Wynnie. Guys who look like Carter aren't exactly thick on the ground around here."

She wanted to tell her sister looks weren't everything, but she knew the advice was unnecessary. Unlike the man in question, Kat wasn't stupid.

"I just don't want you to have your heart broken."

"A broken heart isn't the worst thing that can happen to a person," Kat said.

In an almost involuntary reflex, Wynona looked over at Cade, who was across the patio talking with Marshall with his legs stretched out and an empty plate balanced on his knee. She focused on her sister again, hoping Kat hadn't noticed.

"Isn't it?"

Katrina shrugged. "I'd rather risk a few rips in my cardiac muscle than sit home night after night, waiting for life to happen to me."

Wyn didn't do that. She went out with friends, she attended concerts in Boise, she had season tickets to a theater troupe in Shelter Springs. Okay, maybe she had come to the point where she would rather not date at all than waste her time with someone she knew wasn't a keeper, but that was her.

She wasn't waiting for life to happen to her. She thought of her appointment with her academic adviser in Boise, the stack of paperwork waiting on her dining table at home, the changes she was preparing to make.

"Enough about Carter," Kat said. "What's up with Uncle Mike?"

Wyn shifted her gaze to where her father's older brother was scrubbing the grill. He was the sweetest man, always willing to lend a hand. His wife had died fifteen years ago after a short battle with colon cancer. They'd never had children and after she died, Uncle Mike seemed content to run his auto repair shop in town and restore classic automobiles, including the ancient blue Ford pickup he cherished.

"What do you mean? Nothing's wrong with him."

"He's acting weird, don't you think? And I think he and Mom aren't getting along, for some reason. Before we sat down to eat, I went back inside for the napkins and they looked like they had been arguing. Mom was all red in the face and Mike looked upset."

Come to think of it, Mike hadn't said much during dinner, when he was usually full of fun stories.

"You know how Mom can be. He probably got sick of her asking him for the hundredth time if he checked the temperature of the chicken, so her precious babies all don't get food poisoning."

Kat didn't look convinced. "*Everybody* is acting weird," she complained. "Marshall's mind seems to be a million miles away and Cade has hardly cracked a smile all night."

At the mention of his name, that involuntary reflex kicked in again and her gaze shifted to him. This time she found him watching her in return. They both looked away quickly and she felt her face heat.

"He's checked his watch six times in the last twenty minutes," Kat went on. "Maybe he has a hot date waiting for him at home."

She hated the jealousy that sliced through her like her mom's best paring knife through his sun-warmed tomatoes.

"You obviously have too much free time on your hands during the summer when school's not in session, if you have nothing better to do than speculate on Cade Emmett's love life."

"Are you kidding? Sam and I have great fun watching women throw themselves at him, then trying to guess which ones he's willing to catch." Katrina's mouth twisted into a pout. "It used to be fun, anyway. Lately he's totally boring. It's been months since he even flirted with *us*, no matter how hard we try. Our theory—well, Samantha's, anyway—is that he has a secret love muffin out there somewhere and he's staying loyal to her."

Her stomach muscles tightened. Maybe he *did* have a secret lover. Come to think of it, she hadn't been aware of him dating anyone in some time.

She hadn't heard any gossip among the other officers and hadn't seen him make or receive any furtive phone calls or texts, but that didn't necessarily mean anything. Maybe he was just being extraordinarily discreet.

Would he kiss her with such heat and hunger if

he was hiding a relationship with this hypothetical woman? Maybe that explained why things had become so awkward between Wynona and him, because he was racked with guilt over cheating on the woman he loved with one of his officers.

"Any clues who she might be?" Katrina pressed. "And why he feels like he has to hide their relationship?"

The idea of it made her feel hollow and achy inside and she spoke more sharply than she might have otherwise.

"He's my boss, not my BFF. We don't hang out at the station house in between dispatch calls doing each other's hair and talking about our latest crushes. Unlike you and Sam, we have better things to do."

Katrina's eyes widened with shock and hurt at what Wyn realized was a totally unprovoked attack. Now the ache in her stomach was coated with a slick layer of guilt.

It wasn't her *sister*'s fault Wyn was all tangled up over Cade and didn't know what to do with her feelings and she had no right to take her confusion out on Katrina.

"Yeah. Everybody's in a pissy mood tonight," Katrina said in disgust. "Some party. And now it looks like it's going to rain."

"I'm sorry. I guess I'm a little on edge about going back to work tomorrow."

Katrina frowned. "Just because I don't run into burning buildings like you doesn't mean my life is shallow or that I don't care about important things."

"I know that. Of course it's not! You're a teacher, just about the hardest job out there!"

"That's right. And I kick ass at it."

Despite the lingering turmoil, she had to smile. "You absolutely do."

She adored her younger sister, even if she could sometimes be superficial and a little immature. Sometimes she had to remind herself that Kat was barely twenty-six, which seemed a lifetime younger than her own twenty-nine.

Her sister was also quick to forgive. "We should do something to liven things up," she said after a moment. "Marsh looks like he's going to fall asleep at his own birthday party."

"Any suggestions? And resurrecting one of our old dance numbers is completely off the table."

Kat laughed just as lightning flashed at almost the same moment thunder boomed across the lake.

"Wow! Where did that come from?" Kat asked.

"Oh no," Charlene wailed. "I was hoping that storm would stay away until after we had dessert!"

Mike turned from the grill. "No problem. We can have dessert in the house. Boys, help clean up these dishes."

The *boys*—both over six feet tall, in their midthirties and strong enough together to lift a patrol car—dutifully rose and began piling dishes in their arms just as fat raindrops plopped onto the concrete. Another lightning strike flashed and thunder rumbled just an instant later.

"That's a close one," Marsh said. "The storm front must be passing right overhead."

"Hurry, everyone!" Charlene exclaimed.

Ordinarily, Wyn loved storms, especially those summer thundershowers that churned the waters of the lake and sent boats racing for the safety of the shore. When she was young, she used to love nothing better than to sit in the window seat in her second-floor bedroom and watch dark clouds race across the sky while the waters boiled.

These sudden fierce squalls that seemed to come out of nowhere were something else again.

Wyn grabbed the potato salad and the basket of silverware. In the few seconds it took to carry them in the house, the raindrops began to fall with harder intensity and velocity and she barely made it inside before the clouds completely unleashed. The lightning now seemed to be hitting with hardly a pause in between strikes.

"Hurry, hurry. Get in here!" Charlene stood just inside the back door, ushering everyone into the kitchen as if none of them had the sense to get in out of the rain without her guidance.

"Is that everything?" Wyn's mother asked as Cade hurried inside with his arms full of condiments and salad toppings.

"All I could see."

They were all a little damp as they crowded into the kitchen while the thunder continued to rumble. The adrenaline rush and the crowded conditions left her a little breathless.

"That certainly woke everyone up," Katrina said with a grin. "Too bad I didn't have time to snap pictures of everyone running around like chickens with your heads cut off."

Her mother suddenly looked horror-stricken. "Pictures! Did somebody bring in Marshall's baby album? It was under my chair. I was going to pass it around after we finished eating."

"Thank you, Mother Nature," Marsh drawled.

"Oh, I hope they're not ruined!" Charlene cried. "There are pictures of your dad in there holding you that are just priceless and I don't have copies of them anywhere else. Someday you'll want to show them to your own children."

"I'll get them," Wyn said and headed for the door.

"No, I've got it." Cade pushed past her before she could reach it and ran out into the deluge. He crouched down under the chair where Charlene had been sitting and emerged triumphant with a photo album a moment later. He wrapped it in his arms and hunched the rest of his body over it before he ran back inside.

"Hurray." Charlene looked close to tears as he handed it over to her.

"It should be okay," he said. "The chair seemed to be protecting it from the worst of the rain."

"Thank you, my dear," her mother said. "That could have been a disaster. But look at you! You're sopping wet!"

In just the thirty seconds he was outside going after the album, the storm had drenched him, leaving his dark hair soaked and his blue polo plastered to the strong muscles of his chest and shoulders.

Wyn couldn't seem to take her eyes off him. She

swallowed hard, feeling warm all over. His gaze met hers and something shivered between them, just like those waves churned up by the storm.

"It's fine," he murmured.

"No it is not!" Charlene exclaimed. "Wynona, grab a towel and help him dry off."

Her eyes widened at the order. Why her? Why couldn't Katrina do it?

On the other hand, she didn't want her flirty sister anywhere near Cade and his soaking-wet pectoral muscles.

"There's a clean load in the dryer. You can probably find one of your brothers' shirts in the extras cupboard too."

"I'm not that wet," he protested. "Really. It's a warm evening. I'll be dry before I get home."

"Don't be silly. You'll catch your death. Go with Wyn. She'll take care of you."

She knew better than to go up against her mother, who had ruthlessly raised five children of her own and half the neighborhood too, while her husband was off protecting the people of Haven Point.

"No sense in arguing," Marsh told him. "You can't win."

"Everyone else, take these kitchen chairs into the living room," her mother instructed. "We'll have cake in there."

Wyn led a reluctant Cade down the hall to the laundry room. This had actually once been a small ground-floor bedroom but when the boys started moving out, her mother declared she needed more space than a cramped closet off the kitchen to do laundry. This had become a combination sewing room, laundry, craft room and something of a retreat for her mother.

It smelled of laundry soap, dryer sheets and wet male. She reached into the dryer and pulled out a still-warm towel. "Here you go."

Cade took it from her. "This is stupid. I'm not that wet."

"It's my mom. What are you gonna do? She will expect you to come out at least wearing a dry shirt."

With a sigh, he started toweling off his hair, which left it sticking up in dark, wavy tufts that begged for a woman to reach out and straighten it.

Her fingers twitched but she managed to keep them at her side, though she was suddenly aware of the intimacy of the room. The two of them were alone, truly alone, for the first time since the day he kissed her.

She swallowed her nervousness and headed for the white armoire in the corner. "This is where Mom keeps extra clothes we've all left here over the years for various reasons. She even keeps extras for Kat and me and Marsh, who all live within a six-mile radius. Crazy, I know. I think she has this secret fantasy of all of us being stranded here after Sunday dinner because of a blizzard or something."

His mouth lifted in a faint smile. "She loves fussing over all of you."

"Whether we want it or not."

He smiled again, though she thought there was a bleak shadow in his eyes. "You should consider yourself very lucky."

For most of his life, he *hadn't* had a mother who fussed over him, she knew, and Cade's bastard of a father had basically abdicated any responsibility for his sons.

Cade had been the one who took care of his two younger brothers. He walked them to school, fixed their lunches, helped with homework. Her heart hurt just thinking about it.

"I *am* lucky," she murmured. "Thanks for the reminder."

She turned and rifled through the clothing stacked neatly inside the cupboard until she found a T-shirt she thought would work.

"Here you go. I think this one was Elliot's but it should—"

She turned around and forgot what she was going to say. He had taken off his wet polo and his chest was every bit as hard and muscled as she had imagined.

Not that she would admit to ever imagining it.

She managed to close her mouth—barely—and handed the shirt to him.

"Thanks." He took the shirt and pulled it over his head.

She had always considered her brothers large men but apparently Cade was bigger. The shirt—soft and worn thin from frequent washing—hugged each muscle, each line.

He flexed his shoulders forward and back, as if trying to make more room. "You sure this wasn't yours?"

"No," she whispered. Her voice sounded tight, thready,

which earned her a strange look from him. *Pull it together, Wynnie. You've seen a half-naked man before.*

Just not one who looked like Cade Emmett.

"It's Elliot's, I think," she said, in a voice that sounded much more in control. "Do you want me to look for something else?"

"No. This works."

"Why don't you leave that one here for my mom to wash?" she suggested. "She can store it there in the extras cupboard."

"In case I happen to be having Sunday dinner over here when Snowmageddon hits?"

"You never know. Anything's possible."

He gave that small smile again, the one that made her wonder if he felt as awkward in this situation as she did. "If there's a blizzard in Haven Point, I'll probably be out in the middle of it. I'm afraid I won't have much time for sitting around your mom's fireplace, roasting marshmallows and singing songs."

"You're just like my dad," she said softly. "He could never stay here where it was warm and dry if somebody out there needed help."

For some reason, instead of taking that as a compliment, his eyes grew shadowed. "I'm not at all like your dad," he said gruffly. "He was a hero in this town, beloved and respected by everybody in Haven Point."

"And you're not?"

A muscle flexed in his jaw. "I don't need to be a hero. I just want to do my job half as well as he did."

"You're doing better than that. He would have been so proud of you, Cade."

His mouth twisted and his eyes took on that haunted look again.

"What's wrong? Why do you get so upset when people say things like that?"

"It doesn't matter. We should get out there before people wonder what we're doing in here."

As soon as he said the words, he looked as if he wished he hadn't. Suddenly, the air between them thickened. She knew what *she* wanted them to be doing in here, what she had wanted since she closed the door behind her.

He was staring at her mouth, she realized with a thrill of shock. Was he remembering, too, the heat and the wonder of that kiss? He gazed at her while thick currents seethed between them.

There was no secret mystery woman. Wyn didn't know how she was so sure, but somehow she knew Cade would never be looking at *her* with that raw hunger if he were involved with someone else.

He wanted her as much as she did him.

She swallowed hard. "I haven't been able to stop thinking about the other night," she whispered.

The words were barely out of her mouth before he was there, inches away. How had he moved so quickly? She had only half a second to wonder before his mouth descended on hers and all that heat and wonder roared back.

He kissed her wildly, fiercely, as if he had been storing up the need for days, just as she had, and had to get it all out while he had the chance. Cold metal pressed against her legs, her back, as he captured her between his body and her mother's washing machine, but she didn't care. She barely noticed, lost to everything but him.

Rain pounded against the window and the air stirred with the scent of clean laundry. She couldn't breathe, couldn't think. She could only feel—and right now she felt amazing. Vibrant, feminine, *alive*.

He was aroused. She could feel him pressing against her and he lifted her, raising her high enough so her softness cradled his hardness at exactly the right spot while his tongue teased and explored.

She rocked against him and he groaned.

Oh. Oh my. Yes. Like that. Oh. A little more.

She gasped his name, then instantly regretted it. He froze as if she'd bashed his head against the dryer.

Breathing raggedly, he stared at her. She watched reality crash over him like that thundershower and saw the instant his wild needs shifted to shock and dismay.

He caught his breath and then lowered her feet to the floor again and stepped away, raking a hand through his hair.

"I can't do this, Wyn. I *can't*."

The warm glow, that sweet sense of rightness, seemed to float away like so much dryer lint.

"Why not?" she whispered.

He glared at her, then at the door. "How about we start with the fact that your entire family is twenty feet away?"

Her family.

Charlene, Aunt Jenny, Katrina, *Marshall*.

Her eyes flew all the way open. "Oh. Right."

She quickly stepped back, straightening her skirt out again with a snap.

"Yeah. *Right*."

She didn't want to hear him tell her all the reasons he shouldn't have kissed her. She knew. He was her boss, they worked together, blah blah blah.

"Wyn, I—"

Suddenly she couldn't bear to hear him minimize or apologize for something that had been earthshaking for her. "Be quiet. Do *not* say a word about how sorry you are."

"Why not?"

If he were truly sorry, he wouldn't have kissed her again, would he? Especially not with such enthusiasm and ferocity.

Before she could say anything, the door burst open and she was deeply grateful that she was no longer pressed against the dryer with her legs clamped around him.

He stepped away farther, shielding the bulge in his jeans behind her mother's sewing chair.

"What's taking you guys so long? Mom sent me in to see if you need help finding a shirt."

Kat walked in, a curious look on her face that seemed to trickle away as she looked at the pair of them. Her sister wasn't stupid, unfortunately. Her gaze shifted back and forth between them and seemed to narrow with each pass.

Wyn could tell instantly when her sister's speculation reached the entirely accurate conclusion about what had been taking them so long. Katrina's mouth sagged open slightly and her eyes widened with shock.

Oh crap.

"We're, um, just about ready to sing 'Happy Birthday' to Marsh," Kat said. "Are you guys coming?"

Almost, Wyn wanted to say.

"Yeah," Cade said instead, rather grimly. "We're done."

He headed out of the room ahead of the two of them. Apparently he didn't need much time to get things back in order, while Wyn still felt as if a hurricane had just roared through her.

Hoping her legs would hold her, Wynona went to follow but Katrina grabbed her arm.

"Was that…? Were you…?" Her sister couldn't seem to come up with adequate words.

Katrina would *not* let up if she suspected for a minute that Wyn might have a thing for Cade. She couldn't let it happen. She had to convince her sister she was imagining things. She drew in a breath and forced a smile.

"Sorry to keep everyone waiting," she said, her tone brisk and no-nonsense. "We were talking about a case and lost track of time. It was nothing. Absolutely nothing. Let's go sing to Marsh."

She pushed past her sister and left the laundry room, quite certain she hadn't convinced either one of them.

CHAPTER FOURTEEN

A FEW MINUTES after that stunning kiss, Cade sat on Charlene Bailey's flowered living room sofa eating chocolate cake that was probably delicious, though it had all the flavor and consistency of spackle to him just then.

What the hell was *wrong* with him?

Had he really just been wrapped around Wynona in her mother's laundry room? One taste of her luscious mouth, one brush of her curves against him, and the heat burned away every ounce of good sense he had left, leaving him hot and hungry, consumed with need for her.

All he could think about was exploring that tight curvy body, tasting every inch of her, coming inside her.

Another minute or two and her little sister might have stumbled onto an entirely different scene.

He closed his eyes briefly, aghast all over again at the close call and his own lack of self-restraint. When he opened them, he found Katrina watching him with narrowed eyes, her mouth tight.

Did she suspect something was up between him

and her sister? He didn't want to think so but he had to wonder. He didn't like that speculation in her eyes.

Would Kat mention her suspicions to anyone in her family?

What would Marshall say if he knew even a sliver of the thoughts Cade was having about his sister?

What would her *father*—the man he had loved dearly and respected more than anyone—have thought?

John had always treated him with kindness and respect—far more than he deserved, coming from his screwed-up family. From where he sat in the living room, he had a clear view down the hall to that portrait on the wall, with that stern, unsmiling expression that belied the warmth in those kind eyes.

He remembered that expression the first time their paths had crossed, when John had caught him shoplifting a pound of hamburger at the grocery store. Cade had been eleven and his mother had died a few months earlier and all he'd wanted was a little hamburger to go with the spaghetti he was making for his brothers.

John had taken pity on him and given him a warning—and had ended up buying about eight bags of groceries for Cade's family, groceries that Walter Emmett had refused to let his grieving boys eat. They didn't need to take charity from a pig, he'd told them after John dropped him off in the patrol car.

It was shortly after that when Marshall Bailey started taking an interest in him at school—not that Marsh had ever been mean to him, but though they were the same age, they'd hung with different friends. Suddenly Marsh was inviting him to have lunch at his table, to play ball at recess, to hang out at his place after school. He could bring his brothers too, if he wanted to, Marsh would casually add.

On some instinctive level, he had known the seeds for that friendship had probably been planted by John Bailey but as it turned out, he and Marsh liked the same things, laughed at the same jokes, enjoyed the same sports.

Despite the kindness of the Bailey family and the steadiness of his friendship with Marshall, Cade had been pulled in other directions too. Sometimes walking into the Baileys' warm, comfortable house filled with music and laughter and delicious smells became impossibly jarring and only highlighted the stark contrast with the unrelenting ugliness of his own home life in Sulfur Hollow.

Eventually, he'd started surrendering to that despair and began to slip away from his friendship with Marsh and hang out with other friends—guys who wanted him to drink with them and smoke weed and cut classes. It was an easier path. When he was high or loaded, he didn't have to face the ugliness, the futility of dreaming. His grades had slipped, he dropped off the baseball team, he started making reckless choices. It was as if he led two lives, the Cade he had been at the Bailey house and the bad-seed Emmett boy he was the rest of the time.

That autumn he was fourteen, he'd been caught stealing beer from the Gas N Go one afternoon. The owner hadn't pressed charges—but knowing of his haphazard friendship with Marsh, he did call John Bailey.

John had picked him up in his patrol vehicle. Cade had thought he was going to take him home and maybe have a harsh word or two for Walter, but instead of taking the turn toward Sulfur Hollow, he had driven him to a quiet spot along the lake.

With those stunning blue waters across from them, John had finally faced him and Cade would never forget the raw disappointment in the man's eyes—and the conversation that would change the entire course of his life.

"The way I see it, you're at a crossroads, son." John Bailey looked hard, uncompromising, in his starched blue uniform shirt and his close-cropped brown hair peppered with gray. "Some people want to think you're nothing but trouble, like your father and your uncles and your cousins. You're big for your age and tough and we both know you've got your father's quick temper. It probably wouldn't surprise many people if you took that same road and ended up in and out of prison. You've started down that path already."

John had held his gaze and Cade had been unable to look away, though the two beers he'd already had that afternoon had roiled around his gut.

"You can go ahead and sink to meet their expectations of you. Or you can lift yourself, to meet mine. You can try harder, study more, make different choices. I know what's in your heart and it's not the things you've been doing."

"You don't know anything," he'd snarled, sick with shame and fear and self-disgust.

"You're not the first to think so," John had said, the

first hint of a smile he'd shown since he'd picked him up. "But in this case, I know what I'm talking about. I've seen the way you take care of your brothers, how you help them with their schoolwork and make sure they have clean clothes to wear and healthy food to eat. You even watch out for your father, though he doesn't deserve it. I know you want something better for yourself, but I can promise you this. You won't find it anywhere along that particular path you've started down."

John had been right. That moment *had* been a crossroads. He had taken the man's words to heart and decided, even at fourteen, that he needed to make different choices for himself. He'd knuckled down in school, picked up baseball again, dropped his partying friends. In the summers and after school, he'd taken a job mowing lawns and doing janitorial work at the police station.

Through it all, he'd observed the way John handled his responsibilities as police chief. He'd watched him show caring and compassion in some circumstances and be tough as titanium in others.

He missed him.

A vast wave of sorrow washed over him for John Bailey and the steady presence he had been in his life. Yes, he clearly saw the irony, that he grieved for Wyn's father far more acutely than he had ever grieved for his own. That sorrow was made more acute because of the grim knowledge that John would be here enjoying his son's thirty-fourth birthday if not for Cade's own weakness.

"Do you think that's a concern this year?"

He looked up from his thoughts to find the entire

Bailey clan gazing at him, waiting for his answer to whatever question Charlene had just posed to him.

"Sorry. I was thinking about something else."

Charlene's plump features softened. "That's the same look John used to wear when he was puzzling over a case—the same one I imagine Marshall gets, if he were ever home long enough for me to see it. That rain hasn't let up out there. I asked if you think flooding might be a concern on the Hell's Fury this year, like last summer."

He forced a smile. "That was a fluke, a combination of several days of heavy rains coupled with the dam break upriver. I'm not worried about it. A few hours of hard rain isn't going to raise the water level enough to make it a concern."

Charlene gave a worried sigh. "I just don't feel good about Wynnie being in that house by herself. You'll watch over her, won't you?"

He didn't dare risk a glance in Wyn's direction. "In the very unlikely event we have more flooding on River-bend Road, I'll certainly make sure she stays dry," he answered.

"I don't know what we would do without you here in Haven Point," Charlene said.

"I hope we don't have to find out," Mike Bailey said.

"The town could always use another Bailey as po-lice chief. Why not Wynona?" he suggested.

She looked vaguely horrified at the idea, though he wasn't quite sure why. Before she could answer, Mar-shall's phone rang.

"I've got to take this. Excuse me."

"At your own birthday party?" Charlene asked with

a harrumph, but she had been married to a police officer for years so didn't look genuinely annoyed.

A few moments later, Marsh emerged with the look of a man who already had one foot out the door. He headed to Charlene and kissed the top of her head. "I've got to run, Mom. Big accident from the rain outside of town."

"Oh, I hope no one was hurt."

"Looks like some serious injuries but nothing life-threatening so far. I'll find out soon enough. Thanks for the birthday party."

"You're welcome, sweetheart. Can you take some cake? And what about your presents?"

"I'll stop by tomorrow. Sorry about this."

"Happy birthday," everybody called out to Marsh, who gave a distracted wave as he headed for the door.

His departure seemed to signal the end of the party. Cade rose, seizing on the excuse.

"I should probably take off as well," he said. "I worked a double shift yesterday then ran to Boise and back this afternoon."

"Oh, poor dear!" Charlene fussed. "I imagine you're completely exhausted."

Now that she said it, his eyes seemed gritty and tired and fatigue weighed down his shoulders in the too-tight T-shirt. He wanted to use exhaustion to excuse his behavior with Wyn earlier in the laundry room but he knew that was feeble at best.

He'd kissed her because he'd wanted to, because he hadn't thought about anything else in a week.

"Won't it be a huge relief when you have Wyn

back on the rotation?" Katrina said, giving him a pointed look.

Had Wyn's sister guessed what they had been doing just minutes before she walked in? he wondered again. He couldn't tell.

He forced a casual smile, quite sure he was fooling no one. "Sure," he answered. "We've definitely noticed her absence this week. She's a good officer and the department needs her."

"It's so nice to be appreciated," Wyn murmured, a little caustic edge to her tone.

"Wynnie, didn't you walk here?" Katrina asked with an innocent look. "It's still pouring down rain out there. Maybe you should get a ride home with Chief Emmett. That way no one would have to go out of the way to take you home."

"I don't mind walking," she answered tersely.

To Cade's dismay, Charlene picked up the cue from her youngest daughter. "Don't be ridiculous! You can't walk in that downpour. Cade wouldn't mind at all, would you?"

Cade minded very much, thanks, but he certainly couldn't say that to Charlene. "Not at all," he lied. "It's no trouble."

Wynona gave him a cool look that told him quite plainly that while she didn't want him to give her a ride home, she was also annoyed with him and didn't mind making him uncomfortable.

"Thanks. I appreciate that. I just need to grab Young Pete and the dish I brought over."

"You all should take some leftovers," Mike put in. "Shouldn't they, Char?"

Charlene gave him a flustered look though Cade couldn't tell whether that was because he reminded her of her hostess duties or because he called her by an affectionate-sounding nickname.

"Oh yes. Just give me a minute and I'll find some containers for you."

She headed into the kitchen, which seemed to be the signal for all the women to do the same, which left him alone with Mike.

They made small talk for a few minutes, and then Mike asked, "How's your brother these days? Marcus. I really enjoyed the few years he worked for me down at the auto-body shop after school. He was quite a character, always joking, but I remember him being a hard worker."

He barely contained his sigh as he pictured Marcus as he had just left him, with his mood shifting between anger, defensiveness and unbearable sadness. The afternoon had been a rough one. Marcus was furious at Cade for refusing to pay his bail and reality was beginning to sink through that he was in real danger of losing his family.

He decided not to tell Mike his brother was in jail. "He's been working construction in Boise but got laid off a few months ago. He's been struggling ever since, if you want the truth."

"That's a real shame. He sure knew his way around a car. I might have an opening in the next few months, if he wants to move back to Haven Point. I'd be happy to have him back."

How would that fit into the family's needs? Cade didn't know. If Christy ended up going through with her threat to leave him, the whole situation could implode.

He hated that he couldn't make everything right for his brother but sometimes a man had to find his own way.

"He's got a wife and a couple of kids who are pretty settled in Boise right now. I'm not sure they'd be ready to pick up and move back here, but I'm sure he would appreciate knowing you made the offer."

"You got it. Keep me posted."

"I'll do that."

Charlene came bustling out of the kitchen with her arms full of bags. Though she had been gone for only five minutes, Mike's face lit up at the sight of her like the sun had just come up over the Redemptions.

Yeah, something was definitely going on here.

"Here you go," she said, handing Cade one of the bags, which he now saw was filled with disposable food containers.

"You should have enough there for lunch tomorrow and maybe even dinner. I even added a couple pieces of cake, since I know it's one of your favorite recipes. You can always use a little more sweetness."

Warmth seeped into a cold little corner of his heart at the way she fussed over him, and he didn't tell her he hadn't even noticed the flavor of the cake. "Thanks, but I don't want to take away leftovers that should be going to the birthday boy."

"I've got plenty," she assured him. "Marsh said he'll stop by but I know how busy he is. If I don't see him by the middle of the week, I'll just run it up to the sheriff's office in Shelter Springs."

He could just imagine how much Marshall loved having his busybody mother stop by the county jail. He had to smile as he returned her embrace.

He barely remembered his own mother. The image of her seemed hazy and faint, like a photograph that had been handled too many times.

He didn't remember her being particularly loving or warm. Maybe she had been sick longer than he knew but he mostly remembered her napping on the couch, yelling at him and his brothers for being too loud in the house, leaving for doctor appointments.

He remembered being totally shocked the first time he came to Marsh's house to see Charlene laughing with her children, playing ball in the backyard, bringing snacks even before they asked for them.

He had been fiercely envious of it—and livid whenever Marsh would talk back to his mother, like boys sometimes did.

If not for John and Charlene, his life would have been so different. They'd given him the precious gift of hope, of possibilities, and shown him by example that he could have something better.

He was doing a piss-poor job of repaying them.

"Don't be a stranger, Cade Emmett." Charlene hugged

him. "I hardly ever see you now that we're not meeting in John's room at the nursing home on Sunday evenings."

As much as he missed John, he didn't miss those grim visits to see a man who had become a hollowed-out version of himself.

"I'll do my best to stop more often," he promised, kissing the top of her carefully colored hair.

When he stepped away, he saw Wynona watching him with an unreadable expression that made his chest ache, for reasons he didn't want to look at too closely.

"Ready?"

She still looked reluctant to ride with him. "Yes. Though, really, I don't mind walking."

"Don't be ridiculous," Charlene said. "You practically live next door to each other. Cade doesn't mind a bit, do you?"

"Not a bit," he lied again.

It was only a mile across town, he told himself as they headed out through the steady rain to his vehicle. What could possibly happen?

CHAPTER FIFTEEN

THOUGH IT WOULDN'T be full dark on these long summer days for another hour or so, the rain and thick storm clouds obscured the sunset, making it seem much later as Cade drove down rain-slick streets toward home.

Cade was intensely aware of Wyn beside him—her quiet breathing, the pale curve of her jawline in the low light, the little smile that played around her mouth as she watched her goofy dog in the cargo area move his head back and forth in time with the steady, almost hypnotic pace of the windshield wipers beating back the rain.

"You said earlier that you've been to Boise and back today," she said after a moment. "I guess that means you probably went to see Marcus."

"I did. I wanted to go earlier in the week but didn't have time until today. I'm not on his list of favorite people right now."

"Why is that?"

He shrugged, fatigue and frustration weighing down his shoulders in equal measure. "He's angry that I refuse to bail him out."

"I'm sorry. That must have been tough."

"Just another lovely day with the Emmetts. He'll get

over it. A little more time to straighten out his priorities and think about what he really wants out of life won't hurt him. If he wants to keep his family, he's got work to do. Being in jail at least keeps him off a bar stool."

She smiled faintly. "There is that, I guess."

"Your uncle Mike offered him a place at the shop."

"Did he?" she asked, her smile softening.

"I told him I'm not sure Marcus is ready to come back to Haven Point. They're pretty settled in Boise, as far as I can tell, but it was nice of him to offer."

She was quiet for a few moments, the only sound in the vehicle Pete's breathing and his tires humming on the wet road.

"If I ask you something, will you give me an honest answer?"

"If I can," he said, bracing himself for her to ask him why he kissed her. He would have to lie. Plain and simple. He couldn't possibly tell her all the wild thoughts racing through his mind about her.

To his relief, she didn't take the conversation in that direction.

"You were there tonight," she said instead. "Tell me the truth. Do you think something weird is going on between my mom and Uncle Mike?"

He never would have believed it, but he would actually prefer having to lie to Wyn about his too-active imagination if it meant he didn't have to talk about Charlene's love life. "Something weird?" he said, stalling. "What do you mean?"

She shifted in the leather seat to face him. "I don't know. They were both acting...odd. That's the only word

I can use. Kat was the first one to point it out but after she did, I couldn't help but notice. Something's up. I can't quite put a finger on it but my mom blushed every time she talked to him and they were being almost *too* careful not to look at each other, you know?"

Sort of like Cade did with Wyn? Yeah. He was familiar.

"I don't know," she went on. "Maybe I was imagining things."

He ought to just keep his big mouth shut here. It wasn't his business. On the other hand, if his suspicions were right, she was going to have to find out somehow. Maybe a little warning would be appreciated.

"What are the chances the two of them are…seeing each other?"

She stared at him, her features mottled by the rain streaking down the window. "As in *dating*? Dad's only been gone since January!"

"*Physically*, he's been gone since January," he pointed out, hating that he had to, as familiar guilt and regret pressed in on him. "In reality, your mom has been alone much longer than that."

"But Uncle Mike? That's crazy!"

"Why? He's been a widower for years. They're both still relatively young, not even sixty. They both have a lot of living to do."

"Why do they have to do it together?"

"I don't know if they are. It's just speculation."

Speculation that hadn't been without basis. He had sensed something different between them too, small signs that they were constantly aware of each other, some little shiver vibrating in the air when they were together.

Sort of like the shiver between him and Wynona. He quickly pushed away the stray thought. The situation wasn't the same. He and Wyn weren't *dating*. They just had this...heat between them.

"I don't believe it," she said, but he heard the threads of doubt woven through her voice. "He's my dad's brother! Don't you think that's weird?"

"Why? They've been friends for years. Maybe it just developed slowly over those years."

He refused to think about any more parallels between her mother and Mike Bailey and him and Wyn.

"I can't accept it. Uncle Mike. What is she *thinking*?"

"Wyn, your mom was completely devoted to caring for John for more than two years. You know she was. I doubt there was a single day she didn't spend at least a few hours at the care center with him. He was her life and she cared for him with all the love and concern any man could ask for. But he's gone now. If she has the chance for happiness again, don't you think she deserves that, after everything she's been through?"

She was silent as they drove down Riverbend Road toward home. He couldn't see her expression and couldn't tell if she was angry with him or merely pensive. She didn't speak again until he pulled into the tree-shaded driveway of her grandmother's old stone house.

"I miss him so much," she said, her voice ragged.

His heart ached at the pain of her words and the answering echo in his own chest. What a measure of a good, decent man, that he was mourned so completely.

"I do too," he murmured. "I still can't bring myself to take his number out of my cell phone contacts. Somehow, that seems too final, my last connection to him."

The rain was beginning to ease, he saw. The dying sun peeked between the clouds to send a last glow across the landscape, brushing her lovely features with light.

"He loved you and was so proud of the man you've become," she said with that faint smile again. "During your deployments, he read your emails to the whole family. Kat and I used to watch the clock, waiting for the moment when he would have to stop reading and grab a tissue to wipe his eyes."

He smiled, though he felt funny to think not only about her father becoming emotional at his stupid emails but about her whole family being party to them.

"You know, you couldn't have made him happier when you decided to go into law enforcement after you got out of the Marines," she went on. "And I seriously thought he would bust through the phone with excitement when he called to tell me you were coming to work for the Haven Point PD."

He shifted as that guilt pinched him again. "John always had a warped perspective when it came to me."

She shook her head. "No, he didn't. He always knew you were a good man."

"I'm not," he said, his voice low. "You have no idea."

She made a face. "Oh stop. Who's the guy who goes into the elementary school as often as he can to read to the kids so they don't see the uniform as scary and will trust the police when they need us? Who responds to every single call at every lonely old lady's house in town, even when everybody knows it's bogus, and treats them with the same kindness every time? Who's the only person I know besides McKenzie who can be polite to Darwin Twitchell when he's in a mood? Face it, Cade. You're a good man."

He couldn't let her words seduce him, to work their way to that cold place inside him. It was too dangerous. He wasn't her father, kind and compassionate and beloved.

"If I were a good man," he growled, "would I be sitting here talking about your father and Darwin Twitchell and old ladies on the surface, while underneath it all, I'm stuck wondering how the hell I'm supposed to keep my hands off you?"

Just like that, the mood changed inside the vehicle, as if the storm had returned and another lightning strike had just arced between them. He could almost hear the sizzle of it.

She stared at him, her lips parted and her breath catching a little on the inhalation.

"Oh Cade," she whispered. "Why do you have to?"

It wasn't the answer he expected and now that her words hovered in the air between them along with his own, he didn't know what the hell to do. Why wouldn't she see reason? Why couldn't she understand that he was lousy for her?

He might be the chief of police but some part of him was just as wild and lawless as the rest of his family. Did he really have to prove it to her?

Apparently so. Without thinking beyond that, he made a low sound in the back of his throat and yanked her against him.

As CADE KISSED her again, his mouth hungry and urgent, all the heat from before roared back like they hadn't just spent the last hour apart.

They picked up right where they'd left off, as if both of them had been at a slow simmer and only needed a tiny spark to blaze out of control.

His mouth was warm and tasted of chocolate and caramel from Marshall's birthday cake and she wanted to lick every last inch of it.

She was vaguely aware of the gathering darkness as the sun went down, of the rain that had slowed to a patter, of the wipers still beating it back.

Mostly, though, she was consumed with him, with Cade, this man who had been part of her life forever.

Though the heat was there, midway through their kiss shifted from urgent, needy, to something slower, more deliberate, but infinitely more arousing. He kissed her as if he couldn't get enough, as if he treasured each taste and wanted to remember it always.

All the words she had said about his compassion and decency seemed to slide through her thoughts, jumbling this way and that until they seemed to catch on each other like magnets, forming one overriding thought she couldn't ignore.

She was in love with him.

She blinked with shock as the world came back into focus a little. The realization was still there. Indeed, it seemed to be swelling, expanding, until it crowded out everything else.

She was in love with Cade Emmett.

She probably had been since he was a boy in too-short jeans and a ragged T-shirt working out in her mother's garden in exchange for a bag of green beans or a basket full of corn.

She thought it was merely healthy attraction for a gorgeous man, mixed in with the lingering crush from her childhood, but this was so much more.

Emotion swelled in her throat, thick and hot, and tears burned her eyes.

She couldn't tell him. And how horrible was *that*, suddenly discovering she had this vast reservoir of love inside her at the same time she knew without question he wouldn't want it?

She hitched in her breath, refusing to cry. He might not want her love but it was quite obvious he wanted *her* and she wasn't about to give up this chance to be in his arms.

His fingers traced her face, the curve of her ear, the expanse of skin bared by her summer dress and she wrapped her arms around him tightly, wishing they could keep the world at bay forever.

Amid the warmth they generated between them, she suddenly felt something cold pressed against her shoulder that made her twitch away.

She shifted slightly and came face-to-face with familiar brown eyes, watching the two of them with curious interest.

Her dog.

She eased away from Cade with a breathless laugh. "Pete, you scared me!"

The dog must have climbed over the seat from the cargo area to the backseat. She didn't want to think about the muddy footprints he was probably leaving all over Cade's leather.

"Get down," she ordered. When the dog settled onto the seat, she turned back to Cade, ready with an apology, only to find his features had once more turned to granite.

"I guess that clears things up, doesn't it?" he said, his voice as hard as his expression.

Not for her. Realizing she was in love with him only made everything more murky and confusing. She'd never been in love before. What was she supposed to do now?

"Not really," she murmured. "You kissed me. That doesn't make you some kind of…criminal."

"It makes me just like the rest of the Emmetts, who take what they want without thinking about stupid things like rules and pesky laws—who act first and worry about the freaking consequences later."

He genuinely believed what he was saying. He thought kissing her put him in the same category as his father, who died in prison after being convicted of armed robbery. If she hadn't been such a mess, she might have found it laughable.

"Exactly what are the dire consequences of two unattached adults kissing?"

"You're not that naive, are you? What would happen if Mayor Shaw happened to drive by and caught us steaming up the windows? Or Jane Parker from the *Haven Point Sentinel*? The chief of police and one of his officers found making out in the front seat of the chief's SUV. Great headline, isn't it?"

"Nobody can even see us back here."

"Yeah, it's dark and it's rainy, but people know my vehicle and we're parked in your driveway. They can do the math."

"What does it matter? Nobody cares!"

That clever mouth tightened. "Again, don't be so naive. My job is tough enough without everyone in town gossiping about how I'm banging one of my officers between traffic stops."

"When exactly did we jump from kissing to *banging*? I can't believe I missed that part."

"I'm a guy. In my imagination, that's exactly where we've been since I kissed you the day of the fire—over and over, in every possible position."

Yes, she knew he was being crude on purpose to shock her back to her senses but now her own imagination caught hold and everything inside her ached with yearning. She closed her eyes, wondering how she was possibly going to get those images out of *her* head now.

"Good to know we're on the same page," she finally murmured.

He stared at her. After a long, tense moment, he swallowed with effort and jerked his gaze out the window, where rain continued to trickle down the glass.

"You said your dad believed I was a good man," he said, his voice low. "Someone with honor. I'm having a tough time agreeing with him right now."

"Because you're attracted to me, that makes you without honor?" she whispered.

"If I act on this—if I went inside with you right now and turned my completely inappropriate fantasies into reality—I would be betraying everything I have fought to overcome since I was a stupid kid caught stealing beer at the Gas N Go. I won't do it, Wyn. No matter how badly I might want you."

She let out a shaky breath as the dark conviction in his voice seeped through her jumbled emotions.

"You work for me," he went on. "Don't you see the impossible position I'm in? My job is everything to me and I can't risk it—I *won't* risk it—for something that would just scratch a momentary itch."

She had been about to tell him about her own trip to Boise this weekend, the choices she was considering but his last words made her see how fruitless that would be.

This wasn't about his position as police chief. He didn't share her feelings. He wouldn't *let* himself share her feelings. She folded her hands together at her stomach, wishing she could hold back the icy fingers of reality that were beginning to spread there.

She loved him and he would never love her in return. How pathetic could she be?

"Where do we go from here, then?" she murmured.

"Nowhere," he said firmly. "As far as I'm concerned, tonight never happened. Neither did anything else between us this past week. I'm going to go home and get some much-needed sleep and in the morning I'll have my head screwed on straight again and be able to focus on what's important—protecting the people of Haven Point."

Well, that firmly let her know her place in his world. As long as she wore the uniform, she mattered to him and he refused to let himself have any interest in getting her out of it.

"Fair enough," she said, hoping her voice didn't wobble on the words. "Come on, Pete. Let's go."

She opened her own door and grabbed the bag of leftovers her mother had sent home with her, then climbed out to open the door for Pete.

She heard Cade swear behind her then a moment later he joined her, umbrella opened to keep her dry on the short walk to her front door. That's right. She was a citizen of Haven Point, one of those he had sworn to serve and protect. Right now that particular citizen wanted to shove that umbrella right back in his face.

At the door, he grabbed the leftovers from her while she worked the key in the lock.

Pete immediately pushed his way inside, headed for his food and water. She thought Cade would rush to get away from her. Instead, to her surprise, he followed her into the house and turned on the lights of her small entry for her.

He hadn't bothered with the umbrella himself, she realized, and his hair was slightly damp and curling at the ends. It made him look oddly vulnerable.

"Wyn, I'm not the man you think I am," he said, his voice grave.

"Oh, you have no possible idea what kind of man I'm thinking you are right now," she retorted.

His mouth lifted into a sudden smile she was quite sure surprised both of them but it faded as quickly as it appeared.

"I don't want you thinking this is…any more than a physical attraction. I'm not the sort of man you should lose your heart to."

The organ in question gave a sharp, hard twinge, as if to reinforce that his warning came too late.

"You might be the chief of police for the department where I work, but that doesn't make you boss over my heart," she answered softly.

His gaze sharpened as if he was wondering whether her heart was already involved. For an instant, she thought she saw a fierce joy flash there but it quickly gave way to something that almost looked like despair.

"Don't," he said roughly. "If you knew the truth, you would hate me."

"The truth about what?"

He looked as if he regretted saying anything. Lines of exhaustion had appeared around his mouth and his features were taut with fatigue. He'd already been through an emotional day after a difficult week. She might have been sorry for him, if she had any room left for compassion in her poor battered heart.

"Forget it," he said. "Just forget everything. I'll see you in the morning."

He turned and walked back through the rain without bothering to use the umbrella.

She didn't close the door behind him until she saw his taillights turn into his own driveway down the street.

Forget everything, he said.

How could she? Her entire world had just been up-ended and she felt as if everything stable and comfortable had been shaken to the core. She was in love with Cade Emmett, the stubborn, impossible, wonderful chief of police.

What was she supposed to do now?

CHAPTER SIXTEEN

"I THOUGHT YOU weren't going to be able to make it today!" McKenzie exclaimed when Wyn walked into her store room at Point Made Flowers and Gifts in her uniform a little over a week after she'd returned to work.

"I was able to rearrange my lunch hour but I can't stay long. Looks like you've called out the troops."

Indeed, it looked as if the entire Haven Point Helping Hands had turned out for the emergency meeting called by McKenzie—with the exception of Katrina and Samantha Fremont, who had gone climbing in Jackson with Carter the wonder-boyfriend.

For once, she wasn't sorry her sister was absent. Kat had tried to pin her down repeatedly about that scene she had stumbled onto at Marsh's party. Each time, Wyn had to tap-dance around the interrogations like she had the evasive skills of a hardened criminal. She wasn't fooling her sister. Katrina was certain something was going on between her and Cade—she just hadn't figured out what yet.

"Hi, Wyn." Andrea Montgomery smiled at her and Wyn grabbed the last empty seat at the table, next to her.

She was happy to see Andie looking so much more

relaxed and comfortable than she had when Wyn first met her just a few short weeks ago. It was great to see her here. Apparently the meeting she had attended the week before hadn't scared her off.

"What's the big emergency?" Wyn asked.

"Desperate times, my friend," McKenzie answered. "This is our last chance before the fair this weekend and I'm just not sure we have enough inventory. The library is still trying to replace the books they lost because of the little plumbing disaster in the children's section. We've allocated emergency funds to replace them but Julia Winston says it's not quite enough. I'm hoping we can help make up the difference. I figured one more batch of our special Christmas on the Lake ornaments wouldn't hurt."

"You do know Aidan will help with whatever the library needs, right?" Eliza said.

McKenzie looked grateful. "Ben would too. Trust me, it's nice to know we have a couple of fat-cat donors waiting in the wings."

"And I'm sure they appreciate you calling them that," Wyn said drily.

Kenz grinned. "You know what I mean. We could have them donate but I want the community to feel invested. People care more for something when they have a stake in it. If we can take care of the children's collection at the library without having to call on Ben or Aidan to help, then we can hit them up when we have an urgent need somewhere else."

That was McKenzie. Always thinking. She loved Haven Point almost as much as Cade did.

Wynona gave an inward grimace. She had tried so hard to push the man out of her head this last week. Obviously, she wasn't doing a very good job. He tended to show up there at the oddest moments.

Resolutely, she pushed him out again and plopped into an open seat next to Eppie Brewer and across from Andie and Eliza.

"I'm sorry I missed your self-defense class yesterday," Eppie said. "I had Ronald drive me to the eye specialist in Boise."

Poor Ronald Brewer, who had become the de facto escort and chauffeur for his wife and her sister since his twin brother died a few years back.

"Is everything okay?" Wyn asked.

The other woman made a face. "Stupid cataracts. The only good thing about having them is that when they operate, I can lose the glasses. I'll just need bifocals for close work like this. Did we learn any hot new moves in class?"

"We mostly practiced what I've already taught."

Devin's yoga class had really enjoyed the self-defense lessons she taught during her suspension—which seemed a lifetime ago—and they had asked her back to teach more on a regular basis.

"We've been practicing," Hazel said.

"That's right," Eppie said. "I can't wait for some bad guy to come out of the bushes at me. He'll be sorry he messed with this old broad."

Wynnie grinned, picturing Eppie on the sidewalk in fighting stance yelling, "Come at me, bro" while Hazel cheered her on from the sidelines.

Oh, she would miss them all so much. Hazel, Eppie, Aunt Jenny and the rest.

The familiar mix of emotions of the last few weeks jumbled around inside her again—trepidation, sadness, anticipation, fear.

She still wasn't certain she was making the right choices but at least she no longer felt frozen, suspended in limbo.

Life couldn't stay the same. It was like the Hell's Fury, always changing a little from year to year. She had to shift her own course to change with it. The alternative was unbearable.

The transition would be tough. Just thinking about leaving Haven Point and all her friends made her heart ache, but she couldn't let that hold her back. She didn't want to leave but she knew staying was impossible, especially now.

"Did you still plan to start the self-defense classes that are open to everyone?" Andie asked from across the table.

The question seemed casual but she sensed an intensity in her friend's eyes. Though she had been by several times to visit with Andie and the children, she purposely hadn't pushed the other woman to tell her what had *really* brought her to Haven Point.

"You know, I haven't given it more thought, to be truthful. You're more than welcome to come to Devin's yoga class. We work on self-defense for the last forty-five minutes, from about nine forty-five to ten thirty on Wednesdays at the community center."

"The restaurant has been busy so I haven't had time

to get to your class. What kind of things do you work on?" Barbara Serrano asked.

"Only a few moves that might help you get out of sticky situations. Nothing too elaborate."

"You ought to teach all of us some of those moves," Linda Fremont said. "Do you know someone is sexually assaulted every one hundred seven seconds in this country?"

"I did. Yes."

She had firsthand knowledge of that particular grim statistic, not something she shared with anyone or even thought about much anymore. It had happened. She couldn't change the past but it no longer consumed her as it had once. The course of her life had changed so much, sometimes she thought that day had happened to someone else. She no longer seemed like the same heedless college coed who had been date-raped.

Andie, she noticed, was looking down at her hands and her features seemed to have paled a shade. She frowned, wondering if that was the source of the fear and uncertainty she had sensed in Andrea when she moved to Haven Point. Had she been attacked?

"Every woman should learn a few basic self-defense moves," Wyn said. "They're not always practical to use, but sometimes it can make all the difference. I'm happy to teach a class or two outside the yoga class. Maybe we can reserve the big meeting room at the community center one evening."

"That's a great idea," McKenzie said. "I can check into it."

"You've got enough on your plate, with the wedding and all," Eliza said. "Why don't you let Wyn and me organize it?"

She wanted to tell Eliza they would have to schedule it before the second week of August, when she would be moving to Boise, but now wasn't the time for that grand announcement. She hadn't even told her family yet and didn't intend to until some of her plans were a little less nebulous.

"Sounds good to me. Just let me know when to be there."

"Definitely. We'll spread the word to everyone who might be interested," Eliza said.

The conversation shifted, as these things did, to children and grandchildren and vacation plans.

"How are the wedding plans, anyway?" Barbara Serrano asked McKenzie a few moments later.

"Fine, I suppose. I'm not panicking yet. I have to get through Lake Haven Days and the wooden-boat festival first and *then* I'll start stressing about the last-minute wedding details."

"You know we're all here to help," Wynona said.

"I do. And I'll probably use every one of you."

She would be leaving for Boise just a few weeks after McKenzie's wedding. Maybe by then, she wouldn't be so conflicted about the idea.

"That was a heavy sigh," Andie said in a low voice. "Is everything okay?"

The concern in the other woman's voice touched her. She had been right about Andie. She was a sweet, compassionate woman with a kind heart. Wyn didn't want to lie to her but she couldn't confide in Andie without telling *everyone* and she wasn't ready for that yet.

"Fine. Just fine," she said with a forced smile. "How are things with you?"

"We're starting to settle in. It's only been a few weeks but so far I'm very happy with our decision to move here. Everyone has been so kind to include us in things and help us feel part of the community."

"Haven Point is a nice place. I told you so."

Andie smiled, though the light of it didn't quite push away those lingering shadows in her gaze.

"Where are my favorite adorable little urchins?" Wyn asked.

"They were hanging out here with Jazmyn and Ty Barrett for a while, then they all got bored and begged to go to the park down the street. Letty Robles agreed to take them."

"The woman is a superhero," Devin said. "Talk about saving the day."

Letty Robles was housekeeper to Cole Barrett, Devin's fiancé, who was a single father of two very cute kids in their own right, Jazmyn and Ty.

"I'm sorry I won't have the chance to say hello to any of my favorite children," Wyn said with real regret. "I'm due back at the station in about twenty minutes."

"Then let's see how many ornaments we can finish before then," McKenzie the bossy taskmaster ordered.

She would miss all of them, even McKenzie and her whip-cracking.

A river couldn't stay the same, year after year, and her life couldn't either.

WYN CHECKED HER watch as she parked her patrol vehicle and headed into the police-department offices, in back of the large, graceful city hall with its historic clock tower.

At certain moments when she pushed open the door to the office, she felt as if she had traveled back in time.

When she was a girl, she loved to ride her bike to the library next door on summer afternoons, then stop to see her father after she had checked out her books. If things were slow at the Haven Point PD, she would sit on his guest chair and chatter to him for an hour or more—about the books she had found in the stacks, about her current annoyance with Wyatt, about any trouble she might be having with friends, about her favorite television show.

He had been such a good father, always acting as if he cared, never letting on he might be bored with a discussion about her crush on one of the members of a certain boy band.

John would have been proud of her, working here in the police department he had given so much of his life to—and ultimately given his life *for*.

She hadn't come to work here until after his brain injury, when she felt as if her job in Boise was just too far away for her to be a help to her mother. She wasn't sure just how much her father understood after his injury. He hadn't been able to talk, though she was almost certain he smiled when she would talk to him about working here.

What would he have thought about her recent decision to leave and start a new chapter of her life?

A few weeks earlier, she might have worried Charlene would feel abandoned by her departure. She supposed that wasn't as much of a concern now, with Uncle Mike in the picture.

Mike.

Her mother and Mike Bailey were indeed dating. Twice the week after Marsh's party, she had stopped by the house and found him there both times. Finally Sunday, Charlene had gathered her, Marsh and Katrina together to announce it rather defiantly. She had then burst into tears and run out, leaving Mike to face them all amid enough awkwardness to fill Lake Haven several times over.

Wyn still didn't know how she felt about it. The concept still seemed so strange to her but Cade's words returned to haunt her several times over the last few days.

He was right. Her mother had cared selflessly for her father for more than two years, putting her own life on hold to make sure John felt as happy and safe as he could with his diminished mental capacity.

She loved her mother and she had always adored her kind uncle Mike. If they had a chance for happiness together, Wyn didn't have the right to begrudge them that.

That didn't mean she was ready to throw a party for them yet but she was working on it.

On her own time, she reminded herself. Right now she needed to focus on work.

She headed into the station and any lingering angst about her mother and uncle flew right out of her head when she found Cade leaning a hip against her desk, his arms crossed.

Her heart rate kicked up and nerves danced through her. He was every inch the tough, dangerous lawman— but that didn't stop her from remembering just how sweet and tender his mouth could be on hers.

"There you are."

She blinked at the hard edge to his voice.

"I radioed in that I was taking lunch."

"You did. More than an hour ago."

"An hour and *five minutes* ago," she pointed out. And ten minutes of that time had been spent giving a warning to the out-of-state driver of a big RV that had been parked in front of a fire hydrant, despite the red-painted lines.

Okay, she was late. Until the last few weeks, Cade had always been the best kind of boss but since she'd been back from her suspension, their interactions had been stiff, awkward, tense affairs.

Even after she had been able to make an arrest in the vandalism case that had taken up entirely too much of the department's time, his reaction had been muted. Forget that she had worked her tail off and finally ended up searching through the garbage can of Jimmy Welch's *mother's* house, where she found empty spray-paint cans that matched the color used in the graffiti—with Jimmy's fingerprints on them.

Cade hadn't even smiled, though the other police officers celebrated with her, and Jesse Fisher even brought in a bowl of her favorite gelato from Carmela's.

Another reason she knew she had made the right decision about graduate school.

"What's going on?" she asked now.

"Carrie Anne's babysitter called and one of her kids was throwing up so she had to take off," he said, referring to their receptionist, a divorced single mother trying her best under difficult circumstances.

"Oh, I hope it's nothing serious."

"A stomach bug, as far as Carrie Anne can tell. But I just got a call about a domestic dispute at the marina and Cody is out helping Jim Buttars round up a bunch of dairy cows that broke down a fence in his pasture and are wandering through the neighborhood. I need you to hold down the fort here."

"I can take the domestic disturbance."

He shook his head. "I've got it. I've been in meetings all morning and could use a little excitement. You know how to reach me."

Did she? That was a big part of the problem. She knew his phone number by heart and how to call him on the radio in half a second flat but she had no idea how to *really* reach him.

He took off without another word and after a moment, she plopped down at her desk. For a summer afternoon during the busiest time of year, the phone was surprisingly quiet and she decided to use the downtime to catch up on paperwork that had piled up since her suspension. It wouldn't hurt to clean things out in preparation for leaving.

An hour later, she finished organizing her own files but decided to clear out some of the old folders in her desk, cases dating back to before her time, when this had been Cade's desk.

It was surreal to see her father's handwriting on some of the paperwork, his bold, no-nonsense scrawl. Again, she had that odd sensation of walking back in time, as if she could go knock on the door to the chief's office and find him in there puzzling over a case or talking on the phone to a witness.

She had to smile a little as she leafed through the mostly closed cases of parking violations and a few drunk and disorderlies. Hmm. Most of these should have been filed a long time ago and she felt guilty that she hadn't gone through the drawer before this.

The majority were dated in the weeks just before and just after her father had been shot, when everything here was understandable pandemonium while the Idaho State Police investigated the officer-involved shooting and the subsequent death of the shooter, Joseph Barlow, a drifter who decided to rob the local liquor store at gunpoint for gas money to get him to the next town.

While her father had been fighting for his life, Cade had been named interim chief and probably hadn't had time to organize some of his old paperwork.

She could have handed the work off to Carrie Anne when her kids were healthy again. But since things were slow and her own work was caught up, she decided to take on the task. It was kind of interesting anyway, encountering names of townspeople she knew on old files, and there was a definite sense of satisfaction in putting a little order to the chaos.

She reached the bottom of the pile when she found it.

At first when she saw the name Ronnie Herrera on the form, she thought it was another drunk and disorderly. Ronnie could be a great guy but he didn't hold his liquor well. She had broken up more than one bar fight at the Mad Dog where he had been involved.

As she read further, though, her insides seemed to turn to a block of ice.

Impossible. It must be some mistake.

By the time she reached the end of the form—a witness report, actually—the ice seemed to have crackled out to fill the rest of her.

What was this, and why had it been tucked away under other incident reports in a drawer of Cade's old desk?

She had read every single scrap of paper in the case file about her father's shooting. The state police had investigated it thoroughly—when a police chief was shot and severely injured and the suspect in turn shot by another officer, every stone had to be turned over.

She had never read this particular witness report, though. She was sure of it. Was it possible she missed it somehow?

Her copy of the documents in her father's case file was at home—it somehow had seemed important for her to have a record of the cataclysmal event that changed so many lives—but the original would be just a few feet away in the file cabinets.

On impulse, she made a copy of the witness report for her own duplicate of the official case file, then found the original. She was carrying both to her desk when— naturally—Carrie Anne's phone rang.

She pushed the buttons to pick it up on her desk extension. "Haven Point Police Department. Officer Bailey speaking."

"Hello, Officer Bailey. This is Detective Warren from the Portland Police Department. How are things in your little corner of Idaho this fine afternoon?"

Maybe it was the result of her lingering turmoil from Ronnie Herrera's confusing witness statement, but she took an immediate dislike to the detective's smarmy, falsely jovial, brothers-in-arms tone. She checked the caller ID to verify it did have a Portland area code.

"Fine. Quite busy today. How can I help you, Detective Warren?"

Some of her curtness must have trickled through the phone line. The detective paused for a moment then spoke in a tone that was markedly cooler. "I'm doing an ATL on a person of interest in a case I'm working and got a tip this week that she might be in your area. I'm wondering if you can point me in the right direction."

Typically, the Haven Point PD tried to cooperate with other jurisdictions but something about the detective set her on edge. She didn't want to assist with his attempt to locate but since she was the only one in the office, she didn't know how she could avoid it.

"Haven Point has nearly six thousand residents. I'm afraid we can't know every single person in the city limits but I'll help you if I can. Do you have a name on this person of interest?"

"Yeah. She's a pretty redhead by the name of Andrea Montgomery. She might also go by her maiden name. Andrea Packer."

Wyn froze, suddenly on alert.

Oh Andie. What kind of trouble are you in?

"Hmm. Montgomery or Packer, you said?" She did her best to stall for time while she tried to figure out how to play this.

"Yeah. There's a chance she could be using another alias entirely. She would be new to the area, probably within the last month or so. She's also traveling with two children, a boy who's four but small for his age and a girl who is six."

Who the hell was this detective and why was he looking for Andrea? Was this man part of the reason her friend had been so jumpy?

"Whatever name she's going by," the man went on, "she's about five foot four, a hundred and twenty pounds, with red hair and green eyes. No tattoos, but she does have a small scar at the corner of her mouth, left-hand side, maybe half an inch long."

How would this detective know Andrea didn't have any tattoos? Wyn wondered, all alarms now firing wildly.

"I'm sorry but I'm afraid I can't help you. That doesn't ring any bells for me," she lied. "Like I said, we can't know every single person in town. What makes you think she might be in our jurisdiction? Does she have family here? If so, I can check with them to see if they have any clues to her whereabouts."

"No. No family there. She has a…business connection, but it's tenuous." Frustration crackled through the phone line.

"If you want to send us her mug shot and jacket,

I'll let the police chief know. We can certainly keep an eye out for her." She tried to keep her voice calm and even, hoping he couldn't hear the hard suspicion in it.

"She doesn't have a mug and she's never been arrested before, so she doesn't have a rap sheet."

She did her best to play along. "A slippery one. I get you."

"I do have a snapshot I can shoot you. Do you have an email address?"

"Yes. But first, let me jot down your particulars. What was your name, precinct, phone number and badge ID, just so I can pass it along to my chief? He's a bit of a hard-ass about that kind of procedure."

She had no problem throwing Cade under the bus in this situation, even though her words weren't strictly true. Cade ran a tight house but not to the point of obsession— except when the rule violation involved her disobeying direct orders or the chief of police engaging in extracurricular activities with one of his officers, anyway.

Again, he hesitated slightly and she had the distinct impression Detective Warren would prefer not to divulge all that information but couldn't avoid a direct question.

He recited his necessary identification, which she wrote down carefully.

"Got it. Go ahead and send me what you have and I'll pass it along to my chief and the rest of the department so we can be on the alert."

She gave him a department email address she knew Cade didn't monitor. Until she had a chance to talk to

Andrea, it might be better to keep this information to herself.

"You should have it within the hour."

"Great. We'll be sure to get back to you if anything pops."

"Thanks."

"You mind telling me why you're looking for her?" she asked, trying to weave her question ever so casually into the conversation. "If we've got some kind of a dangerous criminal mastermind in our midst, we would really like to know so our department can be on alert."

Again, he hesitated almost imperceptibly. When he spoke, that smarmy, ingratiating note had returned. "I'm afraid I can't talk about it. You understand. It's an ongoing investigation and I'm not ready to reveal my hand just yet."

Which both of them knew was cop code meaning he didn't have diddly—if there even *was* an investigation.

"Anyway, it's only speculation at this point," Warren went on. "I'm just looking to have a conversation with the woman. But I have to find her first."

Wyn *really* needed to have that conversation first. The only way she could help Andie was if she knew what was going on.

"You go ahead and send me that photograph. Meanwhile, I'll pass this information along to my chief and let him take it from here."

"Chief Hard-Ass," he said, in that jovial tone that grated down her spine like a room full of fingernails scraping down blackboards.

"That's the one. You'll hear from me, either way."

"Thank you for your help, ma'am. I'd like to get down to your neck of the woods someday. I hear it's beautiful."

"We like it," she said shortly. "Thanks for your call. You'll hear from us."

She basically hung up on the man then stared into space. What was Andie mixed up in? And what did this Detective Robert Warren have to do with it?

On impulse, she went to the first line of investigation and Googled him. From the first few links, she was able to get an image of a man younger than she might have expected, maybe late thirties. He appeared to be highly decorated, with several citations she found listed on an online bio.

Maybe she was crazy to be on edge about the phone call and to think that he was somehow connected to Andrea's edginess when she first came to Haven Point.

There was a chance her instincts were totally out of whack. Maybe Andie had committed some heinous crime in Portland and was on the run here. She had a hard time reconciling that idea with the woman she had come to know, but it wasn't the first time that day she had come to question her own judgments.

She had to get the story from Andrea and figure out a way to talk to her friend when she couldn't evade the questions.

She closed the last file just as Cade came back. "Did you get things sorted at the marina?" she asked.

"Yeah. Two brothers fighting over whose turn it was this week to drive the boat they went in on together. I'm guessing they're now rethinking that particular business decision and will likely end up selling the thing."

He glanced down at her desk before she could hide the notebook where she'd jotted down information during her phone call. "Detective Robert Warren from the Portland PD. What did he need?"

She couldn't possibly tell him his neighbor across the street was a person of interest in an as-yet-undetermined investigation. Not until she had a chance to speak with Andie herself.

"Just an ATL. When he sends me the particulars, I'll pass it along."

To her relief, he took that at face value. "Okay. Keep me posted."

"I will."

"Anything else happen while I was gone?"

The witness statement she had found was concealed beneath the thick file into her dad's shooting. Cade, of all people, might be able to shed light on it. He had been there, the other responding officer. It had been his shot that had finally taken out Joseph Barlow during that last, terrible gunfight.

"Something weird." Her stomach was suddenly a tangle of nerves, just talking about that day two and a half years earlier. "I was organizing my desk and clearing things out when I found a form that hadn't been filed under the corresponding case number."

He shrugged. "It happens, unfortunately, though things have gotten better since we computerized more paperwork in the last few years. Just put it in the right file."

She met his gaze. "It's a witness report from the Joseph Barlow shooting."

He froze like a cougar on prey, his features going completely still. Sudden tension seemed to ripple through the room. "Oh?"

"Yeah. Ronnie Herrera. It's the weirdest thing. I thought I knew that case inside and out. I read every detail of it. I never knew Ronnie was down at the marina, sleeping in his pickup truck after he and Elena had a fight."

He nodded, his mouth in a hard line. "Oh yeah. I'd forgotten that. Yeah. He was there."

So why hadn't she ever read that in the case file?

"According to his witness report, he says he woke up when he heard shouting and peered out his truck window just as Barlow was cornered at the lake's edge. He claimed Barlow was the first one down."

CHAPTER SEVENTEEN

WITH EVERY OUNCE of control he'd learned as a boy growing up as Walter Emmett's son, Cade fought to hide his reaction to her words.

He couldn't let her see how rattled he was by her discovery of that witness report. His face felt hot and a slick ball of dread roiled around his insides.

He wished to God he'd shredded the damn thing after the state police took Ronnie's statement. He hadn't been able to bring himself to do that. It was an official report. Instead, he had tucked it away and forgotten about it completely until this moment.

What an idiot.

For two and a half years, he had done his best to keep the truth from the Bailey family—or at least from Charlene and Wynona. Marshall knew. They'd talked in the hospital waiting room in the early hours of the morning after the shooting. He hadn't wanted to but Marshall either suspected something or just knew him well enough to know he was hiding something about that night.

Marshall reluctantly agreed with him, that nothing good would come of full disclosure, especially not when John was fighting for his life after taking a bullet to the brain.

The truth would devastate everyone who loved John Bailey. Charlene, Wyn, Katrina, the whole town of Haven Point, who looked at him as a hero.

Now Wyn was waiting for him to answer, her blue eyes trained on him like a sniper on a target.

He swallowed hard. "You've read the ballistics report. You know it says the round that hit your dad came at him in an upward trajectory, when Barlow was on the ground. You also know your dad got off a wing shot in the firefight."

She pulled out the witness report and held it out to him. His gut clenched when he saw her fingers were trembling. "Ronnie Herrera said here that Barlow had his hands up and was just about ready to set his weapon down when the first shot was fired."

And there it was. The suspicion that haunted him, that kept him up nights, that made him question everything he thought he knew.

He remembered one of his trainers at the police academy telling him that any cop who obsessed about choices he'd made—or hadn't made—in the heat of the moment would eventually turn to booze or drugs or worse.

He was able to close the file on most of the cases he'd worked over the last decade and a half but not this.

Never this.

That didn't mean she needed to carry the burden too.

At the same time, he couldn't lie to her straight up. "Ronnie's version of events didn't match the evidence and since he had a blood alcohol level that was twice the legal limit, the state police investigators chose to disregard his statement."

He took the statement from her and pointed to the signature of the investigating officer. "See? Right there. They talked to Ronnie and concluded his testimony wasn't pertinent to the investigation."

"Not pertinent."

"You know how unreliable eyewitnesses can be. Throw in a dark night and a guy who is drunk and despondent after a fight with his wife and you're not going to get the straight story."

He saw her eyes cloud with doubt. Good.

"You need to let this go, Wyn. That's all I'm going to say. The state investigators did their job. And if I never have to talk about that night again, it will be too soon for me."

Hoping he'd convinced her, he grabbed the statement and carried it into his office, where he shut the door carefully and sat at his desk.

John Bailey's desk.

The man Cade had loved and respected above all others.

He closed his eyes, the memories of that night as fresh as if he had just lived them.

The first call that the liquor store had just been robbed at gunpoint, then the report that someone had seen a possible suspect on foot, heading toward the marina. John had been closer and had a head start and called for Cade to back him up.

Like most stories, though, that wasn't the beginning. To see the full picture, one had to step back and see what had preceded that night.

John had been behaving strangely for days leading up to the incident. Longer, if Cade really stopped to look at small details. He would forget where he left his keys, stop talking in the middle of a conversation to search for an easy word like *sandwich*, become distracted by the strangest, most inconsequential things.

Something was wrong. In another man, Cade might have blamed substance abuse but John abstained from all but a glass of wine at the holidays. He suspected a physical or mental condition—possibly early-onset dementia, though he would never be able to prove it.

He only knew he had concerns her father wasn't fit for duty—concerns he had done nothing about.

That was the burden he would always carry.

He hadn't seen the actual shoot-out with Barlow so he couldn't ever be sure what had actually happened. He only knew what he had heard.

John yelling for Barlow to put down his weapon.

Barlow responding, "Okay, okay. It's going down. See?"

Then a barrage of shots. By the time Cade rounded the corner seconds later, John was down. Cade had yelled at Barlow to put down his weapon but the man continued firing, leaving Cade no choice but to fire back and take him out.

Had John truly fired on a man who was trying to surrender? Or had Barlow only been pretending to lay down his weapon, before he came up shooting?

The only two men who knew the truth to that were both dead.

Cade only knew that if he *had* witnessed the encounter from the beginning and if John *had* fired on a surrendering man, Cade wouldn't have been truly surprised, given John's poor decision-making in the days leading up to the shooting.

He should never have been in uniform.

Could he tell Wyn the truth? All of it? About John's odd behavior, about his suspicions?

She believed her father was the sort of larger-than-life lawman who would do no wrong. She believed John Bailey was a true hero who gave his life to protect his little town.

How could he uproot that idea and plant seeds of doubt in its place? He couldn't. Cade loved her too much to take that away from her.

HAVEN POINT WAS enjoying a beautiful evening—the warmest temperatures of the year so far. As Wynona drove home after her tumultuous day, it seemed everyone was enjoying the summer night except her. The lake seemed packed with watercraft of every sort—powerboats, kayaks, canoes, even stand-up paddleboards.

This was the sort of evening the Lake Haven tourist bureau loved. She waved at her neighbors, Herm and Louise Jacobs, who were each walking with gelato cones from Carmela's in one hand and holding hands with the other. She got a gelato-cone wave in return from each of them and she found it rather sweet that they didn't want to drop hands even to wave back at her.

Despite the tranquillity of the scene, her thoughts hadn't stopped racing all afternoon. Between the phone call from the Portland detective about Andie and that puzzling, incongruous witness report she stumbled onto, she had plenty to stew about.

Had Ronnie really been too loaded to be sure of what he saw? Yes, Cade was right. Eyewitness reports were the least reliable kind of evidence. She might have dismissed it completely, if not for Cade's reaction when she'd shown it to him. He looked almost…guilty.

What was he hiding?

She had thought before that she didn't know the entire story about what happened the night her father was shot. A piece of the puzzle was missing, she'd always believed so. Perhaps it had something to do with that witness report.

She ought to swing by Ronnie's place and ask him. He worked for the gas company and was probably off shift by now.

Ronnie, she knew, lived in Sulfur Hollow, not far from the ramshackle house where Cade had grown up. She could be there in a second. She hit her turn signal and tapped her brake as she approached the road. At the last minute, she lifted her foot from the brake and thumbed the turn signal off.

The past wasn't going anywhere. It could wait.

Meanwhile, she had problems to deal with in the now. She needed to talk to Andie about that unsettling phone call from Detective Warren first.

As she turned onto Riverbend Road, she had to slow down for a couple of kids playing soccer in the street. Out of habit, she waved at them, then at another neighbor mowing his lawn.

When she passed Andie's house and saw her out front with her children, working in the flower garden, she waved but didn't stop. Not yet. Some instinct urged her to think the conversation might go better if she changed out of her uniform into civilian clothes before asking about the phone call from the smarmy detective.

They were friends. She didn't want Andie believing she was visiting in an official capacity.

She hated thinking she might be risking the ruin of their new friendship. She couldn't help thinking about how skittish Andie had been that first day they met, especially after Wyn told her she was a police officer.

She remembered the stark, white face, the fear in her eyes.

Wyn didn't want to do anything that might bring back that fear but she was very much afraid mentioning Robert Warren might do the trick.

Cade wasn't home yet, she saw across the street—at least his vehicle wasn't in the driveway. That didn't really surprise her, since he had been holed up in his office when she left, where he'd retreated after she'd asked him about that witness report.

When she reached her house, Young Pete greeted her with all the energy of his misnomer.

She smiled and scratched his ears. "How was your

day? Did you keep all the nasty cats and squirrels out of the yard?"

He barked an agreement and she had to smile, despite the craziness of her day. "That's my good dude. You're my hero."

She petted him for several moments, in dire need of the calm perspective he always provided.

How would he adapt to living in Boise for the immediate future? Finding a rental close to campus that allowed dogs might be a struggle.

She would figure it out. She was ready for the next stage of her life. Somehow it didn't seem so overwhelming when she considered that at least she would have Pete along for the ride.

After she changed quickly into a T-shirt and shorts, she grabbed the dog's leash and her little pack filled with treats and balls off the hook by the door. Pete could be a good distraction for the children. They would enjoy a visit with him, which might give her a better chance to talk to Andrea.

On impulse, she picked up her gardening gloves and shoved them in her pocket. She'd noticed before that when she worked alongside people, they were often more willing to open up to her—to ask her questions, confide secrets or simply to talk.

Pete trotted outside, tongue lolling with eagerness. On their short walk down the street, he sniffed at every mailbox they passed, every crack in the sidewalk, every tuft of grass.

Andie was still outside with her children but they

had moved to another planting bed along the side of her house. Will was the first to notice her and her dog.

"Pete!" he exclaimed, his adorable features lighting up with glee. With none of the apprehension he had shown earlier in their acquaintance, he hurried over to Pete and threw his arms around the dog's neck.

"Hi, Pete." Chloe hurried over to get her own doggy hugs in.

"Hey, you two. Beautiful evening, isn't it?" Andie said.

"Nothing prettier than a Haven Point summer evening. I thought you might need some help." She held up the gardening gloves.

Andie shaded her eyes with her hand. "Are you kidding me? You must have known I was at the end of my rope. For every weed I pull, it seems like three more grow in its place."

"With both of us fighting them, we might stand a chance," Wyn said, forcing a smile. "Where would you like me?"

"I just started in this bed. If you work on that side and come this way, we can meet in the middle."

"Good plan. I forgot a trowel. Do you have an extra?"

Andie produced one from the bucket nearby and for several moments, they worked in a companionable silence while the children played fetch with an enthusiastic Pete. One good thing about a golden Lab—he never got tired of fetch.

When she was sure the children were on the other side of the yard, she finally addressed the questions racing through her mind.

"I didn't actually come here to weed," she confessed. "I needed to talk to you and I guess I was just looking for an excuse."

"You know you can talk to me anytime but I would be stupid to argue. Anytime you want to use weeding my flower gardens as an excuse, be my guest!"

This was much harder than she expected. She didn't know where to start, reluctant to take away Andie's look of rare contentment.

At the same time, the other woman might be in more trouble than she knew, if Robert Warren had narrowed her location down enough that he had known to call the Haven Point Police Department.

She sighed and set down the trowel. "I got a phone call a few hours ago at the station. What we call an ATL—Attempt to Locate."

"Yes, I'm familiar with most of the police jargon. I helped Jason study for his POST training when we were dating."

Her husband, who had drowned trying to save another man's life. Wynona drew in a breath, hating what she had to do.

"The detective calling was a Robert Warren from Portland, looking for a person of interest in a case he's working."

Andie stared at her for a full thirty seconds as every trace of color seeped away from her features, then she looked away, blinking rapidly.

"Oh? What does that have to do with me?" She asked the question in a falsely casual tone, though she was hardly moving her mouth.

"I think you know the answer to that, don't you?" Wynona spoke gently.

Andie started to tremble, so abruptly that the trowel fell from her hand to the dirt. She covered her face with her hands and sank down to the ground as if her body couldn't support even a kneel.

Little panicky breaths came out of her and for a moment, Wyn worried she was hyperventilating. She went to her and put an arm around Andie's shaking shoulders.

"Why is he looking for you, Andie?" she asked gently.

Andie dropped her hands, her eyes suddenly wild with panic. "What did you tell him? Does he know I'm here? I have to get the kids. We have to…to go. I have to grab their things and go."

She would be caught in a full-fledged panic attack in a moment if Wyn didn't step in. "Breathe, honey. You're not going anywhere. Breathe. That's it."

She stayed beside her, giving Andrea physical and emotional support until the woman's breathing slowed slightly.

"I didn't tell him anything," Wyn finally told her. "He asked me outright if I knew you and I lied to him. I told him the name didn't ring a bell. Yes, that's right. I lied to another officer of the law."

"I… Thank you." Andrea hitched in a ragged breath. "That might buy me a little time."

Wyn slid away. "Time for what? To pack up your kids and go on the run again? What about the flowers?"

Andrea looked at her as if she didn't know who or

where she was. "I can't… He won't give up. I've been so *stupid*."

The bleakness in her voice almost made Wyn shiver despite the warm evening.

"How?" she murmured.

"When I moved away from Portland, I thought it was over. I thought, if I wasn't there, right in front of him, he would…lose interest and move on. But he never will."

"Who is Detective Warren to you, Andie?"

"He was my husband's partner."

Those were the only words she said, which told Wyn exactly nothing.

"And?" she finally prompted.

"And six months ago, he…raped me."

THOSE WORDS. SO STARK and yet so devastating.

"Oh Andie."

Andrea sat in the grass, pulling her knees forward and wrapping her arms around them. She looked dazed, with that shocky look Wyn was used to in crime and accident victims.

"Sometimes I have to ask myself if it really happened. He was Jason's partner. His best friend. He seemed…wrecked by Jason's death."

That wasn't an uncommon reaction for partners, who often ended up blaming themselves when something went south. She would have described Cade the same way after her father was shot.

"After the funeral, I was…lost," Andie went on quietly. "Completely lost. It's humiliating now when I think about it. Jason handled everything around the house when he was alive, you know? The yard, the cars. I didn't even know how to start a lawn mower. Rob could see I was struggling and he...started coming around all the time to help. He mowed for me, he helped with leaky faucets, he cleaned out the gutters that first winter. I was so *grateful* to him at first."

"And then?"

She gazed at her children, who were now wrestling with Pete, oblivious to their mother's trauma.

Andie rested a cheek on her upraised knee, watching them.

"Everything started to change around the holidays last year. I gave him a sweater from me and from the kids. I don't know. Maybe I gave him the wrong signal or something and he got the wrong idea."

"A sweater isn't an invitation to sleep with you," Wyn said gently. Any more than a friendly conversation at a party was a signal that a woman wanted a roofie slipped into her drink.

"He...started to come over more often and wanted to stay later. His wife and I were friends. Our children played together all the time. It didn't seem right to take so much of his time. And things between us were starting to get...weird. He wanted to hug me and touch me all the time, friendly at first and then...more. Finally I told him I had to stop relying on him so much, that he needed to be with his own family. I told him I couldn't let him come around anymore, for everyone's sake."

The controlling men Wyn had known in her career hated being told what to do, more than anything.

"Let me guess. He didn't take kindly to that."

"You could say that. He was so angry. He told me he owed it to Jason to take care of the family he had left behind, that they were brothers. He...told me he was in love with me."

Two high spots of color on her cheekbones showed stark against the pale of her cheeks. "I didn't feel the same way. How could I? He was married to my friend! They had children together, a family, a life. Besides that, my grief was still so raw, even though it had been a year since Jason died."

The children were back to fetch again and Pete was doing a heroic job of keeping them occupied.

"I told him to stop, that I didn't share his feelings," Andie said, her voice so low Wyn had to strain to hear. "It was horribly awkward—especially when he didn't believe me. He said he knew I cared about him too. He wouldn't listen to reason. I didn't know what else to do so finally I told him he had to leave or I would have no choice but to call his lieutenant and tell her Rob was harassing me."

Andrea picked up the trowel and began digging it into the dirt, hacking and hacking at a weed there.

"He got this horrible, ugly expression on his face. He looked like a stranger, not at all the kind friend who was always willing to help. And then he...raped me. I fought and cried but he didn't seem to care. He just kept saying, 'I love you, I love you, I love you.' Over and over."

Tears dripped down her cheeks but still she kept

hacking at the weed, until it was jagged and broken, a pale skeleton.

Andie wiped at her tears with the back of her hand, leaving a little trail of dirt from her glove. "Afterward, he acted like I was the one who instigated things. That we had a…a *relationship* or something. He actually said we would have to keep things secret between us for now."

"I told him there was nothing between us except sexual assault and he laughed. He said I…begged for it. That I seduced him. He said that's what he would tell his wife and his lieutenant and anybody else, if I was foolish enough to say a word."

"You didn't report it." Wyn didn't need to state the phrase as a question. The answer was obvious.

Andie closed her eyes. "I was a police detective's wife. I knew I needed to go to a rape crisis center or the emergency room. That was the right thing to do. I *knew* it in my gut. I even had the car keys in one hand and my cell phone in the other to call a babysitter. But I couldn't. I just wanted it all to go away, you know?"

She did. Oh, she did.

"I completely understand," she murmured, reaching out and covering Andie's hand with her own. She knew exactly what it was like to wonder what she had done to cause this and, afterward, to wonder if she could have fought harder.

"I put my keys and phone back into my purse and climbed into the shower," Andie said. "It was the worst decision of my life. I know that now. I just…didn't have the strength for a court battle."

"Warren didn't go away."

Again, it was a statement, not a question. He wouldn't have tracked Andie to Haven Point if things between them had ended with the sexual assault.

"He sent me flowers afterward. How sick is that? He sent me flowers with a note that said the night had been unforgettable and he couldn't wait to see me again. I thought about taking that to his lieutenant but it only seemed to reinforce his version of events. That we had a *relationship*."

"You don't think his superiors would have believed you?"

"He was a hero in the department. Well liked, well respected. Everybody loved him. He had this humble, happy-to-serve thing going on and I knew people would never believe he raped me. *I* could hardly believe it myself."

Over the years, she had learned how to carefully tuck away her emotions when she responded to any report of a sexual assault. Her experience wasn't important to the victim when they were reliving the trauma, the fear, the helplessness. Though she wanted to tell Andie she understood perfectly what she had gone through, Wyn knew the time for that would come later.

"So what did you do?"

Andie's gaze shifted to her children. When she looked back at Wyn, some of the bleakness had been replaced by cold resolve. "I bought a Taser, changed the locks, installed an elaborate security system, and told him when he dropped by later that week that I was recording every conversation between us and wouldn't hesitate to report him if he ever touched me again."

"Good for you!" Wyn squeezed her hand.

"Except it wasn't. He just found different ways to torment me. He started spreading rumors about me around our circle of friends. That I was sleeping around. That I had come on to him and others. That I had cheated on my husband when he was still alive. Some didn't believe him but enough did that life became…difficult."

"Is that when you decided to move?"

"No. That was later, when he started trying to get to me through my kids. He pulled Chloe out of class one day to question her about some alleged vandalism at the school, which automatically pinned suspicion on her. He started rumors about *them* through his children. Then one day in May, Will disappeared from the play yard at his preschool. For an hour, we didn't know where he was. We scoured the school grounds, looked in all his favorite places. I was just about to call the police when Rob rolled up with Will asleep in the backseat of his car. He said he just wanted to take his old buddy for ice cream and, *oh, did I forget to tell the right people? Sorry.*"

Wyn wasn't a mother but she could certainly imagine how terrifying that must have been for Andie. She had disliked the guy instinctively on the phone. Now she hated just the mention of his name.

"I knew I had to leave. I could no longer stay in Portland, where the situation had become more than I could handle. I thought moving would help us make a new start and we could put all that ugliness behind us. But that's impossible, isn't it? We never will."

"If he's obsessed with you, he's not going to stop looking, no matter where you run."

Her eyes darkened with despair. "So what do I do?"

Wyn knew what *she* would like to do—drive to Portland right now, tie the bastard into knots and toss him off the same bridge where Andie's husband had died.

"Do you still have the Taser?"

"Yes. I keep it in my purse all the time."

"Good. And I saw you installed a security system."

"The landlord agreed to let me upgrade the one that was here as soon as I moved in. It's very highly rated."

"Excellent. You're not going to like my next advice," she predicted.

"It's got to be better than spending the rest of my life on the run."

More color had returned to her friend's face. Coming up with a plan of action was the most empowering thing a victim could do. That's why Wyn had started her own investigation that eventually led to the arrest and conviction of Brock Michaels.

"I think you should get in front of this now. Tomorrow, first thing, we're going to get a restraining order against him. If he comes anywhere near Haven Point, he'll be arrested for violating it. As soon as that's in place, I want you to call him, tell him exactly where you are, but tell him firmly and decisively that you do not want to hear from him and he needs to stop harassing you. Tell him you are good friends with the chief of police and several people in the police department.

Tell him you've told us everything he did and that we believe you."

"Thank you for that," Andie said, her chin wobbling.

"You've got friends here, Andie. Friends who have your back."

Andie started to cry again, silent tears that dripped through the smudge on her cheeks.

"I moved to Haven Point simply because I liked the name," she said softly. "On the surface, it seems like a crazy decision, but I'm beginning to think it was the very best one I could have made."

CHAPTER EIGHTEEN

"THANKS FOR THE HELP, man." Moose Porter with Idaho Fish and Game filled the doorway, holding the copies Carrie Anne had just helped him make containing everything in Jimmy Welch's file.

"We're always willing to lend a hand, but I'll be honest with you," Cade said. "I don't know how much our notes on his vandalism case will help with your poaching investigation. What connection do you see that I'm missing?"

"No connection, really, I'm just thinking it shows an escalating pattern of antisocial behavior in the last month or two. The man has a big chip on his shoulder, that's clear enough. He seems to think the world owes him something. It's not a huge leap to think he might be the one setting illegal traps at watering spots along the lakeshore. All our evidence points to him, anyway—especially considering the trapping has stopped since he's been a guest of Sheriff Bailey at the county jail since you arrested him."

Though his bail had been set low, Jimmy had burned most of his bridges in Haven Point and couldn't raise enough to get out of jail.

"Well, let us know if you need to consult further

before you bring charges. Wyn Bailey was the arrest-
ing officer on the vandalism charges and she's probably the best one to talk to."

"Is Officer Bailey in today? I was hoping to catch
her."

Cade didn't miss the too-casual eagerness in the game
warden's voice and the way his gaze kept darting back
to the squad room of the station, empty now since his
officers were out on assignments.

He had suspected for a while now that Moose had a
thing for Wyn since the man blushed and got tongue-
tied whenever she was around. Cade couldn't help a
pang of sympathy.

Apparently he and Moose both had it bad.

He had missed her that morning. A half-dozen times
already, he had thought of something he needed to tell
her. He'd even gotten up once, before he remembered
her desk was empty.

He needed to cut it the hell out. His only interactions with Wynona Bailey should be related to department business.

He couldn't help thinking Moose was just the kind
of guy she needed. Solid, earnest, hardworking, without the truckload of baggage Cade seemed to cart with
him wherever he went.

"I'm afraid she's not coming in today."

He didn't add that Wynona was scheduled to work
a half-day shift that morning but she'd called him and,
in a terse exchange, told him she needed to take time
off to handle some personal business.

She had hung up the moment he agreed. She hadn't

told him why she needed the time and the curiosity was driving him crazy. A few weeks ago, before her suspension, she'd asked for the afternoon off on this date so she could get things ready for a bridal shower she was throwing for McKenzie Shaw later. Maybe she'd run into some kind of party-related crisis, but that didn't seem like Wynona.

"Okay. Well, I guess I should have called first."

"That might be a good idea, next time."

"Okay. Well, if she comes in, tell her I said hi, okay?" Moose asked, his hands fidgeting with the file.

What was this, junior high school? Next the guy would be asking him to slip a note in her locker for him.

Cade forced a smile. "Sure. No problem."

"Thanks, Chief. Appreciate it. I'll see you later."

Moose took his time walking out of the station, as if he hoped Wyn might magically appear on his way out. He stopped to talk to Carrie Anne for a minute then left, with that hopeful look still on his broad features.

When Moose was gone, Cade settled back to take care of the paperwork that always seemed to pile up in a small-town police department when he handled everything from human resources to public relations to parade permits.

After a few minutes, he had to accept that his concentration was shot. Thanks to Moose, now he couldn't stop thinking about Wyn and wondering again why she'd needed that extra time off.

Was she ill? Was it a problem with Charlene? Did she need help with something around her house?

This was getting ridiculous. It wasn't any of his

business. Personal leave was just that. Personal. He was her boss and he needed to keep that front and center in his mind.

What the hell was he going to do?

He was in an impossible situation, through nobody's fault but his own. If he hadn't kissed her that day after the fire, everything would be the same as the past two and a half years. They both had always worked well together and were able to socialize comfortably. He considered her a good friend, someone he could confide in, count on.

Now this awkwardness seemed to permeate every interaction.

Their lives were connected on so many levels, it seemed impossible to extricate her from his mind and heart. He couldn't seem to escape her, no matter what he did or where he went.

She was his neighbor, his best friend's sister, his late mentor's daughter, his best police officer.

He was in love with her.

The realization had been seeping in slowly for weeks; now it was like the raging flood that had threatened the houses along the Hell's Fury last summer.

He was in love with his best officer. His best friend's sister. His mentor's daughter.

He probably had been for a while now but Cade had never been in love before. At first, he hadn't recognized this soft tenderness, the desire to be with her all the time, to make her smile and try his best to make everything better for her.

He was in love with her and if she knew what he

had done—or *failed* to do, more precisely—she would despise him.

Did her personal-leave request have anything to do with that stupid misfiled witness statement?

While he was dealing with the shock and dismay of realizing he was in love with her, Cade had also decided something else while he was tossing and turning in the early hours of the morning.

He had to tell her the truth.

Maybe not today, maybe not even this week, but he needed her to know.

All this time, he'd told himself he was protecting her but he had come to accept that he was really trying to protect himself.

She wanted to know and he had to figure out a way to tell her without shattering every single ideal she held sacred.

He did his best to focus on necessary paperwork for another hour. Just when he was feeling restless and ready to climb out of his skin, he heard a familiar voice then Carrie Anne's response.

"Don't you look nice, all dressed up," Carrie Anne exclaimed.

A man who knew what was good for him would just keep on working—would maybe even be smart enough to close the blinds in his office so he couldn't see her.

Apparently he didn't have the first idea what was good for him.

He looked up and saw Wynona smiling at Carrie

Anne and showing off a pair of sandals that made her legs look long and luscious.

She had on one of those soft, feminine dresses she wore in her off-hours, this one a pale lavender with an abundance of lace. Over it, she wore a light short-sleeve sweater in a darker shade of purple. Her hair looked different, soft and pretty, curled into waves that she held away from her face with a jeweled clip.

Longing was a hard, sharp ache in his gut.

"I had to go with a friend to see Judge Jenkins," he heard her say.

"That old lech." Even from here, twenty feet away, he could see Carrie Anne roll her eyes.

"Right? Yes, I know it's a huge step back for the movement but I figured, use what you've got. He's a chauvinistic pig but we needed his help and I guessed correctly that a little primping would only work in our favor."

What friend of hers needed a judge? And why? More important, why hadn't she told him what was going on?

He was her boss, he reminded himself, not her confidant. He didn't have the right to know every single thing going on in her personal life.

"Nice strategy. Did it work?" Carrie Anne asked.

"Perfectly." Wyn smiled. "We got just what we asked for. How have things been here? Has it been busy?"

"Not at all. Moose Porter was in about an hour ago, asking Chief Emmett about you."

"Was he?" Wyn glanced briefly toward his office and, caught, he couldn't look away quickly enough. Their gazes met and color rose on her cheeks. Was it because of Moose Porter or because she caught him staring at her like they really *were* back in junior high?

"He's so cute, like a big old cuddly teddy bear," Carrie Anne said, a wistful tone in her voice. "And he's always so sweet with my kids whenever we see him. He'll be a great dad someday. I don't get why you don't go out with him."

Yeah, Wyn. Why not?

"Moose is a great guy. He's just not…" She hesitated and though he was now pretending to concentrate fiercely on the papers spread out on his desk, he was almost certain she looked into his office.

"He's not what I need right now," Wyn went on, her voice firm. "But you should totally go for it, Carrie Anne. He really is terrific."

What *did* she need right now?

It certainly wasn't him.

"Anyway, I only have a minute, then I'm out of here again," Wyn said. "During one of my breaks last week, I bookmarked a couple of ideas for the games we're playing tonight and I didn't pin them or email them to myself. For some reason, I can't find the links again so I just need to go through my browser history and email them to myself."

"Don't you hate that? I can't wait for tonight. This shower is going to be epic! My mom is babysitting for the kids and I told her to just plan on sleeping over, since I didn't know how late we would be."

"I really hope it lives up to everyone's expectations," Wyn said.

Cade was aware of her heading in his direction and

he held his breath until she took a detour to her own desk. He did his best to ignore her. Really, how were they going to keep working together when he had all the concentration of a flea with ADHD when she was around?

After a few moments, he risked a glance up again, just in time to see her heading for his office with a stack of files in her hand.

"Yesterday when I was going through some files in my desk, I found some that still need your signature."

"Thanks. You can add them to the pile."

She set the papers down and turned to go but he wasn't ready to lose this brief connection. She looked so lovely and he ached to have the freedom to tell her so. To wrap her in his arms and press kisses to the back of that soft, sweet-smelling neck and listen to her breathy sighs…

"I heard you tell Carrie Anne you had to go before Judge Jenkins this morning," he said.

She turned around, releasing the delicious scent of citrus and vanilla. A cop wasn't supposed to smell so good, damn it.

"Yes. Thanks for giving me the personal leave."

"It's your leave. And things have been miraculously slow again today. That will all change tomorrow when Lake Haven Days start, but we're good for now. George is following up on a property-line dispute and Jesse's out on patrol."

"He's coming along, isn't he?"

"Yeah. He was a good hire." He didn't want to talk about his newest officer. Finally, he decided to come right out and ask the question he had told himself all morning was none of his business. "So what's the story? Why did you need to see the judge today?"

She paused and for a long moment, he thought she wasn't going to answer, but she finally sighed. "I guess you probably should know what's going on since she's your neighbor and since you're chief of police. The truth is, I was helping Andie Montgomery petition for a protective order against someone."

"Oh?"

"Her husband's former partner, actually, in Portland."

The pieces clicked into place. "Let me guess. The detective who called the station yesterday? Warren, wasn't it?"

Her mouth twisted into a sour look. "Right. That's him."

Apparently she had been keeping a few things from him. "And why did Andrea feel she needs a protective order against him?"

"It's a long story and some of it is…private and personal in nature. She has decided not to press charges over some of the things he's done because she has no physical evidence to prove it. I don't feel right about sharing details without her permission. But I believe everything she says and so does Judge Jenkins. Suffice it to say, the man abused his position in the worst possible way and then he became obsessed with her to the point of stalking her. That's the reason she moved to Haven Point."

"And why she was so jumpy and afraid of the police when she first moved in," he guessed.

"Exactly. She's had a rough time of it. She thought Detective Warren would lose interest if she moved away but when he tracked her here yesterday, she knew he was both obsessed and determined."

Wyn had been right. Something *had* been off about their new neighbor. Her instincts, as usual, had been stellar. Stalking. An obsessed police detective who abused his position and tormented the widow of a fallen fellow officer.

He hated thinking that someone who had sworn to uphold the law would twist it to suit his own purposes but it wasn't the first time.

"She kept some threatening text messages she had received from him. That and some other evidence she had might have been inadmissible in a criminal trial but, combined with her testimony, it was enough to convince Judge Jenkins the order was warranted."

"That's great."

"And then I gave Andie moral support while she called Detective Warren to inform him of the order and to tell him in no uncertain terms to stay away from her. Just in case he wasn't convinced, I took the phone and told the son of a bitch that if he ever came to Haven Point, he would be arrested and prosecuted to the full extent of the law."

The sheer satisfaction in her voice—and her rare profanity—made him smile, despite his own emotional upheaval.

"You love sticking it to the bad guys, don't you?"

"When they have it coming, absolutely," she said. "Anyone who thinks he has impunity to attack or torment someone smaller and more vulnerable deserves every possible punishment and I'm happy to be on hand to help deliver it."

"It's what makes you a good cop, a dogged investigator, especially in cases where there is child abuse and neglect or sexual abuse of any sort."

She blinked. "I… Thanks."

Something he had wondered about for a long time made its way to the surface of his brain. For a brief second, he considered ignoring the impulse to ask her, but somehow the moment seemed right. His instincts were sometimes spot-on, too, and he decided not to question them in this case.

"Tell me something. Did you become a cop because of Wyatt's death or because of what happened to you in college?"

She stared at him for several long seconds then she sank into a chair as color flooded her features in a hot tide. "You…know about that?"

"I've known since before I hired you. I did a complete search, Wyn. You think I wouldn't find out you were one of the key witnesses in the trial of an accused serial rapist who preyed on college students in Boise?"

She drew in a deep breath and then another and he was in awe all over again of her strength and her courage. She refused to be a victim. Instead she was tough and smart and completely dedicated to helping others.

"You've known, all this time, and you never said anything?" Her voice was a mix of shock and disbelief.

"You just said it, when you were talking about Andrea," he murmured. "Some things are private and personal. If you had wanted to talk about it, I figured you would have."

Why he had asked her now, after avoiding the question all this time, he wasn't sure but he still wouldn't regret it. This was all part of the package that made her the strong, courageous, amazing woman he loved.

"Does my...family know?"

His throat ached at her question and what it implied. He had read the transcript of her testimony. Like her, he hated when anyone vulnerable was hurt or abused in any way but it was so much worse when that person was someone important to him.

"Not from me," he answered gruffly. "You mean you never told them? You carried this burden alone? Didn't you think you needed their love and support?"

"Yes," she said, her voice low. "But I also know it would have killed Dad to know how stupid I was, how I foolishly ignored all the things he told me about protecting myself. I went to a party by myself at the home of people I didn't know, I didn't watch my drink closely, I let a strange guy drive me home. Stupid, from beginning to end."

"You do know it wasn't your fault, right? You were drugged and sexually assaulted without your consent."

"I know that *now*. I had an excellent rape counselor and that made all the difference. But right afterward, all I could see were my own stupid mistakes. I was afraid to tell my parents at first. After Brock Michaels was arrested and charged, I was getting up my nerve to tell them I would be testifying at his trial and then Wyatt died and…it didn't seem important. They were already grieving so much for him. I didn't want to add more hurt to their hearts."

She had chosen instead to walk the difficult road on her own. He couldn't imagine what that would have been like. Testifying without the support network of friends and family, being forced to relive the ordeal again and again.

How had she found the strength to get through it, at the same time she would have been lost and grieving for her beloved twin as well?

Her dad used to tell him that some people had grit and other people had grace. Wyn had both and contrary to what she thought, John Bailey never would have thought her stupid or weak. He would have been nothing but proud of her.

Was it any wonder Cade was so deeply in love with her that it seemed to fill every single empty space inside him?

He knew. All this time.

As the police station faded in her rearview mirror after her stunning conversation with Cade, Wynona shook her head, still reeling. Cade knew about her attack, about her testimony in the trial, about the events of one stupid night that had changed her life.

She didn't know what to think.

Why hadn't he said anything over the years?

He had spoken about it so matter-of-factly, as if it

was one of those things that just *was*. She could only believe her past had never mattered to him. She had worked for him for more than two years and he had never treated her like a victim, someone fragile or damaged.

She drove toward Riverbend Road with her thoughts as twisty and wild as the Hell's Fury.

Ahead of her, a couple of kids were riding long boards. They turned into Sulfur Hollow, shoulder-length hair flying in the wind behind them. She lifted her foot off the gas and on impulse clicked her turn signal on and followed after the kids.

She waved at the boys but they just glared at her. She wasn't in uniform and she wasn't driving her department vehicle but people here knew who she was.

Sulfur Hollow always seemed…different from the rest of town. If she combed through the police department's statistics, she would suspect they had almost twice as many calls to this particular neighborhood as any other area of town, far out of proportion to the number of residents who lived in the cluster of twenty or so small, run-down homes.

She passed the house where Cade had lived as a boy, a small, boxy ranch-style house that had once been covered in peeling gray paint but now was tidy with new siding and fresh-painted shutters.

Another family had moved in since Walter Emmett died in prison. She had never met anyone in the family—probably a good thing, if they were staying under the police radar—but she knew the father worked as a laborer in Shelter Springs and the mother was a teacher's aide at the elementary school. She saw a couple of bikes on the lawn and had a fervent wish that those children were enjoying a much happier childhood than Cade had in that house.

A wave of tenderness washed through her, huge and deep.

Cade was a good man. He had been a tough, emotionally starved boy who had grown into a tough, hard police officer.

It would have been so easy for him to take a different route—his father's way, always thinking life owed him something and if it didn't deliver, he could go out and take it.

Cade could have followed his father's footsteps into a life of crime. In her experience, these things often ran in families. If members of one generation were convinced they were above the law, they usually taught that philosophy to their offspring.

What made Cade take a different path?

John Bailey.

Her father had reached out a hand and lifted a struggling boy out of the squalor and hopelessness and showed him something better.

She wanted to do the same. That was the reason she was finishing her degree. Police officers certainly could make a real and permanent difference in the lives of those they encountered. She had known many dedicated, passionate people in the law-enforcement community who tried diligently to impact their communities for good, starting with her father right on to Elliot and Marshall and Cade and on to Wyatt and Andrea's husband, Jason, who had both given their lives trying to help someone else.

Too often, though, people's brushes with the law were punitive and came too late, when ingrained habits made it too difficult to divert them from their troubled road.

It might be idealistic, but she wanted to help stop problems before they began.

How would talking with Ronnie Herrera help her with that new plan for her life? It wouldn't. But she knew something else had happened that night, something Cade wouldn't talk about. He knew all her secrets, apparently. Why wouldn't he tell her the truth about the night her own father was shot?

She wanted to snip the dangling thread before starting the new phase of her life.

She would try one time to talk to him. If he wasn't home, she would forget the whole darn thing and she wouldn't come back again.

When she pulled up to the house where he lived with Elena and their three children, though, Ronnie was outside with the hood up on his old wood-side Jeep Wagoneer.

Hoping she wasn't making a huge mistake, she turned off her SUV and climbed out. A dog barked in a dyspeptic sort of way and she heard a radio somewhere nearby playing some '80s hair band. Ronnie sang along in a surprisingly good baritone.

"Hey, Ron," she called out loudly. She had learned early that it was best not to sneak up on people in this neighborhood. Most of them had some kind of weapon at the ready, even if it was just a makeshift rock sap.

He knew who she was—and though she was dressed in civilian clothes, he managed to look both resigned and suspicious.

"What do you want? Did that bony-assed witch next door call and complain about the noise? That's a classic, man. Nobody can belt it out like Axl Rose."

He reached down to the boom box on the ground next to him and turned up the volume. "How do you like that, bitch?" he yelled in the general direction of the house next door. A curtain twitched and Wyn wondered if she would have to go apologize to Dolores Hammond, who likely had no idea what was going on.

"I'm not here about the noise, Ronnie," she said.

"No?" He turned down the tunes. "Then what? I ain't doing nothing wrong. It's my own damn yard. I'm not breaking no laws."

She decided not to mention the senseless murder of the English language going on here, since that wasn't important. "I'm actually not here in any official capacity. See how I'm not wearing a uniform?"

He narrowed his gaze and seemed to accept that. "Then what do you want? Can't you see I'm busy? I got to change the clutch in this stupid thing again, third time in two years. I can't seem to make my kid understand she needs to take her foot off it sometimes, that she will only burn it up when she rides it constantly."

She had done the same thing with the old manual-transmission pickup truck she and Wyatt had traded driving when they were teenagers.

She was stalling. Maybe she didn't really want to know what happened that night. Maybe she should just tell Ronnie she had made a mistake, jump back in her vehicle and leave Sulfur Hollow for good.

No. She was here. She should follow this through.

"I need to ask you a question on an old case you might have information about," she said, before she could lose her nerve.

He scratched his cheek, avoiding her gaze. "Yeah, you're probably gonna have to be a bit more specific than that."

Under other circumstances, she might have smiled. She had always liked Ronnie, even though he was one of those guys like Walter Emmett who always seemed to slip in and out of trouble. Ronnie, though, didn't have a malicious bone in his body—unlike Walter Emmett, who had seemed filled with them.

She didn't smile, though. There was nothing amusing about this conversation she suddenly wished she had never started.

"I'd like to talk about the night my father was shot."

"I don't know how helpful I can be. That was a long time ago."

Two years, six months. But who was counting?

"The thing is, I was going through some old files and found a witness statement signed by you that seems to run contrary to the official report."

"Like I said. A long time ago."

She had interviewed enough reluctant eyewitnesses to recognize that Ronnie didn't want to talk to her. "This might jog your memory. See your name down there? That's you, right?"

He squinted at the copy she had made of the report for a minute then busied himself wiping a rag across the screwdriver in his hands.

"A lot of water has flowed under my bridge since then, ma'am. I can't be sure."

"You seemed pretty sure of what you said that night," she pressed. "You wrote in this statement that you were a hundred percent certain the first shot came from the two officers, that the suspect was preparing to surrender and had even laid his weapon down when he was shot."

Ronnie released a long breath. "Here's the thing. I was pretty drunk that night. Me and the wife had a big fight and she threw me out. That's why I was trying to sleep in my pickup down by the dock, even though it was colder than a witch's, well, you know."

He shrugged. "Some investigator with the state police threw out my statement, said I wasn't a credible witness."

"Ronnie, I need to know, straight up. Were you telling the truth as you knew it in this statement?"

He scratched his cheek. "Why you have to dredge all this up again now? Your dad's dead. Why go messing around in the past? Things that maybe ought to be left alone?"

She needed to let this go. What did it matter who shot first?

She thought of her father his last difficult two years, unable to speak in complete sentences, unable to dress himself or even use a knife and a fork.

Her heart ached at the hard memories. John Bailey would have pushed to know the truth. He wouldn't stop until he had the answers he needed, even if the truth was hard.

"Ronnie, you said your statement was thrown out by the state police but you didn't say it was inaccurate. I need to know what you saw that night. Did the police fire on a man trying to surrender?"

He dropped the rag to his side. "I don't know. Wish I could say yes or no a hundred percent, you know? Like I said, I was drunk. But seems to me, that's what happened. One minute the guy was going to his knees with his hands up, the next I saw a flash then heard the shot and him yell out a second later. He went down, then scooped up his gun and started firing. It was like a movie, you know? A real shoot-out. I ducked down out of the way and crouched on the floor of my pickup. Not ashamed to say it. I was scared as shit. The whole thing lasted maybe two, maybe three minutes and when the shooting stopped, I saw both your dad and that punk from California on the ground with Cade Emmett yelling into his radio while he did CPR on your dad."

Wyn let out a breath. She was gripping her car keys so hard the cuts were gouging into her skin and she forced herself to relax her fingers.

She had interviewed many witnesses in her years as a police officer. She liked to think she had developed a pretty good internal polygraph over the years. Though she certainly wasn't infallible, Ronnie's words rang with veracity.

He believed what he had originally said in his statement. He believed that one of the officers had fired on an unarmed man who was in the process of surrendering.

"Could you…tell which officer it was?" she asked. Her voice sounded hollow and thin, as if she were trying to talk at high altitude without quite enough oxygen.

He shifted, his expression now filled with discomfort. "Don't know. It was dark and pretty rainy. I know what I think I saw but how can I be sure of anything? Maybe I'm crazy."

She didn't think so. Something else had happened that night but she wasn't any closer to figuring out what.

"Your dad was a good man, Wynona. I always said so. He was never anything but kind to me, even when I didn't always deserve it. Same goes for Cade Emmett, come to that. He's always done right by me. Does it really matter exactly what happened? Your dad's in the grave now and so is the son of a bitch who put him there."

He was right. She shouldn't have come. She should have let it go, just as Cade had told her to do.

If you're gonna go pokin' at a wasp's nest, make sure you're ready for the swarm.

Yeah. That was another of her dad's sayings, one she should have remembered before she turned into Sulfur Hollow. Sometimes asking one question only seemed to stir up a hundred more.

CHAPTER NINETEEN

FOUR HOURS LATER, she still couldn't shake the questions buzzing through her head like those angry wasps she'd been thinking about.

Was Ronnie right? What really happened? Had her father or Cade fired on Joseph Barlow as the suspect was surrendering?

She was sorry she had ever picked up that damn stick and poked the nest. Yes, she'd had questions before about what happened but they didn't fill her with this ball of angst in her stomach.

She couldn't spend all afternoon stressing about it. In two hours, she had thirty-five women showing up to her house for McKenzie's bridal shower and she still had to finish hanging all the heart streamers around her patio overlooking the river. With extreme effort, she forced the questions away, locking them away until she had time to face them.

This was *not* one of her skills.

McKenzie was far better at decorating, with her floral and craft skills and she had actually offered to come early to help. As tempting as that was, Wyn finally decided it probably wasn't really fair to put the guest of honor to work designing table-scapes and blowing up balloons. Devin and Megan Hamilton were supposed to be helping her but Devin had a patient go into labor and Megan was running late.

Wyn had always figured she'd missed the whole what-looks-good-where gene somehow. Oh, she had created a comfortable space for her house and loved walking through the door at the end of a long day. In her grandmother's day, she had loved this house but it had always seemed small and cramped to her. Once she'd cleared out all the clutter and little knickknacks and repainted the dark, close rooms, the house seemed to open up and become warm and comfortable.

It wasn't designer-worthy but she liked it.

She hung the last streamer and was arranging the tablecloths on the extra tables Megan had dropped off earlier in the week when her doorbell rang.

Young Pete lifted his head, mildly curious, then let it fall back onto his front paws. She envied him that insouciance. She would give anything for a ten-minute nap right about now, though even if she had the time, she would never be able to sleep with all her thoughts and worries chasing each other.

The doorbell rang again and she hurried through the house toward it. It was probably Katrina and Samantha Fremont, who were supposed to be dropping off the sugar cookies they'd been making, stacked and decorated to look like little wedding cakes—at least according to the social-media pictures they'd been posting all afternoon.

Apparently Pete decided maybe something interesting might be on the horizon after all so he lumbered to his feet and padded after her just as she reached the door.

"Isn't it just like you to show up when the work is almost done?" she said as she opened the door. Her words faltered when she found not her sister and friend on her doorstep but a big, tough, gorgeous man.

A big, tough, gorgeous *angry* man, she amended. She had worked closely with Cade enough to pick up the signs: the hard, uncompromising jawline, the glitter in his eyes, the tension in his shoulders.

After their last conversation at the station—his shocking revelation that he knew all the difficult pieces of her past and his matter-of-fact acceptance—she found this shift jarring.

Had he somehow found out she had talked to Ronnie? What was he hiding?

She took a breath through lungs that suddenly felt tight and achy. "Sorry. I thought you were Kat and Sam. They were coming by to help me decorate for McKenzie's bridal shower."

"Were you ever going to tell me?"

She swallowed at his clipped, furious words. She had a feeling he was upset about something else entirely. She had barely talked to Ronnie two hours ago. It didn't make sense that he would phrase the question that way, if he was upset about her following up with the man.

"Tell you what?" she asked carefully.

He made a rough noise in his throat and stalked into the house without waiting for an invitation.

"I just had an interesting phone call with your

graduate-studies adviser at Boise State. Apparently she couldn't reach you on your cell and thought she could reach you through the police station. Carrie Anne sent her to me."

That ball of angst expanded in every direction and her fingers and toes suddenly seemed cold. This wasn't the way she wanted him to find out she was leaving. She had a whole speech memorized—about opportunities and possibilities and all—but just now she couldn't remember a bit of it.

She swallowed. "Oh. Did she…have a message?"

His glare would have caught Darwin Twitchell's barn on fire all over again. "You'll be happy to know not only that all your previous credits have been accepted but she was able to obtain permission for you to waive two of the required classes because of your work experience so you'll be able to be that much further along when you start classes on campus next month."

A few more days and she would have been much better prepared for this. Not now, when she was already emotionally wrung out, first from the appearance before Judge Jenkins, then Cade's startling revelations and finally the conversation with Ronnie.

"Well. That's good news."

"Isn't it?" he agreed, though his tone made it clear it was anything but. "Here's the funny thing. I had no idea you were starting classes on campus next month. You're leaving Haven Point and you didn't have the balls to tell me?"

See, that was the whole problem between them. She

didn't happen to *possess* that particular set of accou-
trements.

"I was planning to tell you. Do you think I would
just not show up for my shift one day and send you
a text or something? *Moved to Boise. Later, sucka.*"

"I don't know what to think. I didn't even know
you were considering a change! What the hell, Wyn?
I thought you were happy in Haven Point. You've got
a house here. A life."

She had a job, she had a house, but her life wasn't
what she wanted anymore.

"I was ready for a change. I want to go back and
finish my master's degree and maybe do something
else with my life."

"Besides police work?" He seemed completely
stunned at the very idea and she didn't know how to
explain it to him.

"I can't give speeding tickets and chase moose out
of Aunt Jenny's yard the rest of my life," she began.

"What's wrong with that?"

"What you do—we do—is important and necessary.
I know that. I grew up with nothing but respect for
the uniform and the people with the guts to put it on."

"Then why leave?"

She sighed. "You asked me today why I became a
cop. It was both of those things we talked about. After
Wyatt died and I was…assaulted, I was lost and grieving. I felt completely powerless. There's no other word
that fits. The world suddenly seemed like this terrifying, senseless, unreliable place and I didn't know what
to do. The only thing that made me feel…stronger was

when I helped police identify and investigate the man who attacked me."

His frown turned even more fierce. "Helped them how?"

She decided not to tell Cade about the wire she had agreed to wear or the chances she had taken meeting with Brock Michaels the night he was eventually arrested.

"It doesn't matter. But I realized through that process that I couldn't let what happened to me become my identity. Going through POST seemed the next step—a way to honor Wyatt's legacy and at the same time prove I knew how to take care of myself." She paused, then added softly, "But being a police officer was Wyatt's dream and my dad's and Marshall's. And yours. It was never really mine."

"I thought you loved your job."

"I love parts of it. I do. I love solving problems for people. Finding stolen property or helping someone after a car accident or stopping an underage kid from buying beer. Solving the mystery. But face it. For the most part, our job is triage. We might help people with an immediate problem but we don't do much to address long-term solutions."

"And you really think you'll be able to do that with a master's degree in social work?"

"Yes, actually. I'd like to be a counselor of some kind. Maybe at a youth treatment center or a sexual or domestic-abuse crisis center. I just want to do something that will make a difference."

"Why do you have to go somewhere else to make

a difference? You're doing it here! People connect to you. You're invaluable to the department."

His words jabbed at her sharper than a shiv. The department. That was all Cade cared about—all he would *let* himself care about.

"It's not enough for me anymore."

"What do you need? I can maybe squeeze a little more out of the budget for a raise. Not much of one but a little. Maybe we can put you in more of an outreach capacity. Working resource at the high school or teaching drug prevention classes. You can't leave, Wyn. You're my best officer."

Out of nowhere, anger flooded her. She was furious, suddenly. "How can that possibly be the truth, when you don't trust me?"

He blinked, obviously taken off guard by the attack. "Is this about the fire again? We talked about that."

"No. It's not about the fire. It's about my father."

All the turmoil she had shoved down after talking to Ronnie came roiling back, stirred up by her anger and her frustration and her overwhelming sadness that Cade would never let himself truly see her.

"Your father? What does that have to do with anything?"

"I've worked beside you for two and a half years, Cade, and you've been lying to me for all of it, haven't you?"

"Lying about what?" he asked, but she thought she saw just a flicker of unease in his eyes. The same shadow she saw there whenever anyone brought up the Joseph Barlow incident.

"You know what I'm talking about. I want to know what really happened the night my father died. An hour ago, I had a really interesting talk with Ronnie Herrera."

His mouth thinned. "We talked about this. Ronnie was drunk, it was dark and rainy. You need to let this go."

"I can't," she whispered.

She didn't know for sure why she was pressing this so hard. On some level, she sensed she really wouldn't want to know, especially since he was so hell-bent on keeping it from her.

She also had a feeling that this secret, whatever it was, was one of the reasons Cade kept this careful distance between them and wouldn't admit he had feelings for her. He blamed himself for something that happened that night and would never be able to open his heart if he didn't tell her about it.

"It doesn't matter. Your dad is gone now. Why dredge it all up again?"

"I have to know. Please, Cade. Tell me. What happened that night?"

He shouldn't have come.

After that phone call from the university, he should have just waited for her resignation to show up on his desk one day. The minute he hung up, though, he had been so filled with betrayal and loss and hurt that he hadn't been thinking, he just grabbed his keys and stormed out of the office.

She was leaving.

His heart ached so badly and all he wanted to do was wrap her in his arms and beg her to stay. The urge was so deep and so huge, he was having a hard time keeping his thoughts together around it.

"What happened?" she pressed. "Ronnie said the shots came from the police first. He is certain he saw Barlow lay down his weapon and start to raise his hands and then he heard shots fired and the suspect went down."

He couldn't tell her, for a hundred different reasons. But how could he continue to keep her from the truth?

"Just tell me!" she cried. "What are you hiding, Cade? Why did you stuff that witness report away? What really happened?"

He drew in a harsh breath. "Your dad was shot in the head and died two years later. That's what happened. Twenty-four freaking months of a long, lingering, horrible death without dignity or grace, when he couldn't walk or feed himself or remember his own name. If I hadn't shot that son of a bitch Joseph Barlow, he would be facing first-degree murder charges, two years after the fact. Your father was the best cop I knew—the best *man* I knew—and he didn't deserve that."

To his dismay, his voice wobbled a little on the last words and he drew himself up, wanting to punch something. He was aware of Pete whimpering a little, coming to stand beside him, but mostly of the vast, searing ache in his chest.

Wyn was leaving, like his mother, like John.

How would he bear it?

She stared at him for a long moment, those blue

eyes that could always see too much narrowed with anger and confusion.

"You're protecting my father," she finally said, her voice thick with shock, sadness and perhaps even resigned understanding.

For the first time since she came to work at the department, he was sorry she was such a dogged investigator. She left him with no other choices.

"Maybe I'm protecting myself," he countered. "Maybe I shot the bastard. He was laying down his weapon but he'd already fired a shot. I was hopped up on adrenaline and thought he was palming it, ready to come up shooting, so I tried to wing him before he could and I missed. He shot your dad and I had no choice but to take him out."

He saw just a sliver of doubt in her eyes before she shook her head. "Nice try. I read the ballistics report. You fired only one round, the shot that killed him."

Tears welled in her eyes and she swallowed hard and dashed them away. "He was surrendering, wasn't he? Barlow put his gun down and had his hands up and my father shot him before he could. I think I accepted that the moment I read Ronnie's statement. I just didn't want to."

He thought his heart couldn't rip apart any more but the tear sliding down her cheek showed he was wrong. Why did she have to push and push and push? He had hoped she never had to know the truth about the man she had idealized—or the sins on his own head.

"What happened, Cade? Please. I need to know. Did my dad shoot an unarmed man?"

He raked a hand through his hair, wishing he could wrap her in his arms and tuck her cheek against his chest. "You know how things can be in the heat of the moment, Wyn. Maybe John saw the guy reaching for his gun again, I don't know. I have to think maybe he saw something I didn't."

She let out a shaky breath. "He fired on a suspect while the man had his hands up in the air and his weapon on the ground. How could he?"

He couldn't stand the appalled hurt, that sense of innocence lost in her voice. He had to tell her, no matter the consequences. "Don't blame your dad. It wasn't his fault." He faced her squarely. "It was mine."

She stared at him, that tear still trickling down her cheek. He longed to wipe it away but knew she wouldn't welcome anything from him now.

"What are you talking about?" she whispered.

Here it was, the real reason he had kept the truth from her. Marshall knew. He had asked him outright, after the shooting, and Cade hadn't been able to lie to his best friend. Marshall hadn't blamed him but he wasn't sure Wynona would see things the same way.

"Your dad wasn't fit for duty. He hadn't been for a couple of months before the shooting."

She stared, her eyes huge. "He…what?"

"I should have reported him. I should have talked to the mayor, the city council, the sheriff at the time. Even your mom. But I didn't. I tried to protect him and did my best to cover for him as much as I could. I tried to talk to him about it, to tell him he needed to see a doctor. He…wouldn't listen."

He didn't tell her of the growing rift between him and John the last few months, how the man he loved and respected like a father had started to make cruel comments, belittling Cade just like his own father had.

He should have stepped up then, knowing that wasn't the John Bailey he knew, but he hadn't been able to see past his own hurt at the time. If he hadn't been so self-absorbed about that part of things, he might have noticed earlier that John had started making serious procedural mistakes.

Wyn's features had paled and she grabbed hold of the table in her foyer as if she wasn't sure her legs would support her.

That stupid witness report. He thought again that he should have shredded the damn thing when he'd had the chance, then he wouldn't be here having this horrible conversation with her.

"What are you saying?" she asked.

"It doesn't matter now, Wyn. Please. Just let it go."

"Tell me! What do you think was going on? You think he was…impaired or something? How? He didn't drink or take any medications, as far as I know."

She sounded like a lost, frightened girl, and he couldn't fight back the need to touch her any longer. He reached out and took her hand in his. It was cold and her fingers trembled slightly.

"I can't prove any of it, especially now, years after the fact, but… I believe your dad might have been suffering from a physical or mental condition. Maybe the beginning stages of some kind of early-onset senility, like your grandmother."

She stared blankly. "Alzheimer's?"

"It's a theory, anyway. The brain injury sort of covered any symptoms that might have shown themselves later. I only know John was…not himself for weeks before. He was suddenly mean-tempered and he would get confused at the simplest of tasks and then lash out at me or one of the other officers if we tried to help. I covered for him the best I could, started picking up the slack, while I tried to convince him to see someone."

"Alzheimer's."

She sounded numb, her voice hollow.

"I'm sorry. Now you see why I wanted you to let this drop. You didn't need to know."

"Did my mother know? Anyone else in my family?"

"I don't know about Charlene. Marsh and I talked about it. He suspected something was wrong but couldn't put a finger on what. Please don't cry, Wyn."

Her tears ripped at his heart, because they were so very rare. He had seen her cry at Wyatt's funeral and at John's but otherwise she always seemed so strong.

He thought of what courage and strength it must have taken her to be a witness in the trial of her rapist. He suddenly remembered another incident a few months after she came to work for the department, when an unrestrained baby had been killed in a car accident they both had responded to. She had dealt with the investigation in a brisk, no-nonsense way but had escaped to her patrol vehicle at the first opportunity.

He hadn't dared look then because he had known in his heart she would be weeping.

He couldn't look away now.

"I'm sorry," he murmured, finally pulling her into his arms. "I'm so sorry. It wasn't his fault, it was mine. Don't you see that? He wasn't fit for duty and I should have reported him. I've regretted it every single day of these last two years. I should never have let my love and respect for him interfere with my duty. If I had acted, he could have gotten help, maybe. Delayed the onset of the symptoms a little. He might still be here."

"Why didn't you tell me? Did you think I wasn't strong enough to take it?"

"How could I ever think that? You're the strongest person I know, Wyn." She had testified in a rape trial, had survived losing her twin, had watched the father she loved spend two agonizing years in a nursing home.

"Then why try to protect me from the truth?"

"It wasn't about protecting you. I told myself it was but I was really protecting myself. I didn't want you to blame me."

He regretted the words as soon as he said them, afraid they revealed far too much about what was in his heart. Her gaze lifted to his and the moment seemed to stretch and thin between them. He did his best to keep his feelings for her locked away but he wasn't sure he was completely successful.

She let out a shuddering little breath. "You weren't responsible for what happened that night, Cade. You can't think that. Joseph Barlow was the one who robbed the liquor store then shot at the pursuing officers. If he hadn't, none of this would have happened. You loved my father and tried to do everything you could to protect him. I know that."

Her words soaked through him, sweet and cleansing, and he felt as if a weight the size of the Redemptions had been lifted from his shoulders.

"Thank you for telling me. I know it was…painful," she murmured. She stood on tiptoe and pressed a soft kiss to the corner of his mouth.

He wanted to hold her tight, to dry every tear, kiss away every pain, but he knew he didn't have that right.

She was leaving. The reminder sliced through him.

"I don't want you to go, Wyn," he said, his voice low, when she stepped away. "You're my best officer. You're vital to my department."

"I don't *want* to be vital to the department," she answered solemnly. "I only want to be vital to *you*. I'm in love with you, Cade. Don't you get it?"

Her words quivered between them, vibrating like a plucked bowstring, and he felt as if the arrow had lodged right in his chest.

She couldn't be. It was impossible. Emotions seemed to tangle his thoughts and his words—joy, terror, happiness, despair.

Before he could sift through them all to come up with an answer, he heard women's voices then laughter outside, just before the doorbell rang.

Some instinct for self-preservation had him stepping away just an instant before her sister, Katrina, came through the door without waiting for Wyn to answer, followed closely by Sam Fremont.

Katrina stopped the moment she spotted them and her expression tightened with the same suspicion from that day at her mother's house.

Sam snickered. "Ooh, you didn't tell us you were hiring a male stripper for the bridal shower. Smart move, Wynnie. The hot-cop thing always works for me." She held her arms out in front of her, palms up. "You'd better arrest me, Officer. I've been *so bad.*"

Katrina smiled at her friend, but Cade noticed it didn't quite hit her eyes. Her gaze continued to shift between them and he was quite certain she noticed the tear tracks on Wyn's face.

Despite them, Wyn looked lovely, her eyes huge and dewy, her color rosy, soft. He wanted to drag her away from the other two women and have this out, once and for all, to tell her all the hundreds of reasons she couldn't be in love with him.

He couldn't do that now, with her sister and Sam watching both of them with such avid interest. Wynona was supposed to be hosting a party in a few hours, a celebration for her dear friend, and he had selfishly burst in here without thinking and dragged them both through an emotional bloodbath.

"I should…go." Despite his two tours of duty and the years he had put his life on the line as a police officer, apparently he was nothing but a lousy coward, at least when it came to Wynona Bailey.

"Cade," she began, her voice small and uncertain. She hadn't met his gaze since her sister walked in.

"We'll talk later," he promised. "Maybe after your guests leave."

She swallowed and nodded. Pete padded after him to the door and Cade stopped to pat the dog one last time before he slipped out.

As he walked to his car, her simple yet earthshaking words seemed to echo through his head. *I'm in love with you, Cade. Don't you get it?*

He wanted, more than anything, to tell her he felt the same. She had told him she didn't want to be vital to the department, only to him. He wanted to tell her she was more vital than oxygen or water or food, that he needed her desperately.

He just wasn't sure if he had her kind of courage.

CHAPTER TWENTY

WELL. THAT WAS FUN.

Wyn felt battered and achy, as if she'd just survived a long run through Class 5 rapids on the Hell's Fury.

I don't want to be vital to the department. I only want to be vital to you. I'm in love with you.

Had she really dared to say those words to him? She wanted to cringe, to grab a kayak, jump into the river and just keep floating to the ocean.

Why on earth had she blurted them out like that? One moment, they had been talking about her father and his behavior before the shooting, and then next she was flapping her stupid lips about things that never should have been spoken.

He had just been so tender with her, holding her with sweet gentleness while she grieved all over again for the father she had loved. She had wanted to stay in his arms, safe and warm, forever.

And then she ruined everything.

She had completely stunned him. His eyes had widened with shock and he had stared at her as if he didn't quite believe what he'd just heard—though for a moment there, she thought she'd seen something else, something hot and blazing and filled with joy. She wasn't sure if she had imagined it, though, because Sam and Kat had burst in right after that.

What had she done?

She was going to have to work with him for at least another month, unless she took all the vacation she had accrued. How could she even face him again for five seconds, forget about day after day of having to talk to him about arrests and cases and paperwork?

The words were out there and she couldn't take them back.

We'll talk later. Maybe after your guests leave, he had said.

Great. She only needed to throw a party for three dozen women, and then she had *that* to look forward to.

"What did Cade want?" Katrina asked. Her sister hadn't stopped frowning since she walked in.

"Police business," she answered shortly. It wasn't really a lie. Everything between them seemed to come down to the job.

"He seemed upset," Kat pressed. "You do too. Were you having a fight?"

A fight? No. If he was upset, it was probably because she had just bared her soul to him.

Not initially, she reminded herself. He had stopped in the first place after learning her plans to return to Boise State. She had been wrong to keep her intentions a secret, from Cade or from her family.

"He just found out I'm moving back to Boise to finish up my degree," Wyn said. "He's a little annoyed with me for leaving him shorthanded."

It took Kat about five seconds to process the news.

"What?! You're moving to Boise? Why didn't you tell me?"

"I just did," she pointed out.

"Does Mom know?"

That was another bridge she would have to cross. "Not yet. Please don't say anything until I have a chance to let her know."

"What will you do after school?" her sister asked.

"I don't know yet. Not police work."

Kat nodded as if it didn't surprise her. To her gratification, her sister hugged her. "You'll figure it out and it will be the perfect thing for you."

Katrina's faith in her almost made her cry all over again.

"I'll miss you tons," her sister murmured.

"I'll miss you too. But I'm not going anywhere for a month and it's only until next spring. Besides, Boise's not that far away and I'll be back and forth for a while. I might even be able to find a job somewhere around Lake Haven after I'm done."

"What about your house?" Kat asked. "Are you going to sell it?"

She hadn't thought that far ahead. She loved this house and had been so excited to buy it from her grandmother's estate after she moved back to Haven Point.

"I don't know yet. I'm sure I can rent it out until I figure that out. It's not something I have to figure out right now. Classes don't start until August so I've got time to look at all my options. Meanwhile, we've got a shower to throw, right?"

Katrina smiled and hugged her again, though she

had a feeling her sister wasn't quite convinced that was the only reason for Wyn to be upset.

WYN DID HER best to ignore Katrina's worried looks throughout the evening as she set out food and organized games and helped McKenzie keep track of her gifts.

It was harder to ignore the echo of her own words and the cold dread in her gut that she had ruined everything.

I'm in love with you.

She was so *stupid* and right now she would give anything to go back in time and swallow those words.

She would have time to fall apart later. For now, her focus needed to be on making sure everything was perfect for her dear friend.

Finally, the last gift had been unwrapped, the last wine bottle opened, the last bawdy innuendo from the Brewer sisters delivered—wink and all—and the party started to break up.

McKenzie hugged all of her friends on their way out but saved her biggest hug for Wynona. "Thank you so much for everything. This was the best shower *ever.*"

"You are welcome, Kenz. You and Ben are going to be so happy."

"We all left a mess," Devin said, surveying the patio. "We'll stay and help you clean up."

"You will not," Andie Montgomery said sternly. "Neither one of you is lifting a finger. *I'm* staying to help clean up. I already told Katrina and Sam to take off."

"We're happy to," Devin protested. "I'm the maid of honor. I was supposed to be throwing the shower anyway. I owe you for taking over. If it had been left to me, we might have ended up having it at the hospital cafeteria."

"You helped tons with the food and the party planning," Wyn said. "Somebody needs to drive Kenz and her gifts home. That's you. Anyway, you have enough to do, planning your own wedding."

It took a bit more wrangling but she and Andie were finally able to persuade the Shaw sisters to leave.

"Whew," Andie said after she closed the door on them. "Getting the two of them to finally leave was harder than that crazy honeymoon trivia game you made us play."

Wynona managed a smile, though now that the urgency of throwing the shower had passed, she could feel the emotion and uncertainty pressing in again.

Andie must have picked up on it. "What's wrong?" she asked softly, her pretty features concerned.

Wyn couldn't help noticing the other woman had a new calm about her. Even though she had relaxed the last few weeks, obtaining the protective order that morning seemed to be empowering for her. She was no longer skittish, anxious. She seemed…serene, somehow.

Had it really been just that morning? It seemed a lifetime ago. So much had happened, *Wyn* didn't feel like the same person.

She forced a smile now. "Nothing's wrong," she lied. "It's been a long day."

"Why don't you go to bed and let me clean this up?"

"Forget it," she exclaimed. "My house, my mess. It

looks worse than it really is, anyway. We mostly just have to throw away the garbage and take down a few decorations. Sam and Katrina did a good job of keeping up with the dishes throughout the night. It shouldn't take us long."

Her words turned out to be prophetic. Between the two of them, they set the house and patio to order in less than half an hour.

"You need to take some of this leftover food home to your kids," Wyn said as they were finishing up in the kitchen. "Oh, and don't forget your pickles."

Andie made a face, looking at the gigantic gallon-sized jar of dill pickles she had received as a gag prize for winning one of the shower games.

"You can keep it. Really. I'm never going to eat this many pickles. Take it down to the police station with you and give them out to people who come in with complaints or something."

"You're too generous. I insist. I'll even carry it home for you. I'm in the mood for a walk."

Somehow she was going to have to come up with the strength to talk to Cade. Better to take the initiative and stop in at his house, rather than to let it fester between them, making them forever awkward with each other.

She would just tell him, yes, she was in love with him and she understood he didn't feel the same. She would get over it once she moved on with her life.

It was a lie, but with a little work she could probably sell it.

As she might have expected, Pete perked up at the

magic word *walk* so she grabbed his leash, picked up the giant jar of pickles, then headed out into the summer night beside Andie.

"I didn't have the chance to talk with you about this earlier, but who's babysitting Will and Chloe?" she asked, as they passed the Jacobses' home and the sweet, elegant scent of roses growing along the fence.

"Barbara Serrano recommended her youngest daughter. She seems like a nice girl."

"Parker. She really is. I used to babysit *her*, before she could even talk. That makes me feel old."

"You're not old. Trust me. Wait until you have kids, then you'll feel old."

Wynona did her best to ignore the clutch in her stomach. Maybe she wouldn't have children. She had given her heart to a man who didn't know what to do with it.

Stars spangled the sky overhead and she could hear the river gurgling beyond the trees. Oh, it would be hard to leave this place she loved so much.

"If I haven't said it today, thank you."

At the words, Wyn looked over at the woman walking beside her. Andie seemed to be much lighter of step, despite the packages of food she carried.

"For?" she asked.

"*Everything.* This morning, standing by me. Inviting me tonight. Making me feel so welcome here in Haven Point. Being my friend. Most of all, I guess, for giving me hope again that I can move past everything and get my life back. Between the restraining order and our phone call, Rob has to know I'm not going to sit by anymore and play the victim. You gave me the courage to do that."

"No, you had it all along," Wyn insisted. Andie had only needed someone to help her uncover it from beneath all the rubble of her pain. She had done the same, after her attack followed so closely by Wyatt's devastating death. Moved forward. Surely she could recover from this too.

"I made an appointment to see that counselor you suggested," Andie said.

She managed a smile. "I'm so glad."

"You were right. I was giving someone else too much power over my life, even though I moved five hundred miles away from him. No more."

"Good for you," Wynona said as Pete led the way up the steps. The dog paused at the door, sniffing the air, probably on alert for one of the Jacobses' cats, who tended to wander.

"I don't hear any chaos from within, so I guess Parker survived the two-kid demolition team," Andie said.

This time Wyn's smile was a little more genuine. "Your kids are the sweetest. Now, if you want to see a two-kid demolition team, you should check out Lindy-Grace's boys. Just ask Darwin Twitchell, if you don't believe me."

Pete growled and she frowned at his unusual behavior. "Hey. Behave yourself. Children are sleeping inside."

He wouldn't go anywhere without her, she knew, but

she still looped the leash around a newel on the porch steps while Andie unlocked the door.

"Parker," she called softly. "I'm back."

No answer greeted her and the lights were out.

"They must have completely tired her out," she said with a laugh.

She flipped on the living room light and then made a small, terrified sound and dropped the bowl she carried. It clattered to the floor, spilling bits of pasta salad everywhere.

All the color leached from her features like a photograph exposed to harsh sunlight and the other woman's gaze fixed on the man who sat on the living room sofa, with a sleeping Will curled up against his chest.

"Hello, Andrea," he said with a smile that sent jagged icicles down Wyn's spine.

He had sandy-blond hair and a cop's mustache and she knew instantly this had to be Rob Warren.

The son of a bitch.

How dare he show up now, when the only weapon she had was a gallon-sized jar of pickles?

He held a finger to his lips. "Shhh," he said, with that cold smile she wanted to smack away. "You don't want to wake the little guy."

"Wh-where's Parker?" Andie said, her eyes frantic.

"I sent her home," he said, still with that smarmy smile.

"And she just…left?"

"I paid her. Don't worry. Very generously, actually. She didn't want to leave without calling to check with you first but I convinced her she would ruin my big surprise if she told you I was here. The kids were both so happy to see me."

Wyn's brain felt foggy, numb, as if she'd had far more than one glass of wine, but she forced herself to assess the scene. She could see a black handgun on the table next to him. With Will sleeping in Warren's lap, Wyn could think of no possible way under the circumstances to disarm the other cop safely.

She needed backup and she needed a weapon.

Cade. He would have a spare weapon and extra ammunition. She could have him here in two minutes, and then both of them could arrest Robert Freaking Warren.

"Who's your friend?" he asked.

Andie didn't say anything, her features pale as skim milk.

Wyn knew in an instant she couldn't tell him her real name. He would connect it with the female officer who had spoken with him earlier that day, when she had warned him in no uncertain terms never to come to Haven Point.

He struck her as a cornered rat, dangerous and canny, and she decided her best play was to keep her true identity a secret.

"Samantha Fremont," she said, putting her best drunken giggle into her voice. "I've got pickles."

"Yeah. I see that."

"What's your name?" she asked, injecting a little flirtatious note, even though it made her want to vomit.

He looked mildly amused. "Rob. Andrea and I go way back. Isn't that right?"

Andie looked as if she might fall over with a puff of air but she nodded stiffly.

"That's great. So great. Old friends are the *best*." Wyn giggled a little more and ended on a slight belch. For the first time in her life, she was grateful for three brothers who taught her to burp on command from the time she was in preschool.

"Sorry. I think I *might* have had a few too many margaritas tonight. That was some shower."

She gestured blindly behind her. "I'll just, you know, leave the pickles and let you two catch up."

"Wh-what?" Andie turned, her eyes huge.

She tried to send a message to her friend, to assure her she wasn't abandoning her.

"Yeah. I've got an old friend too. He lives just across the street. He's sooo cute. Think I'll drop in and say hi," she said with what she hoped looked like inebriated infatuation. "I'll see you soon."

She gave Andie a hug. "Get Will out of here," she whispered. "Whatever you have to do."

She caught a quick flash of understanding and gratitude in Andie's eyes and hoped that Warren didn't see it.

"Nice to meet you, Robby," she lied with another boozy giggle, then let herself out the door.

She wasted precious seconds fumbling to unhook Pete's leash. At least that fit with the role she was playing. Just in case Warren was watching from the living room window, she forced herself to walk slowly and a little wobbly across the street, as if she had nothing better to do than drop in on a cute neighbor at ten on a Thursday night.

She could only pray that Cade was home and that he would help her keep Andrea and her children safe.

CHAPTER TWENTY-ONE

I'M IN LOVE with you.

Wynona's words rolled around his head in an end-less refrain.

He had tried to shove his emotions aside as he went through the final police-department plans for Lake Haven Days, due to start the next evening and into the weekend, but now that he was home, he couldn't seem to stop thinking about that scene at her house and the one earlier in his office.

She thought she was in love with him but he instinc-tively wanted to tell her she couldn't be, that she was too smart to make that kind of mistake.

At heart, he still felt like one of the outlaw Em-metts, which he knew was a completely ridiculous reaction after all his years of public service, but it was hard to shake something imprinted on him when he was a kid.

His family was still a mess. His mom had died of liver failure, his dad had died in jail, and his brother wasn't speaking to him, as he waited in jail on a DUI charge.

He wasn't his family, though. Hadn't he been fight-ing to prove that since John Bailey took him under his considerable wing? Through his teenage years and his adulthood, he had done his best to show he wasn't defined by DNA, by his family's criminal tendencies, his father's disregard and contempt for the law.

He had been a damn good police chief since John Bailey had been shot. He worked hard and he cared about his community, which he hoped was evident in the performance of his department.

Yeah, he might be an Emmett, but it was only a name. How ironic, that the one person he was having trouble convincing after all this time was himself.

Wynona Bailey loved him. He didn't know how or why but it seemed a miracle, somehow, an amazing, precious gift that he had decided he would be an idiot to turn away.

While he didn't want her to leave the department and would miss her terribly, that was yet one more obstacle between them that had been removed. A month from now, she wouldn't be working for him. If they could hold off for that month before slipping into a full-fledged relationship, he would be over that sticky conflict.

He loved her. He meant what he said to her. She was the strongest person he knew. She was brave and smart, funny and compassionate.

How could he *not* love her?

He laughed a little for the first time all evening, wishing he dared go to her house right now. He had told her they would talk. After they did, he would have to do his best to stay away from her for another month, to keep things light and casual until she actually resigned from his department.

He wouldn't sneak around with her. Those things never ended well.

It would be the hardest thing he ever did, though.

What he needed right now was a good swim in the bracing waters of Lake Haven but he decided a cool shower would have to do. He had just turned on the water and taken off his shirt when he heard a frantic banging on the door. Three knocks then two more then three more, interspersed with his doorbell.

He didn't stop to think, he just rushed to the front door, picking up his sidearm as he went.

He forgot he'd left his shirt in the other room until he yanked the door open and found Wyn on the other side wearing one of her pretty, feminine sundresses and holding tightly to Pete's leash with a wild look in her eyes.

She rushed inside and let go of the dog. "I need your clutch piece now! Where is it?"

She looked around frantically, as if she expected him to leave his backup gun lying on a side table.

"Why?"

"My weapon's at home and I don't have time to get it. I need that Glock 27 you keep in your boot. You've got mags for it here, don't you?"

"Of course."

"Where is it? I need it. Grab yours too. And a shirt."

He had seen her in tight situations before but he'd never seen that tight, frightened look on her face.

Something was very, very wrong. Ice crackled through his veins.

"Wyn, slow down. Tell me what the hell is going on."

She was close to hyperventilating but she drew in a deep breath and then another, fighting for control. After the second breath, the raw wildness in her eyes clicked down to panicked urgency.

"We don't have time to chat. The bastard cop who raped Andie is sitting in her living room right now."

"What?"

"Rob Warren. The one we had Judge Jenkins sign a restraining order against today. I'm guessing he didn't take kindly to being served because right now he's in her living room holding her sleeping son with a SIG Sauer P226 on the table next to him. I need to go back there but I can't take him on by myself, unarmed."

He had time for only an instant of fierce gratitude that she hadn't tried before he grabbed the nearest shirt he could find, a T-shirt off the stack of clean laundry on his kitchen table he hadn't yet had time to put away.

He opened the drawer where he kept his extra weapon and leg harness and handed it to her.

"I don't have anywhere to put a weapon in this dress and I don't want him to know I'm armed. Do you have a sweatshirt or something with a pocket I can conceal?"

He grabbed the closest one he could find out of his closet. It swamped her, made her look even more small and fragile. He suddenly wished he had a closet full of Kevlar too.

"I'm calling for backup. Jess and Cody are on."

She nodded. "Fine, but have them come in dark. We need the element of surprise on our side."

He made the call before they left the house, explaining to his officers that he didn't know the situation inside the house yet and ordering them to stand by at the end of Riverbend Road.

"Stay here, Pete. I'll be right back." She patted her dog, who whined a little but settled onto the rug by the door.

As Wyn opened the door Cade looked out carefully. Across the street, he could see only thin slats of light on the edges of the tightly closed blinds. No shapes or movement made it through. He wanted to beg her to stay at his house and let him handle the situation but he knew that wouldn't be fair or right. She was a trained officer and he trusted her to know how to handle herself.

"What's the play?" he asked. "How do you want to get inside?"

She tucked her arm through his and headed across the street. An interesting approach, but he wasn't about to argue when every instinct warned him to tuck her against him and keep her safe.

"I didn't want him to know I was the officer he spoke with earlier in the week. He thinks I'm Samantha Fremont and I'm drunk from the bridal shower. Let's use that."

"Fine," he said. Before they reached the steps, he stopped and kissed her hard.

"FYI, I love you too."

She stared at him, her eyes huge in the moonlight. "Now? You're throwing that at me *now*?"

"I just wanted you to know. Be careful. I want the chance to show you how much." He kissed her fiercely once more before releasing her.

She let out a ragged breath, shook her head, then squared her shoulders and turned toward the house.

How could he help but fall in love with her all over again?

Wynona was a trained police officer. She was excellent with a firearm and she could kick the ass of any one of his officers at hand-to-hand combat, himself included.

She had this.

She knocked on the door. "Andie? It's Samantha again."

He didn't know how she did it, but Wyn somehow made her voice sound drunk, ditzy, like she was trying—and failing—to whisper.

"Andie? Open the door!"

There was no answer for a long moment and he kept watch, aware every moment of the solid weight of his service weapon at the small of his back.

"Andie? Andie? Are you in there?" She pitched her voice a little louder. "Please. It's an emergency."

"Come in," a voice said faintly.

Wyn's gaze met his for a brief instant, then she tried the knob. It turned easily and she pushed open the door.

The room was lit by only a small lamp beside the sofa. Cade did a rapid-fire assessment of the scene. Andie's little boy was no longer in the room, as far as he could tell. Neither of the children was there. That made things a little less complicated.

A guy roughly six feet, two hundred pounds with sandy-blond hair and a mustache sat beside Andie with his arm around her. Her eyes were red and swollen and she had the beginnings of a black eye and red mark on her cheek where it looked as if she had been back-handed.

Fury roiled through him and he wanted to grab the guy and shove his head against the wall, but Wyn had told him the man had a SIG Sauer. He couldn't see it right now but he didn't doubt it was close by.

Wyn maintained her pretense that she was a tipsy Samantha Fremont.

She wiggled her fingers in a vacuous sort of way. "Hi. Sorry to interrupt your little reunion. Hi."

The guy assessed Cade. "Who's this?"

"This is my friend. Isn't he cute?"

She did sound a little like Samantha Fremont, the big flirt. Or how he would imagine Sam might sound if she were plastered, which he had never witnessed. Much to his relief.

Wyn looked around. "Where's that adorbs little Willie? Is he in bed? I wanted to give him a good-night kiss."

"Yes," Andrea said stiffly. "He's in bed."

"Oh, too bad," she said, though Cade knew she meant exactly the opposite.

"Do you mind?" Rob said, his voice hard. "We're kind of in the middle of something here. What's the big emergency?"

For a brief instant, Wyn flashed him a look of such naked hatred that Cade sincerely hoped the guy didn't pick up on. She hid her slip quickly behind a boozy sigh.

"I can't find my cell phone *anywhere*. Did I leave it in here when I brought all your stuff over earlier?"

"I...don't think so," Andie said. Her hands were trembling as much as her voice, he saw.

"Are you sure? I'm positive I had it with me when we left the house."

"It's not here," Warren snapped. "End of story. I'm sure you'll find it at home. Good night."

"Maybe we should try calling it," Cade suggested.

Wyn looked at him like he was the smartest male on the planet. If she ever wanted a job with the Haven Point community-theater troupe, he could highly recommend her. "Great idea," she exclaimed, as if he had just invented the microwave. "Andie, where's your phone? Is it in the kitchen? Can you help me find it?"

"She's fine," Warren growled. "Your phone is not here, lady. Give it up. We're going to have to ask you to leave now."

"It has to be *somewhere*. Why not here? Come on. Be a pal. It will only take a minute. Come with me to get your phone, Andrea."

That might have been a little *too* blatant or her drunk act was beginning to wear thin. Whatever the reason, Warren's gaze sharpened on Wyn and his gaze seemed to land on the suspicious-looking bulge in her hoodie pocket. Cade saw the man's hand flex at his side. Where the hell was the SIG Sauer? His own fingers curled, ready to draw.

"Wait a minute," Warren snapped, holding Andrea's arm to keep her from getting up. "What did you say your name was again? And your friend's?"

Wynona's gaze darted to his and Cade could see she also sensed the tide was shifting.

To her credit, she tried to play it through. "Samantha Fremont. And this is my boyfriend Moose." She hiccuped. "That's his nickname. Not his real name."

"No," he bit out, though he still didn't produce the weapon. "I never forget a voice. You're that bitch cop. Bailey. Not Samantha Fremont, or whatever the hell you said your name was."

"I'm not—" she started, but Warren didn't let her finish. He obviously had the smell now, maybe because of Cade's alert stance or that bulge in Wyn's pocket.

"You're both cops. I'm guessing this is the hard-ass chief you were telling me about."

The situation was quickly spinning out of his control and he needed to act fast. "I'm Chief Cade Emmett. Are you Detective Robert Warren?"

"Yeah. That's right."

He pulled his service weapon at the exact same moment Wyn did, as if they'd rehearsed.

"Sir, you are in violation of a protective order. Do you have any weapons on you right now?"

The man's gaze darted among all three of them and

Cade could almost see him trying to spin the situation to his advantage.

"This is all a big misunderstanding."

"I'm sure it is," Cade lied. The only one misunderstanding anything was Warren, who must have thought he was dealing with a couple of hayseed small-town cops. "You can explain it to us all night long if you want, down at the station. I need you to show me your weapon right now."

Warren tried one last time, putting on a bluff, hearty smile. "You're making a big mistake, Chief, Officer. I don't know what lies you've heard from this grifter here, but we're on the same team. I'm working an extensive fraud case in Portland that crosses state lines and Andrea Packer or Montgomery or whatever name she's using is a prime suspect. I've just placed her under arrest and I need to transport her back to my jurisdiction. Right now you're interfering with a criminal investigation."

Andie made a small, frightened sound, her gaze darting to the hallway where her children slept.

Wyn didn't give Cade a chance to reply.

"That's bull," Wyn snapped, all trace of the ditzy drunk gone from her voice. "There's no criminal investigation, except the one we're going to be opening into your activities in the last year, especially your sexual assault against Andrea Montgomery six months ago."

Warren looked at Andrea with pure hatred. "Sexual assault? Is that what she said?"

"It's what she testified under oath before a judge this morning. He believed her and so do I."

"You stupid bitch," he snarled. His hand twitched as if he wanted to backhand her again. Cade still couldn't see his firearm but he knew it had to be close.

"Detective Warren, this is your last warning," he said, his voice as hard as his Glock. "You are in violation of a protective order and you are under arrest. Let go of her now and raise your hands where we can see them. I will not ask again."

"You stupid bitch," he snarled again at Andie. "You ruined *everything*. If this is the way you treat the men who love you, it's no wonder Jason jumped off that frigging bridge."

Before either Cade or Wyn could react, the man pulled out the SIG that had been concealed by Andrea's skirt, yanked her head back by the hair with one hand and shoved the gun under her chin.

She whimpered, tears dripping from her eyes.

"Here's the way this is going to go down. You two are going to put your weapons down and let me walk out of here, unless you want me splattering her brains all over this nice furniture."

"You shoot her and you'll be dead a half second later," Wyn promised.

"Do you think I care about that right now? She ruined everything. My career is ruined. My marriage is ruined. You might as well shoot me, but I'm taking this bitch out first."

"Mama? What's happening?"

While Cade's attention had been caught by the bastard with a gun to Andrea's head, her daughter had apparently awakened. She stood in the doorway, eyes huge and terrified.

What happened next probably took only two or three seconds out of his life but Cade died a thousand deaths.

Like the rest of them, Warren turned at the girl's voice and Wynona—his brave, amazing *foolish* Wynona—apparently thought that was her moment to act. She surged forward, likely intending to disarm him with one of her tough-girl Krav Maga moves, but the detective's instincts had been honed as tautly as theirs. He reacted just as quickly and fired before she could reach him.

Her head flew back and Cade saw blood spatter and it was like her father, just like her father, only a billion times worse as his world imploded.

The little girl screamed, high and loud. Though he was sure he was howling inside too, somehow his own instincts kicked in and Cade fired on the man. He wanted to keep firing and firing, to blast him into nothing, but he charged him instead, kicking the weapon away as he dragged him from the sofa, shoved him to the ground and handcuffed him with the detective yelling and cursing in pain and the girl screaming on and on.

With the threat neutralized two seconds too late, Cade raced to Wyn, whipping out his cell phone to call in the backup while he crouched beside her. She was deathly pale, still, bleeding copiously from her head, but she was breathing.

He bit out the ten-code for officer-involved shooting. "I need an ambulance and all available units. Call Sheriff Bailey immediately. It's his sister. Wyn, baby, wake up, come on. Come on."

Andie, he saw, had grabbed her daughter and held her tightly.

"Honey, I need you to go to Will's bedroom," she said. "We're safe now, I promise but I need you to go to your room and shut the door and stay there until I come to get you."

"Is Officer Bailey going to die like Daddy?"

No. No. No! He wouldn't let her!

"Come on, Wyn. I love you. You can't die. Don't leave me. Come on."

He felt ripped apart, his insides jagged and raw. He didn't know what he said, he only begged her not to leave him as he applied pressure to the wound at her temple and prayed harder than he ever had in his life.

WYNONA AWOKE GRADUALLY, feeling as if the world around her was caught in some slow-motion video feed. At the perimeter of her vision, she caught blurred movement, distant voices, someone crying.

She was lying on a hard floor and someone was kneeling beside her, begging her to come back.

I'm right here, she wanted to say but her throat wouldn't cooperate.

As consciousness gradually returned, vague impressions filtered through the haze. Shock, pain, fury. What happened? Why was she here? Why did her head hurt so badly?

Memory returned an instant later. Andie with a

black eye. Cade, standing shoulder to shoulder with her, weapons drawn. That moment of distraction when Robert Warren had turned away and she stupidly thought she could disarm him.

Seriously? That ass-hat really shot her?

He must have. She felt as if somebody had jabbed a white-hot marshmallow roasting fork into her skull and was twisting it around and around.

"Please don't die, Wyn. You can't leave me. Please, baby. Don't die. I love you. I love you."

The light jabbed painfully at her eyes but she managed to prop one open enough to see that the voice belonged to her big, tough, wonderful police chief. Cade looked…shattered. His eyes were haunted, devastated, his hands covered in blood.

As she became more aware of her surroundings, Wyn heard a woman speaking. Andie. It must be. "What can I do?" Andie asked.

Cade's voice sounded ragged. "Make sure the door's unlocked for the first responders. My officers should be here any second. And I called her brother."

Marshall? He called Marshall? Crap. She would never hear the end of this.

The barn fire was bad enough. Her mom was *really* going to freak about her being shot. At least she might be a little more receptive when Wyn told her she was leaving police work and going back to school.

Harsh curses and moans were coming from the corner, out of her visual range.

"What about me?" she heard a man cry out. "I'm dying here. I need bandages or something before I bleed out. Did you hear me? Is anybody listening? I need medical attention right now!"

"Oh, shut the hell up," Andie snapped.

Wyn blinked at the ferocity in her friend's voice. Even though her head hurt like a son of a mother trucker, she wanted to clap. She lost that instinct when she realized Cade was still beside her and the pressure on her hand was his fingers squeezing her tightly, as if he could hold her in place by sheer will.

"Wyn, baby, wake up. Please. I need you here. I love you. Don't leave me."

Even though she wanted to lie there all night and listen to his impassioned words, she loved him too much to let him suffer.

"I'm not dying," she croaked out.

He let out a long, slow breath and she opened her eyes just in time to see him close his and whisper what appeared to be a prayer of gratitude.

He brought her hand to his mouth and the tenderness there just about made her pass out again.

"Did Warren really shoot me?" she mumbled.

"I think maybe the shot went wild and he just grazed you. I can't seem to find an entry wound but you're bleeding like crazy."

"It hurts," she complained.

"I'm sure it does. I'm sorry. So sorry."

Already, though, the pain was beginning to fade.

Cade loved her.

The words were the best analgesic she could imagine.

He loved her. Nothing else seemed to matter.

"EMTs are on the way. They should be here any minute. Just hang on."

"Okay." Shock was beginning to set in. She knew that was the reason the searing pain had started to recede. She would pay the price for the burst of adrenaline that was carrying her right now but she decided to ride it through anyway.

"Cade Emmett. You used the L word. I heard it."

He gave a rough laugh and she managed to prop both eyes open enough to see the tender smile on his face and the naked relief he didn't bother to hide. "Yeah. You're right. I did."

"Several times."

"Not enough," he said gruffly. "It can never be enough. I realized when I saw you go down that nothing else matters. Not the job, not your family. Nothing. I love you. I'll go work somewhere else if I have to. Maybe once your brother is done being pissed at me, he can hire me on as a deputy at the jail. I'll work as a traffic cop if I have to, as long as we can be together."

His arms were around her and she felt safe and warm and cherished, despite the pain that was making her giddy.

"You don't have to give up the job you love, remember? I'm leaving. Six weeks from now, I'll be back in graduate school."

"Then I'll come to work in Boise."

They could work all this out, but it wasn't necessary for him to leave his job. She was only going to be in school for eight months and her classes were only an hour and a half away. The idea of a long-distance relationship wasn't at all appealing but they could survive a short separation.

She'd apparently survived a gunshot wound, hadn't she?

Oh, she loved him, this tough man who needed more lightness and joy in his life. She murmured the words to him again and his arms tightened.

"I don't understand how, but I'm not stupid enough to argue," he said, his voice low. "I love you. You told me earlier today you wanted to be important to me, not to the department. I couldn't say it then, but I am now. You are everything to me, Wynona Bailey."

She squeezed his fingers. "You better not be lying. I hear my brother's on the way and he has a bigger gun than you."

He laughed roughly. "Oh, I doubt that."

"Kiss me. Right now."

"You just got shot in the head, Wyn. You're delirious."

"I don't care. Kiss me. Please?"

He willingly lowered his head and barely pressed his mouth to hers. The gentle tenderness made her throat ache almost as much as her head.

She heard others coming in, brisk official voices, but still Cade didn't release her.

He loved her.

If she had any doubt, that kiss here, now—when his officers and the EMTs and her brother, of all people, were beginning to crowd into Andrea's small living room—would have removed the last of it.

He loved her and he needed her. She didn't question it.

This was the path her life was intended to take—the twisting, turning road that led her here, to this man she had loved forever and a future that promised more than she could ever imagine.

EPILOGUE

"ARE YOU SURE nobody can see anything?" Wyn pressed, turning her head back and forth in the mirror over her bedroom dresser.

She had never considered herself particularly vain but she had spent more time in the last three weeks feeling self-conscious than at any other point in her life—and that included the year she was thirteen, when she suddenly went up three bra sizes in a matter of months.

A big white bandage on a girl's head tended to stand out even more than a C cup.

"I promise, honey." Charlene fussed around her with a curling iron and comb in a cloud of hair spray. "If I didn't know you had eight stitches there, I would never be able to tell. The jeweled clip completely hides it."

"Whew. That's a relief. McKenzie will be very happy about that."

"She won't care a bit," Charlene assured her. "Though why you had to go and get shot three weeks before you knew you were going to be a bridesmaid for her and Ben, I'm sure I don't know."

A few weeks ago, Wyn would have rolled her eyes

at that sort of comment from her mother. These days, the world was too bright and beautiful and full of promise for her to do anything but smile.

"It was quite thoughtless of me, wasn't it?" she agreed.

Charlene huffed. "Yes. And reckless and foolhardy too. You're so much like your father and brothers."

"I'm a Bailey, through and through."

Charlene gazed at their reflections in the mirror, her eyes unmistakably misty. For a brief moment, her mother rested her cheek against Wynona's. "It was also incredibly brave of you, darling," her mother said in a low voice. "When I think of that man hurting and threatening sweet Andrea Montgomery, it just makes me sick."

That, at least, was something about which she and her mother could agree. "He's in jail now and won't be going anywhere for a long time."

Robert Warren was being held without bail in the Lake Haven County Jail, facing a long list of charges including kidnapping, assault and attempted murder. The case against him was so strong, she had every belief he would soon realize he had no choice but to plead guilty and serve prison time.

By the time he got out, Andrea's children would be grown and possibly having families of their own.

She smiled, thinking of those cute kids. Because of them, she knew Andrea would be okay. Her friend was resilient. In a short time, she already seemed like she had been an important thread in the fabric of Haven Point forever.

"Still," Charlene said with a sniff as she made a few more passes with the comb and hair spray, "I don't know what Cade was thinking, to let you get shot! I hope he takes better care of you, now that the two of you are dating."

Was that what they were doing? She had to smile.

"Trust me," she said blandly, "Cade takes very, very good care of me."

"Bragger." Katrina wandered in from her own preparations in the bathroom just in time to hear. "It's so unfair that you won't even give details!"

"Someday I hope you'll meet a man worthy of a little discretion," Charlene said pertly and Wyn grinned at her sister, who, despite her teasing, seemed thrilled about the two of them.

Her sister acted as if Wyn's new relationship with Cade had been Katrina's idea all along.

The rest of her family was a little harder to read. The details of the shooting were still a little hazy, though she vividly recalled her first glimpse of Marshall after he rushed to the crime scene, only to find his sister bleeding copiously from a head wound and Cade kissing her. She imagined it was the same expression Marsh would probably wear if somebody knocked him over the head with a bo staff.

Marsh seemed to have come around, though the few times she had seen him since then, he'd appeared startled all over again, as if he couldn't quite reconcile the idea of his best bro and his pesky little sister being in love.

Elliot had made a video call from Denver to check

on her the day after the shooting, when she was still in the hospital. Cade hadn't known she was talking to her brother when he walked into the hospital room and straight to her bedside to kiss her fiercely, as if he'd been away for months instead of a few hours.

She smiled a little now, remembering how mortified Cade had been when Elliot cleared his throat and he'd turned to find her brother's face, eyebrows raised, watching them from her tablet. Elliot hadn't seemed particularly surprised, though, so she assumed Marsh had passed the juicy info along already.

As for Charlene, her mother seemed to have taken things in stride since she'd shown up near hysterical at the hospital emergency department that night and found Cade refusing to move from Wyn's side. Other than one shocked look, her mother seemed to accept the new state of affairs with equanimity—or maybe she had just been so relieved that Wyn's gunshot wound had been relatively minor.

Wyn *thought* she had accepted things, until Cade told her with bemusement a few days after the shooting that Charlene had stopped by his house to warn him in no uncertain terms that if he hurt her daughter, Charlene would find a hundred creative ways to make him pay—including, but certainly not limited to, pulling up every single vegetable he ever tried to grow for the rest of his life.

A wave of warmth and love for her family washed over her. She would miss them all so much when she left for graduate school—but she would come back on weekends and holidays and they could talk and Skype all the time.

Though the thought of being ninety miles away from Cade right now made her throat ache and tears threaten the careful job she'd done on her mascara, she was determined to earn her degree.

You can do hard things, my dear, her dad often told her.

She could. This was important to her, a chance to reclaim the person she had been and the dreams she'd envisioned for herself before that horrible winter when she was attacked and Wyatt was killed.

When she graduated in May, she could come back to Haven Point to work. She'd already had an offer from the director of an at-risk youth program.

Maybe this time next summer, she would be planning her own wedding.

Her face felt hot at the idea but somehow once it took root, she couldn't seem to shake it. She loved Cade Emmett. She wanted nothing more than to be able to spend the rest of her life showering all the love and tenderness on him he had lived so long without.

"Okay, hair done, makeup done. Let's get you into your bridesmaid dress," Charlene said.

Wyn hurried to her closet and pulled out the dress, an elegant confection in the palest mint green. It flattered her coloring and her figure. Finally, after so many stints as a bridesmaid, she could come through the experience with a dress she might actually wear a second time.

"Oh, you're both so beautiful," Charlene exclaimed after zipping Wyn into it. "I need a picture."

She grabbed her little camera and shot a few frames of Wynona and Katrina together, then Kat shot a couple of selfies with her phone of the three of them.

When they finished, Wyn hugged her mother. Yes, Charlene could be exasperating sometimes with all her fussing and fretting, but Wyn wouldn't trade her for the world.

"Thanks again for helping me, Mom. You always do such a great job and make me look far better than I could do alone."

"Maybe the next time I help you with your hair for a wedding, your dress will be white," her mother said, an unmistakably wistful note in her voice.

"The next wedding will be Devin and Cole's," Wyn reminded her. "I *hope* Dev doesn't pick white for her bridesmaids. That would just be weird."

"Okay. The one after that," Charlene said.

"Maybe that one will be *yours*," Katrina teased.

"Oh stop," Charlene said, her cheeks suddenly pink.

Over the last few weeks, Wyn had become far more accepting of the idea of her mother with Uncle Mike. He was a good man and her mother did deserve to be happy again. It didn't mean any of them would ever forget John Bailey but he was gone now and wouldn't want his widow to spend the rest of her life grieving and alone.

Mike and Charlene were quite sweet together, anyway, like a couple of awkward teenagers not quite sure what to do with themselves.

"We should probably get moving," Charlene said. "You'll want to see if McKenzie needs any last-minute help, of course."

"Is Cade still picking you up, or do you need a ride with us?" Kat asked.

The doorbell rang at that precise moment and Pete, from his spot on the floor watching the proceedings with interest, lumbered to his feet and headed toward it. He adored Cade almost as much as Wyn did.

"That should be Cade," she said, unable to control the little kick in her pulse rate. "He was able to arrange with other officers to cover the shift but he may have to leave the reception early."

"We'll see you there, then," Charlene said.

The two of them opened the door and Cade stood on the doorstep looking incredible in a close-fitting blue suit she had seen him wear only a few times.

She had left him just a few hours before but joy bloomed through her all over again.

"Oh, look how handsome you are," Charlene exclaimed.

He kissed her cheek and then looked embarrassed and pleased when Wyn's mother straightened his tie a little and adjusted his collar.

"Seriously, Cade, you should wear a suit every day," Katrina said, with a slightly dazed look. "I would consider that part of your sworn duty to the women of Haven Point."

He shook his head and kissed her cheek too, holding the door for both of them.

"We'll see you two there," Charlene said.

"Hate to break it to you, but you two really don't have any time to, um, dawdle." Kat gave her a meaningful look over their mother's shoulder as they headed toward her completely impractical sports car, and it was Wyn's turn to flush.

"Goodbye," Wyn said firmly and closed the door behind the two of them.

As soon as they were blessedly alone, Cade pulled her into his arms.

"I missed you," he murmured and Wyn gave a happy sigh and kissed him.

So what if she had to redo her lipstick? It was completely worth it.

"Kat's right," she said regretfully after several long, delicious moments. "We don't have time to, um, dawdle."

"Too bad," he answered, his mouth warm and tender against hers.

He loved her. She still couldn't quite wrap her head around how huge and humbling and amazing that was.

With a sigh, Wyn finally pulled away. "I really do have to go. McKenzie would never forgive me if I missed her wedding and she would know just who to blame."

"Yeah, you're probably right. And our mayor is not a good person to cross."

He gave her one last kiss brimming with so much

sweetness it made her throat ache all over again, then helped her out to his car.

They would have time later, she told herself. They had tonight, tomorrow and the rest of their lives.

She couldn't wait.

* * * * *

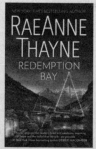

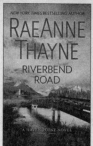
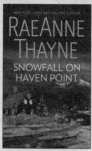

HARLEQUIN®

SPECIAL EDITION

Life, Love and Family

Save $1.00

on the purchase of ANY Harlequin® Special Edition book.

Available wherever books are sold, including most bookstores, supermarkets, drugstores and discount stores.

Save $1.00

on the purchase of any Harlequin® Special Edition book.

Coupon valid until October 31, 2016. Redeemable at participating outlets in the U.S. and Canada only. Not redeemable at Barnes and Noble stores. Limit one coupon per customer.

52614066

5 65373 00076 2   (8100)0 12197

SECOUP0716

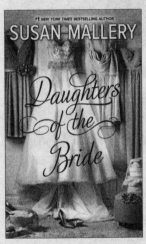

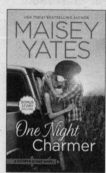
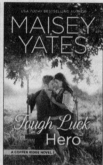

REQUEST YOUR FREE BOOKS!

2 FREE NOVELS
FROM THE ROMANCE COLLECTION
PLUS 2 FREE GIFTS!

YES! Please send me 2 FREE novels from the Romance Collection and my 2 FREE gifts (gifts are worth about $10). After receiving them, if I don't wish to receive any more books, I can return the shipping statement marked "cancel." If I don't cancel, I will receive 4 brand-new novels every month and be billed just $6.49 per book in the U.S. or $6.99 per book in Canada. That's a savings of at least 19% off the cover price. It's quite a bargain! Shipping and handling is just 50¢ per book in the U.S. and 75¢ per book in Canada.* I understand that accepting the 2 free books and gifts places me under no obligation to buy anything. I can always return a shipment and cancel at any time. Even if I never buy another book, the two free books and gifts are mine to keep forever.

194/394 MDN GH4D

Name	(PLEASE PRINT)

Address	Apt. #

City	State/Prov.	Zip/Postal Code

Signature (if under 18, a parent or guardian must sign)

Mail to the **Reader Service:**
IN U.S.A.: P.O. Box 1867, Buffalo, NY 14240-1867
IN CANADA: P.O. Box 609, Fort Erie, Ontario L2A 5X3

Want to try two free books from another line?
Call 1-800-873-8635 or visit www.ReaderService.com.

* Terms and prices subject to change without notice. Prices do not include applicable taxes. Sales tax applicable in N.Y. Canadian residents will be charged applicable taxes. Offer not valid in Quebec. This offer is limited to one order per household. Not valid for current subscribers to the Romance Collection or the Romance/Suspense Collection. All orders subject to credit approval. Credit or debit balances in a customer's account(s) may be offset by any other outstanding balance owed by or to the customer. Please allow 4 to 6 weeks for delivery. Offer available while quantities last.

Your Privacy—The Reader Service is committed to protecting your privacy. Our Privacy Policy is available online at www.ReaderService.com or upon request from the Reader Service.

We make a portion of our mailing list available to reputable third parties that offer products we believe may interest you. If you prefer that we not exchange your name with third parties, or if you wish to clarify or modify your communication preferences, please visit us at www.ReaderService.com/consumerschoice or write to us at Reader Service Preference Service, P.O. Box 9062, Buffalo, NY 14240-9062. Include your complete name and address.

ROM15

Turn your love of reading into rewards you'll love with

Harlequin My Rewards

Join for FREE today at
www.HarlequinMyRewards.com

Earn **FREE BOOKS** of your choice.

Experience **EXCLUSIVE OFFERS** and contests.

Enjoy **BOOK RECOMMENDATIONS** selected just for you.

PLUS! Sign up now and get **500** points right away!

Earn
FREE
REWARDS
Join!
Today!
HarlequinMyRewards.com